Highlander's Hidden Castle

Loved by a Highlander

Book 3

by Debra Chapoton

ISBN: 9798394148859

Imprint: Independently published

Books by Debra Chapoton

The Highlander's Secret Princess
The Highlander's English Maiden
The Highlander's Hidden Castle
The Highlander's Heart of Stone

Second Chance Teacher Romance series written under pen name
Marlisa Kriscott (Christian themes):

Aaron After School
Sonia's Secret Someone
Melanie's Match
School's Out
Summer School
The Spanish Tutor
A Novel Thing

Christian Non-fiction:
Guided Prayer Journal for Women
Crossing the Scriptures
35 Lessons from the Book of Psalms
Prayer Journal and Bible Study
Prayer Journal and Bible Study (the 4 Gospels)
Teens in the Bible
Moms in the Bible
Animals in the Bible
Old Testament Lessons in the Bible
New Testament Lessons in the Bible

Christian Fiction:
Love Contained
Sheltered
The Guardian's Diary
Exodia
Out of Exodia
Spell of the Shadow Dragon
Curse of the Winter Dragon

Young Adult Novels:
A Soul's Kiss
Edge of Escape
Exodia
Out of Exodia
Here Without A Trace
Sheltered

Spell of the Shadow Dragon
Curse of the Winter Dragon
The Girl in the Time Machine
The Guardian's Diary
The Time Bender
The Time Ender
The Time Pacer
The Time Stopper
To Die Upon a Kiss
A Fault of Graves

Children's Books:
The Secret in the Hidden Cave
Mystery's Grave
Bullies and Bears
A Tick in Time
Bigfoot Day, Ninja Night
Nick Bazebahl and Forbidden Tunnels
Nick Bazebahl and the Cartoon Tunnels
Nick Bazebahl and the Fake Witch Tunnels
Nick Bazebahl and the Mining Tunnels
Nick Bazebahl and the Red Tunnels
Nick Bazebahl and the Wormhole Tunnels
Inspirational Bible Verse Coloring Book
ABC Learn to Read Coloring Book
ABC Learn to Read Spanish Coloring Book
Stained Glass Window Coloring Book
Naughty Cat Dotted Grid Notebook
Cute Puppy Graph Paper Notebook
Easy Sudoku for Kids
101 Mandalas Coloring Book
150 Mandalas Coloring Book

Non-Fiction:
Brain Power Puzzles (11 volumes)
Building a Log Home in Under a Year
200 Creative Writing Prompts
400 Creative Writing Prompts
Advanced Creative Writing Prompts
Beyond Creative Writing Prompts
300 Plus Teacher Hacks and Tips
How to Blend Families
How to Help Your Child Succeed in School
How to Teach a Foreign Language

Chapter 1

THE AUGUST SUN did its best to take the edge off the cool morning. Jack McKelvey finished his practice at the hammer throw and moved on to the caber toss. Sweat dripped down his face and his thick black hair fell across his forehead in stringy locks. He was determined to master both events, events which his older brother, Keir, had won the previous year. His arms were going to feel like rubber after all this lifting and straining, but a dip in the cold pond behind the stables would set things right later.

His older brothers, Keir and Logan, didn't spend half the time practicing that Jack did. Of course, they had other obligations. As married men these last two months of summer, they spent much of their time with their new wives. The castle's atmosphere had changed considerably with the last of his sisters now gone and the presence of three new women in her place, Eleanor and Hannah, and Eleanor's mother Mary. At least Jack wasn't considered the youngest anymore with the addition of Mary's adopted son, Colin, a boy of twelve.

1

Och, and here comes the lad now.

"Guid mornin', Jack," Colin ran up, eyed the hammer on the ground and the caber at Jack's feet. "Are ye practicin' fer the games?"

It was the same question he'd asked the last three mornings and Jack gave him the same answer that made Colin laugh each time. "Nay," he said with a smirk, "I'm figurin' how to build meself a cabin."

Colin did laugh, but this time he said, "I reckoned how to help ye. We need to cut down more cabers." He nodded at the Scots Pine pole on the ground.

"Mm hmm," Jack put his hands on his hips, his kilt slapping at his knees. "I'll give ye me axe and ye can go off into yon woods and cut a few more."

Colin plopped himself onto the ground next to the hammer. He ran his fingers over the heavy metal ball and the wooden handle it was attached to. "I was jist watchin' yer brother Logan practicin' the sheaf toss and the axe throw behind the barn. He says he won them both last year."

"Aye, he did. But I'll be strengthenin' me skills in those areas, too. Tomorrow. With any luck and more effort than me brothers, I'll take the prize in all four events."

"I'll be rootin' fer ye." Colin looked up. "Let's see if ye can pitch the caber all the way over today."

Logan huffed and walked to the narrower end of what was, a week ago, a tall tree with branches. He'd axed off the branches himself and dragged it to this spot. Now he picked up the end and walked it upright, took a deep breath and bent down to the thicker end, the pole tilted on his shoulder, wedged against his jaw. The aromatic pine sap sticking to his cheek. He clasped his hands around the bottom, and lifted. A short grunt escaped his lips as he took off running. He stopped at twelve strides, drove upward with his legs and hips and pushed with his hands as he released the caber. It flew into the air, but failed to turn end over end, thumping to the ground with a double thud.

"'Twas jist me warm up," Jack said. He motioned for Colin to get up. "I need ye to help me get it balanced against me chest. The heavy end needs to be up. 'Tis harder that way and the judges will demand it."

2

Colin helped him practice for half an hour, during which Jack managed to toss it seven more times, but never succeeded in making it complete a revolution.

"Thank ye, Colin. Ye're a good lad. I'm goin' to toss meself now, straight into the little loch."

He started off and glanced back when he realized the boy wasn't following. Colin was twirling the hammer over his head. When he let go, the ball flew out, handle trailing like a solid tail feather, and landed a fair distance away. The lad had promise. Jack walked on alone.

As he drifted around the cool pond, Jack dreamed of all the lassies that would fawn over him when he took the prize in several events. All he had to do was keep practicing and lengthen the hours of practice. With no other obligations, he could do that. His arms felt rejuvenated already. He waded near shore, scrubbed his hands and cheek with sand to remove the sap, then dried off in the sun, and redressed.

He was still in his self-centered glory, with smug smile on his reddened face and feeling thoroughly refreshed, as he entered the castle. Two of the maids passed him, carrying bed sheets and ladies' dresses. They each curtsied as well as they could with their arms loaded. The younger one, Elspeth, openly smiled at him. He noted her admiration and smiled back. And why shouldn't the lass find him attractive? He had the McKelvey build, strong and tall, with dark hair—thick and unruly—and sparkling eyes, a brilliant shade of green, glittering like emeralds and framed by dark lashes his sisters envied. He was aware that his gaze could be mesmerizing, at least for the two maids here. He'd tried his best at the beginning of summer to draw Hannah in, but it was obvious she was already smitten with Logan. These lasses slowed their movement past him and once they'd rounded the corner and gone down the steps to the kitchen, he could hear them twittering about him. He rather enjoyed the momentary attention.

He checked the library hoping to speak to his father, but it was empty. Laird McKelvey was no doubt out with Mary, traversing their lands or checking on the workers he was employing to restore the Strathnaver Castle. Jack found it odd that his father intended to marry this widow and set up an entirely new household there, leaving Castle Caladh to Keir and Eleanor. Of course, he and Logan could remain here as well; there was space enough for several families. And now that they employed a second cook and three new servants, bringing the staff to twelve, there was no reason not to think that Jack would live here with his bride—whoever that might be—and raise a family.

He was a bit concerned about who his bride might be, though. Logan had teased him a while back that their father was negotiating a dowry with the McDoons to betroth Megan and Jack. She'd come with her brothers to Rory's wedding and left with one brother while the other, that rascal Dylan, had gotten himself drunk, slept on the floor of the portrait room, and then stolen away the next day with one of their horses and Hannah. That whole incident was serious enough to put some strain on the relationship between his father and ole McDoon. He wasn't sure if his father would be doing any business with the McDoons let alone allowing one to marry into the family.

No matter, really. Megan McDoon wasn't who he was interested in. Not that she wasn't attractive, she was ... in a healthy sort of way. Her hips were generous, and her bosom, too. He'd heard cook say she was made for child-bearing. At Rory's wedding feast, Jack had escorted her to a table and sat with her. She had a warm and generous personality, laughing at all he had to say, and only offering kind words when he tried to get her to agree with his harsh criticism of a rival clan.

Jack entered the portrait room and found it also empty. He took a seat across from the painting of his mother. He missed her tremendously. As the youngest in the family, he believed he'd been her favorite. He was prone to getting into mischief and she was more tolerant of his mishaps than she was of his older brothers' troubles. He'd fallen from trees, scraped himself climbing the towers, tumbled down stone steps, and even almost drowned once. His mother used to insist he come with her as she did her visits to the neighboring clanswomen. She needed to watch him more closely than any of her other children.

He stared at the portrait and a long-forgotten memory flashed to mind. He couldn't quite get the whole picture to form in his head, but bits and pieces arranged themselves. A long horseback ride sitting in the saddle in front of his mother ... a steep incline ... and the further they went, the more the landscape changed. The trees grew thicker, and the terrain became rockier. They eventually reached a plateau, and there before them ... his childish mind believed it was a haunted palace ... but remembering it now, he was sure it was an abandoned castle.

4

He snapped his fingers, jumped up from the seat, and spoke to the portrait. "Mother, I'm off to find our secret place." He had the strangest feeling that she'd taken him there for a reason. Perhaps it was where she had grown up. There'd been no contact with her people ever. He wondered why.

No sense thinking of maids and maidens if there was an adventure, a mystery to solve. His only question was whether to bring along Logan or Keir. Or Colin. No, this would be a journey for one; he'd go alone.

He asked the new cook, a portly woman named Mildred, to pack him a pouch of scran. She gave him such generous portions that he'd be set for a two-day trip if he wanted. He considered taking a bag of oats for his horse, Soldier.

He told his plans to the stable lad as he saddled the horse for him. The boy always knew where each member of the family was, based on the use of the horses, carriage, wagon, or cart. Jack learned that his father and Mary where, indeed, off to Strathnaver Castle in the small carriage, Keir and Eleanor were riding to Rory's cottage at Branaugh, and Logan was fetching his horse, Toaty, from the low pasture.

"And Hannah? Isn't she going to ride with him?"

"Nay, master Jack, yer brother says she's feelin' poorly this mornin'. Can't keep her porridge down."

Jack dismissed that bit of knowledge as simply the poor health of fragile lasses. His sister Rory had a similar malady the weeks before her wedding. Well, it sounded like the castle would be empty of all but one female voice this day. Perhaps he should have Colin accompany him.

He tied two sacks onto Soldier's saddle and mounted him. He trotted him out of the barn and into the bright sunlight. Soldier was keen to get going. Ah, the beautiful McKelvey lands were a sight to behold. And there, where he'd left him, stood Colin, still twirling and throwing the hammer.

"Och, I'll leave him to it, aye, Soldier? The lad'll be worn out afore long."

He continued talking to his horse as he considered which direction to strike out in. It had been a good ten years or more since he'd been a small lad riding double with his mother, but one thing he remembered: she liked to start by riding alongside the creek and cross over where the purple saxifrage was abundant. He smiled to himself that he could remember this little fact. Perhaps more memories would surface on this trek.

***

ANABEL MACLEOD WALKED slowly, her feet sinking into the mossy ground. The morning fog had burned off before she had gotten half way here. Once the grey light of dawn had pushed away the darkness of night, she had risen and started off on her journey to this, her secret place, where she spent hours exploring an ancient castle. Her family thought she was visiting the McDoons or the Campbells or the Stewarts, families that had young women her age with whom she'd spend time sewing or embroidering or knitting while one of them read aloud or practiced an instrument. But not today. Her brother Alpin was tasked with escorting her, but they, by design and secret agreement, went separate ways for the day, planning to meet up again in the late afternoon to arrive at the gates together.

The castle, well-hidden from the lanes and cart paths, was old and crumbling, but Anabel felt a sense of peace here. She'd stumbled upon it the time she'd run away from home. She liked to make up stories of things that might have happened here, sometimes whispering them to see if any ghosts would confirm her imaginations. Today she started at the overgrown back entrance and walked through, trailing her fingers over stones, wondering how many other hands had touched them. Once there must have been a laird and lady living here, with ruddy-faced bairns, laughing children, and a host of servants. A big family, she presumed by the number of rooms the castle had, more than the MacLeods had, but not as many as at Castle Caladh or Beldorney Hall.

She ambled through the kitchen, rubbed her nose, and imagined the scent of yeasty bread, fresh-baked and too hot to cut. She found the ballroom and her thoughts rambled back to the ball at the Beldorneys' nine, ten weeks past. She wasn't the most important guest at the ball, no, that was princess. She pirouetted a couple of times, imagining the musicians playing familiar tunes.

The princess only danced with two of the McKelvey heirs, but Anabel danced with nearly every lad and eligible bachelor who attended. That ball should have been for her and, in fact, she had twirled around the dance floor with her partners, pretending all the fuss was just for her.

She left the large room and strolled down a hallway that stank of something putrid, a dead rodent, perhaps. She didn't want to think about that, instead she pondered her own self-worth. Her beauty was acclaimed by all, though she knew she was ugly on the inside. She couldn't always control the mean streak that sneaked out of her in words and deeds. She regretted most things she thoughtlessly said. She meant to treat the servants better; she tried, but whenever someone touched her, she often recoiled. But not at the ball; everyone was happy at the ball. When unhappy people touched her, she felt things: she felt their aches and pains, their sorrows and melancholy, their maladies and unbalanced humours. She dared not tell a soul. They might torture her or execute her as a witch.

Anabel eventually reached a large wooden door, and pushed it open. Inside, she found a dark and damp hallway she hadn't yet explored. Despite the darkness, Anabel could feel the history here. She could almost hear the whispers of the past echoing off the walls. She walked further into this wing of the castle, exploring the empty chambers. She eventually reached a large room with a fireplace and some furniture, including a few chairs. She sat down in one of the chairs, carefully as it looked unsteady, but it held her light frame easily. She looked around. The stone walls were decorated with moth-eaten tapestries and ancient portraits. The faces were, of course, unfamiliar and utterly uninteresting.

Except for one. The portrait of a young girl with deep blue eyes and hair like ripe strawberries hung slightly askew. Anabel stood and walked up to it, stared, and let her mind go blank. On a whim she reached up and touched the paint on the subject's cheek. She felt nothing. No strange vibration or sense of illness, no premonition of death, or vision of past life. Nothing ... except ... where had she seen those eyes before? Not on her intended, that handsome Keir McKelvey, who had jilted her to marry that Sassenach, Eleanor. She'd met Eleanor who they claimed was a princess and then, at the ball she seemed quite different. No matter, her father and the others hushed up all talk of royalty and connections to court and such. She was Keir's wife now.

Was Anabel jealous? No, heart-broken though, in the sense that she'd been deprived of her due of happiness, for surely marrying into the McKelvey clan would have made her a hundred times happier than she was now.

She pulled the portrait off the wall and went back to the chair, the soft whisper of her slippers on the stone floor the only sound in the high-ceilinged room. She sat with the picture on her lap, dust marking a line across the lap of her dress, more dust tickling her nose, and studied the face. Her imagination failed her. She couldn't invent a tale for the lass, just as she couldn't imagine a reason for the abandonment of this fine structure. There was no evidence of fire, no collapsed roof, though she'd been here in the rain once and found it wet and drafty, and no sign that the tenants had been forcibly removed. She knew the McDoon brothers had evicted people from their homes and they boasted as to not leaving a chair or bed unbroken. Here the furniture was intact and there was plenty of it. Her eye went to the sagging bed in the corner of the room. Ragged drapes pooled on the floor beside it.

Oh! All of a sudden, a mouse scurried along the wall, drawing her attention.

She lifted the picture off her lap, intending to rehang it and leave. As she did so she noticed a scrawl along the back, a name … Nella.

"Who were you, Nella?" And then she noticed the date … 75 years past.

Anabel was pleased to know this bit of history. A young woman named Nella, she looked to be around Anabel's seventeen years, had lived in this castle ages ago. What had become of her? Had her family all died of some plague, or gone off to America, or been killed in one of the wars?

Were there descendants living in Scotland still? Some great-grandchild with those jewel-like blue eyes? … hmm, she had an inkling that she'd danced with someone at the ball with eyes that shade, but she'd been a proper lady that night fluttering her lashes and keeping her gaze mostly on her toes.

***

MEGAN MCDOON HATED her brothers, especially Dylan. Dylan was unpredictable. He'd driven her half the way to Clara Campbell's home and then unhitched his nag from the cart wagon. He hurriedly told her he'd be back in a couple of hours and to walk herself the rest of the way. Before she knew it, he cantered off bareback to do the devil knew what.

She sat fuming. She was quick witted, confident, and even-tempered, but wholly at a loss for words to reprimand her retreating sibling. She sat there a moment more, angrily scrunching fistfuls of her simple blue dress, her freckled cheeks growing redder, and her ire getting the best of her usual kind disposition. And then she saw what had made Dylan take such a sudden leave: a McKelvey had crested the far hill and now trotted slowly toward her.

Which McKelvey? He wasn't riding Toaty, the mare she was so fond of that Dylan had lost in a bet to Logan McKelvey. No, it wasn't Logan … it was Jack. Her breath caught and she pulled the cap around her neck back up and over the red bun of hair she'd so hastily made. She smoothed her brown skirt and sat rigid on the wagon bench, suddenly aware of damp perspiration under her arms. She held her chin high and her elbows firmly against her hips, hands in her lap. It would be but a few minutes and he'd reach her. She'd be blushing soon and her freckles would stand out. She already caught a whiff of her own salty and musky aroma.

She looked away when he got nearer. The sound of his horse's hooves changed from soft thuds on the grasses to louder clops as he met the road and walked his horse straight up to her.

"Ye're blockin' me way, Mistress Megan." Jack doffed his hat and grinned, stopping his horse to face her a mere three feet away. "Ye ken, doan ye, that 'tis easier to move the wagon if ye hitch a horse to it?"

She blew her held breath out and laughed, maybe too loudly. Her eyes met his. "Ye must teach me brother such wisdom, as he's left me here and I must walk the mile or so Clara Campbell's." She looked for a proper way to descend without the help she needed.

"Well, m'lady," Jack teased, "I must insist ye move yer lovely carriage. Can ye nay pull it yerself?"

Megan relaxed at his humor. She'd enjoyed his company at the wedding feast, had hoped there'd be a marriage proposal coming, but had lost that hope in the intervening two months. Dylan had spoiled relations between the clans, but now, since Jack seemed friendly enough, perhaps things could be mended.

She decided to joke along with him. "Well, m'lord, I tried just that, but 'tis hard to drive the cart and be the one pullin' it at the same time. Could ye mayhaps hitch that worthy stallion of yers to the cart and ride with me to Clara's? I'm sure she'll have plenty of pastries to reward ye." She relaxed a bit more, pleased with herself for her bold response.

9

"I'm sorry, m'lady," he bowed his head, "but the street is crowded and I doan want to run over any of the laddies that are playin' here."

"Well," Megan desperately tried to think of some humorous response, "let's see if I can get them to move." She rose in the cart and waved to phantom children. "Get along, children. Off to yer homes ye go." She sat back down, worried she'd acted with too much impertinence. "There. Ye see, I've scared them all away. I'd be much obliged if ye could hitch yer horse now. I must get to this party."

Jack gave a good-humored chuckle and dismounted. He backed Soldier into position, glancing often at Megan as he did so. "A party, ye say? I remember me sisters havin' parties. Sewin' parties. I was always warned to stay away or I'd risk bein' pricked by their needles."

"Ye'd be welcomed at the Campbells, especially fer doin' this good deed." She hoped her blush had left her cheeks by now. She watched him finish hitching the harness over the saddle then coax his horse forward. The animal did not balk, but pulled the cart with ease. "Will ye nay sit beside me?"

"Soldier has nivver pulled a wagon before. I best walk alongside 'im and hold the reins."

Megan bit her lip and tried to think of something clever to say. Nothing came to mind. They traveled on in silence until the Campbell lands came in view.

"Well, m'lady, 'tis been a pleasure to serve ye." Jack smiled back at her as he stopped the horse and wagon in front of a large stone dwelling. He unhitched Soldier and started to mount, then stopped, dropped the reins, and strode quickly up to Megan, raising a hand to help her down. "Forgive me."

She took his hand, but faltered. There was no easy way to get off. Her brother always jumped down and then put his hands on her waist and lifted her off, always grumbling about her weight. Jack was not going to be so bold, she thought. She frowned at him.

"Have ye nivver helped a lady off a wagon, Jack? One o' yer sisters?"

His eyes widened. "Och, forgive me ag'in. 'Twas always Keir or Logan or me father who ... och, may I ... er, is it proper fer me to touch yer waist?"

She bent at the knees and put her hands on his shoulders, wondering if he was as nervous now as she was. "'Tis allowed if ye're brief aboot

10

it." A thrill coursed through her, but not entirely of excitement. She was anxious that Jack might make a comment as Dylan always did, that she was heavier than a wagon full of firewood—or worse, detect how much she was perspiring.

Jack lifted her up and forward and down. Gently. With a smile, she noticed. And he didn't grunt as Dylan always did. Her face grew warm when he didn't let go of her as fast as Dylan would. He settled her to the ground and made sure she was firmly balanced before dropping his hands. Then he did something unexpected. He lifted the hand he'd held before and brought it to his lips, lightly brushing her knuckles. She murmured, "Thank ye," as he let go.

Jack replied, "Farewell, Mistress Megan. I am sure we shall meet again."

"Oh, ye cannae stay? I'm quite sure Clara would welcome ye."

"Aye, ye've made that clear, but I've a wee journey to make before dark and I'm nay sure of the way. I best be goin'." He turned back to his horse, caught the reins, and mounted.

***

JACK SANG OLD songs he learnt from his mother, hoping they would jog more of his memories and also hoping they'd make him choose the right paths to find the place he indistinctly remembered. By noon the sun shone brightly in the sky and as he passed the second loch of the day, that rich summer light reflected off its glistening waters. He reined Soldier toward the loch and both animal and man drank their fill. Something seemed familiar. He scanned the north side of the loch and beheld the beauty of the far shore. Again, his insides tickled with a vague and hazy memory. He felt moved to venture off the beaten path here, and follow the shore around, keeping his horse in the shallows, though it sometimes got as deep as his horse's knees.

Soldier splashed on, ears flicking back and forth, listening to Jack talk of his mother.

"'Twas an old tale, aye, that me mum told of a hidden castle in the Highlands. Her castle, she called it." He tensed in the saddle and Soldier nickered. "Och! I recall it now. How she brought me here." He shook his head, stopped the horse as if he had to remember the tale right here, right now, or moving on would cause him to lose the thought and scatter the bits of memory.

"'Twas only once we came," he said, "and she told me it was where she was born. She was happy there until the English drove them out. Aye, 'tis comin' back to me now, Soldier." The horse neighed and swished his tail. Jack laughed. "We're close." He tapped his heels against Soldier's sides and mumbled, "We're lookin' fer a rock, where a rock shouldna be."

The far edge of the shore was overgrown, but Jack spotted it and remembered: a rock the size of a ram, wedged between two tree trunks that had grown around it and now rotted against it. He clucked at Soldier and guided him past the rocks and into a maze of trees, an old forest with no axe marks or signs of human paths, not even deer runs or rabbit trails. Soldier flinched as branches snapped against his shoulders, withers, and rump, but he didn't spook. Jack held back the branches he could catch, but a couple smacked him anyway before they came out of the woods and into an overgrown garden maze.

"Aha! Soldier, we've found it. 'Tis as I remember. Me mum said to always turn right and we'd wind our way out in no time." He laughed out loud and urged Soldier on.

A hidden castle in the Highlands ... Jack was more determined now. He stopped looking forward and glanced up. There it was. Ancient. Crumbling. Another turn and they were out of the maze. A single, massive spire reached heavenward at the back of the immense structure. Three rounded rooms loomed in front with arched windows, a second story, and maybe a third judging by the small windows near the roof. The rest of the castle, he was sure there was more, stretched beyond his view.

"I found it!" He rose in the saddle and hooted. Soldier whinnied and Jack laughed again. He stared up at the dark windows and ... *what was that? A moving shadow? Was someone there?*

It seemed as if no one had been here in many years. That had to be his imagination. Jack approached the castle with a sense of excitement and trepidation. He had no idea what he might find inside, but he was determined to explore. He found a small door in the side of the castle and pushed it open.

"Hey-o! Hullo?"

Chapter 2

ANABEL DUCKED DOWN and moved away from the grimy window when she saw a horse and rider outside. She realized now the strange sounds she'd heard had been a shout and a laugh. Who was this person? All the times she'd come here, she'd never seen a footprint or heard a voice or even spotted an animal.

Now what should she do? Did he see her at the window?

She cringed when a male voice echoed up from below. *Should she crawl under that bed?*

She stayed perfectly still and listened.

The horse made sounds outside.

The man made sounds inside, huffing and hollering and weirdly calling out to his mother. Anabel's heart began to race. She tiptoed to the bed, crouched down, and put her hands to the floor. *How awful*, it was layered with dust. At that moment, with her head close to that filthy floor and her body about to slide under the ropes that held the straw mattress, she saw the swept-clean path her skirts made across the room. Any child could follow her trail.

The footsteps grew louder. She could only hope that whoever it was would be more interested in the portraits on the wall and not notice the evidence of her intrusion. She crawled beneath the sagging bed, the ropes catching on her bonnet.

Once completely under, Anabel held her breath, dared to peek out, and fixed her gaze on the threshold. If she pressed her face against the floor and ignored the pebbly feel of mouse droppings on her cheek, she could see most of the man who now stood at the entrance. Fine boots. Red stockings. A familiar plaid on his kilt. An axe, a dirk, a sporran hanging from a wide belt. Hands clenched and then opening as he stepped in.

A voice. Soft and gentle.

"Ah, 'tis as it was, I remember this room." The voice mellow and distant.

The boots traced their way to the very portrait Anabel had just rehung. *Would there be smudges from her hands along the frame?*

He moved to the center of the room and faced the fireplace, turned and faced the window, turned again and faced the bed.

Took a step toward it. She gulped. Closed her eyes and willed him to be gone.

That devil of a rodent skittered over her arm and Anabel let out the faintest of squeals.

"Who's there?" The voice deepened, full of a sense of power and authority. "I said, who's there? Show yerself. I mean ye nae harm."

Suddenly a handsome face with chiseled features appeared sideways opposite Anabel's. He had bent low and now … an arm reached under, a hand grabbed her wrist and pulled. She slid out in a plume of dust and filth and once on her feet she immediately lost her balance and fell backwards onto the mattress. The ropes gave way and the bed collapsed.

The man howled, threw his head back, and clutched his sides. His entire body shook with each bellow and his eyes squinted shut.

Anabel, however, was not amused. She stared instead at her wrist, rubbed it gently, and tried to understand what she'd felt from his touch. She could always feel when someone was sick, but he wasn't ill. Or if someone was in pain; but he had none. Or if someone harbored some melancholy or ill will or devilish mischief. This man had a wee tendency toward mischief, but there was nothing evil in his soul.

He stopped laughing. "Did I hurt ye? I'm most sorry. Can ye speak?"

She lifted her chin and wiped the grime from one side of her face.

"Anabel? Anabel MacLeod? Whyever were ye here ... and under the bed no less?"

"Jack." Her heart caught in her throat as she realized the last of the sensation she'd felt at his touch. She knew him. She knew him very well.

Jack sobered from his laughter and offered both hands to help her from her heap of skirts and bedclothes and well-chewed pillows.

"I dinnae mean to laugh at ye. I was jist relieved ye weren't a ghost or worse ... and when ye broke the bed, it added to me amusement. Are ye all right, lass?" He still held his hands out for her to take. "Can ye stand?"

Normally she'd refuse an ungloved hand, but she wasn't afraid of his touch now. She put both hands in his and came off the bed rather fast. Her feet scuffed the floor, but she rose smoothly and stood looking up at him. And into his incredibly blue eyes. Her breath caught.

"Your mother," she said, then wished she hadn't spoken. "Um, ye called out to her." She lowered her gaze and groomed as much dust as she could off her shoulders and then gave her skirt a shake.

"Aye, she brought me here once when I was a wee lad. Do ye ken who used to live here?"

His hand went to her bonnet and he brushed the edge and straightened it.

"Nay, 'tis abandoned." She stepped back. His act was far too intimate; they weren't betrothed. Why, her father and brothers would never touch her ... oh! and she should not be alone with him here, unchaperoned. She should dart for the door and ... it suddenly hit her how inappropriate it was that she hid herself under a bed and he found her. They were not children playing a game. If anyone should find out ... she gulped.

Jack turned to stare at the portraits.

Anabel felt the tears well up. She clenched her jaw, determined not to let her emotions take over.

"I remember that picture. I think me mum told me 'twas me great-grandmother." He turned back to her, still pointing a finger at the portrait Anabel had examined. "What's wrong? Did ye hurt yerself?" He brought

15

his hands to her head again. His brows nearly touched as he frowned at her.

Her own fists were tight balls, but at his touch she relaxed them, brought them up to cover his hands and felt so much sorrow through his skin that she blinked repeatedly and let the tears fall.

"I'm all right … but ye … ye've a pain that's deep … ye miss yer mother." She watched his Adam's apple bob.

His brows went up. "Are ye readin' me mind, Anabel MacLeod? Be ye a good fortune-teller or a witch?" He pulled back his hands and the laugh that followed was short and not at all one of amusement. He let his hands fall to his sides.

She pressed her lips together tightly and twirled away from him, started for the doorway, and said, "I must leave. 'Tis improper to be here, alone with a McKelvey."

He caught her arm and spun her toward him. "Och, 'tis a wound yet unhealed, aye? That me brother Keir negated yer betrothal by marryin' another? Did ye love him?"

She looked from the hand still clasping her arm to his face and those amazing eyes and tried to flash her sudden anger at him through her own. "Love? Ye cannae love a man ye've spent nary a moment with. Besides," she threw her shoulders back, "there are men at me father's door every day, askin' fer me hand. Good day, Jack McKelvey."

***

AMUSEMENT RETURNED TO Jack's eyes. Why, the lass was not so high and mighty as he thought. His impression of her had always been one of admiration; she was the great beauty of the Highlands. He didn't disbelieve her claim of many suitors. Perhaps he could woo her, too … but no, she'd once been betrothed to his brother; it seemed a wee bit incestuous to pursue her.

"I'll see ye safely home then."

"Ye needn't be so chivalrous. I can get meself home. I come here alone often."

"Ye do? Then mayhaps we'll meet here ag'in."

She stopped and looked at him. "This was me only place to sit and have a think undisturbed by pestering servants, but as it must belong to yer mother's clan, I'll nay come back."

16

Jack didn't want her to leave. "Pestering servants?" He sat himself down in one of the chairs and challenged her to stay. "I remember well how ye berated one such servant as we left the Beldorney Hall the morning after the ball." She stopped at the door, as he hoped she would.

"She kept touching me and I couldnae abide it."

He cocked his head and pressed some more, "Ye also unleashed a wee bit o' fury on me brother, Logan. Now I can understand ye bein' outraged wi' Keir, but—"

She twirled on him and marched up to his chair. "Aye, 'twas humiliatin' if ye must ken and Logan was there, Keir was gone. So I chose to berate him in Keir's stead."

Jack quickly ran a sleeve across the adjacent wood chair, relieving it of as much dust as he could. "Please sit. I'll hear ye out. Ye can rebuke the McKelveys 'til me ears turn red as a beetroot."

She took in a deep breath and let it out in a shuddering sigh. A new thrill went up Jack's middle. This was a special day; first he'd rescued Megan and now he had a chance for a real conversation with the bonniest lass in the country. He'd mocked his brothers and his sisters' husbands for succumbing to feminine persuasions.

But ... he glanced at the portrait of his great-grandmother and recalled something his mother had said: a man is nay a man until he has a woman at his side.

Anabel stood trembling, but didn't sit. After a moment she seemed to still herself and said, "Please, wait here." She swished her skirts and walked out of the room. He listened to her steps fade, heard his horse knicker as she must have passed him. Ah, he thought, she's looking for the jakes. He hadn't noticed an outhouse when he rode up. He wondered how long he'd have to wait.

***

MEGAN MCDOON GOSSIPED with Clara Campbell and two other young women, Orla and Shona, who lived not far and arrived before Megan. They'd expected Anabel MacLeod to join them, but it was not unusual for her to miss one of their parties. They didn't mind; it was Anabel they most liked to gossip about anyway: what their brothers said about her, what their mothers whispered, what they themselves had noticed when her behavior challenged good reason.

"Ah, Megan, come sit. We were jist remarkin' on Anabel's beauty and charm." Clara, unfortunately burdened with a crooked nose, beady eyes, and a wide, down-turned mouth, indicated a chair with one hand and with the other waved off the servant who brought Megan in.

"Charm?" Orla huffed. "I saw her make a disgusting face and turn away last week when Shona touched her arm to steady her on the steps."

"'Tis true," Shona chimed in. "I wasna feelin' well to begin with and her act of shunnin' me brought on me monthlies, I swear."

Orla tisked her tongue and drew a hand across a patch of pimples on her chin. Clara smirked. The ladies were off on a series of gripes and complaints about their beautiful friend's 'charms.'

When they exhausted those stories, they turned to comments on each other's brothers, or their brothers' friends, or the scant male population between the river and the town. Twice Clara had to shoo her younger sisters out of the room.

And then, Megan titillated them with her encounter with Jack.

"Me rude brother, Dylan," Megan began, then took a long sip of the fresh cider Carla had refilled moments before, "ye'll nay believe how he stranded me. Why, if it weren't for Jack McKelvey, the verra most handsome of the McKelvey men, I mayn't have arrived here at all today." She sighed with great effect and left off telling more.

Clara leaned forward, her interest piqued. "Aye? Ye were stranded, ye say? How?"

"Mm," she reached for a second blueberry biscuit and took the tiniest of bites, "with a great distance yet to go, Dylan up and stopped the horse, unhitched it, and rode off on it without a word." She pretended to fan herself. "I was left to sit upon the hard boards until his return or walk all the way here."

Shona frowned, making deep wrinkles on her forehead. "He left ye without a word? Was he punishin' ye fer some misdeed?"

Orla came to Megan's defense. "What misdeed would Megan do? Why, she's the sweetest sister Dylan could ever have."

"Thank ye, Orla." Megan flicked a crumb from her lap. "I think me brother is afraid of the McKelvey clan. He did somethin' that brought about their indignation. 'Twas months ago … at the weddin's, ye ken, Rory's and Keir's, when Dylan stayed behind. Me other brother brought me home, complainin' all the way that Dylan would shame us fer sure

18

by drinkin' all the McKelveys' good ale." She took a bigger bite, tasted a hint of cinnamon, and wondered how Clara's cook added such depth of flavor.

The ladies shook their heads, swaying in sync.

Megan enjoyed a burst of juicy sweetness in the next bite before setting the rest of the biscuit back on the tray. She swallowed slowly and said, "And before that I kent that there were words between me father and Laird McKelvey concerning Jack and me, but after that …" she shrugged her shoulders slightly "… me mother says I mustn't worry aboot marryin' as I willna be considered over-ripe fruit for another summer or two."

The other three's wagging chins changed direction to nod up and down in agreement and words like 'old maid' and 'thornback' crossed their minds.

"Ye mustna fash, Meg, ye'll have numerous suitors," Shona sang out. "E'en me own mother says ye've the best chance of any of us because—" she eyed Megan's wide hips "—because ye appear more likely to bring male bairns into the world … with ease."

"Thank ye, Shona."

"But Jack? Ye say he saved ye?" Clara's small eyes narrowed further.

"Aye," Megan smiled at the memory. "He was ridin' 'cross the heathers. Dylan musta seen him from afar and dinnae want to meet him. Jack came up and hitched his steed, walked along the cart, and there we were …"

"A'courtin'," Carla said.

"A'cartin'," Orla said with a laugh.

Once the laughter settled Megan picked up her biscuit again and said, "I have me hopes on Jack, I do."

***

ANABEL SNEAKED OUT of the castle, passed Jack's horse, and then turned back to it.

She stood admiring the animal's fine form, how healthy it looked, and the sheen of its coat.

"Easy now," she cooed as she inched toward it, holding a hand out, and watching its ears flick at her words. One more step and she could touch it. First, though, she looked up at the castle windows. She exhaled

19

and wondered how long Jack would wait for her. She didn't intend to go back inside.

She touched the horse, noticed how wet its legs were. Her spirit lifted as she stroked the warm flesh. She loved to pat a dog's head or feel a horse's muzzle or run a hand along a cat's tail. Animals shared their peaceful moods with her. This horse had a bit more of a steadying feel to it. For an instant she imagined climbing up into the saddle and riding away on him. But, no, she was no thief. The horse nickered and she glanced again at the windows. It wouldn't do to have Jack see her tarrying here.

"Maybe I'll see you ag'in," she murmured, giving the horse a final pet. She glanced at the maze behind the horse and realized that Jack must have conquered it to find his way here. Perhaps he'd leave the same way. She would not chance another encounter with him.

She lifted her skirts and made her way through an old cook's garden, noticing a few thriving vegetables pushing past the weeds. She started to run away from the ruins of the castle, toward the woods. With Jack inside, the beautiful old structure was filled with danger for her. Not that she thought Jack was dangerous, but what she felt when they touched … well, she was confused and she did not like being confused.

Her feet pounded the ground and she was barely aware of the branches slapping her head and arms until a patch of thorns tore at her dress and scratched her face. She put a hand to her face and it came away with drops of blood. When at last she made it out of the woods and into the heathers, she stopped to catch her breath. The purple and pink petals of the heathers provided her with a sense comfort and home. She walked more slowly the rest of the way to where she had to wait for Alpin.

"Sister!" Alpin's face went white when he arrived an hour later. "What happened to ye? Ye look like ye've rolled in the mud with the dogs."

Anabel rose from the rock she'd been sitting on. "'Tis nothin'. I tangled wi' some briars and got dirty pickin' berries. As I dinnae have a basket, I used me frock to gather 'em."

Alpin's face turned to a scowl. "I doan believe ye. Were ye attacked? Is that blood I see?" He stepped closer, put both hands out beside her shoulders, but didn't touch her. He'd been scalded by her outbursts before. Few had been the times he'd laid a hand on arm or hand and not been dressed down for taking such liberties. He took a deeper breath to calm himself before ever so gently resting one hand and then the other on her upper arms.

"Anabel, I ken ye get upset when folks touch ye, intentional or otherwise. Has someone taken advantage of ye whilst ye were alone here or wherever 'twas ye went off to?"

She disliked the vibrations coming through his fingers, but they were tinged with concern and brotherly love. She'd allow it for now. She answered truthfully, "Alpin, I am fine. 'Tis an old frock I'm wearin' and nay worth a penny. The scratches will heal. I am fine." She turned her head slowly to look at one of his hands. He removed them both. "And ye?" She went on, "Are ye dirty and scratched from heaving those poles ye think ye can lift?"

"Aye," Alpin said, looking down at the smudges of debris on his kilt, "the caber toss is one event I'll nay lose to a McKelvey this year. Me practice with Quinn went well. I'll be goin' back on the morrow."

Anabel blinked toward the path she'd come down. Surely Jack would not return so soon. She needed to go back to the castle and take a final look around. There was still one area she hadn't dared to explore: the tower that led to the spire.

21

Chapter 3

THE NEXT MORNING found the McKelvey brothers practicing for the Highland games together.

"Are ye sure?" Jack slapped Logan on the back again. "Good on ye, brother. Ye must be proud indeed. With Rory's bairn comin' soon and then Fenella's, why yer wee heir will have no shortage of cousins to play with at horseshoes or huzzlecap."

"Och," Logan grunted, "but I fear fer Hannah. She's been feelin' peely wally morning, noon, and night. How can a bairn grow in her if she cannae eat?"

Jack shook his head.

They stood behind the stables, twenty paces back from a tree that couldn't take much more punishment from their axe throwing. Jack had joined Logan and Keir in their practice and was pleased to keep up with his older brothers.

Keir came walking back with all three axes. "Yers stuck the best, Logan. One more throw like that and ye'll split the old oak in two." He passed them to walk another ten paces further to where they'd marked the next throw line.

22

Jack whispered to Logan, "And no news of bairns fer Keir and Eleanor?"

Logan lifted both eyebrows and shrugged.

The three brothers attempted the greater distance, but only Keir could hit the target. They kept at it for quite a while and then switched to the sheaf toss, pitching bales of hay with their pitchforks as high as they could. Again, Keir consistently outperformed his brothers.

"Come try the caber toss, Keir," Jack said. "As ye won it last year, I was hopin' to learn yer secrets and beat ye this time."

Keir only smirked. They walked through the bailey and out the gate. Yellow stalks of grass swayed in the breeze, a pleasant complement to the far-stretching blue sky, dotted with fluffy clouds. The air was filled with the sweet scent of hay and sunshine, fertile soil and wildflowers.

Colin came running up behind them. "Are ye all practicin' for the games?" The lad was out of breath. "I've been watchin' ye from the tower, throwin' the axe and tossin' the sheaves. I saw ye headin' out here." He stopped abruptly at the caber and reached for the hammer that lay on the ground next to it. "So I ran down to show ye. I can throw the hammer." He held the ball in one hand and the handle in the other. The loop of chain hung freely between them, swaying. "Ye best stand back."

The brothers eyed one another. Jack nodded at Keir, his eyes twinkling with amusement. Logan and Keir raised their brows, a silent understanding passing between them. All three took two full strides away from Colin.

The lad took a ready stance, gripped the hammer in one hand and bounced it slightly as if feeling its weight. He took a deep breath, focused on some spot in the distance, and narrowed his eyes. He took a few steps back and the brothers did, too, not wanting to be too close when he began to twirl the weapon. He spun the hammer around above his head in a near perfect circular motion, once, twice, three times, then he released it with a grunt. The ball sailed through the air, arcing over the end of the caber and continuing on another twenty feet or more.

"Aye, the lad has style," Keir said.

"And the distance is nay doubt farther than Jack can throw," Logan teased.

Jack smirked. "Aye, then ye won't mind standin' where ye be whilst I go fetch it and throw it back this way."

23

Keir and Logan laughed. "Is that the only hammer we have at Caladh? Where's the one I used last year to win the hammer throw?"

"That be it," Jack said. He started walking, counting aloud his steps till he reached the hammer. "Twenty-two paces," he shouted. "A good throw for a lad. Colin, when ye reach the proper age ye can be on the McKelvey team."

The boy blushed and withdrew a round stone from his breeches' pocket and started rubbing it. "And can I wear a kilt? A McKelvey plaid?"

"Ye're welcome to our clan, laddie," Keir smiled at him. "Now let's see if Jack can throw it back." They all stepped off to the side and watched as Jack impressed them with a throw of nearly thirty paces.

"Well," Keir addressed both brothers, "with Logan throwin' the axe so well, and Jack equally notable with the hammer, I best do a good trick with that caber. Help me get it up, lads."

He walked along it to the narrower end.

"Now doan ye strain yerself, brother," Logan teased. "Save some strength and favor fer yer bride."

Keir furrowed his brow and pursed his lips. "Ye cannae offend me, Logan. The bairns'll come to us in the good Lord's time. Up, up with it, now."

They walked the pole to its vertical angle and Keir lifted. He took off running and when he tossed the unwieldy thing into the air, it made a cooperative rotation and landed with an earth-shaking thud.

Jack stroked the hair on his chin, took a deep breath, and said, "I saw how ye depended on yer largest muscles. Let me try."

***

"BUT FATHER," ANABEL protested, "Kilmahew Castle is far to the south, almost to Eng—"

"I willna be defied, daughter," Bram MacLeod slammed a bony fist down on the table. Both his daughter and her mother jumped. "Ye shall marry the youngest son of the Kilmahew clan and that is final. Ye're most fortunate he took a shine to ye at the Beldorney ball and dinnae ken ye were rebuffed by Keir McKelvey."

Anabel set her jaw. She remembered quite well the Kilmahews. They were rich from their devious schemes, promoting foolish gambling games among the people who worked their land, raised their crops, and tended their herds. Their servants were sad, wretched souls who thought they could rise from their poverty through betting what little they had on anything from when it would rain to who would win the tug of war at the Highland games. The Kilmahews had taken in more coin collecting debts at past games than the host clans had gained in fees.

"I ... I have bad feelings for him. I danced but once with Hamish Kilmahew at the ball. He said rude things to me. Bold, he was." She pushed her bottom lip out and threatened to pout. "I do not understand why I must marry against my will. At least the McKelvey heir had a pleasant look about him," her thoughts went to the equally handsome brother, Jack, "but Hamish is ill-favored with a monstrous nose and simple chin. I could only bare to glance at him once or twice."

Her mother put a soft hand on Bram's. "Husband, tell us, what has this Kilmahew done to deserve her hand?"

"'Tis nay what he's done, but what his clan will do if this alliance is not forged by a contracted marriage." He turned his attention back to Anabel. "It be yer duty as a daughter to obey me. I decide yer future ... and it will be so. 'Tis final."

He put his fingers around her wrist and she understood from more than the tight squeeze that there'd be no winning argument to prevent this union.

But Anabel had a plan. It sprang to mind fully developed. Her father let go of her and strode out of the room, her mother following.

She had little time to collect what she needed and she could not depend on Alpin or Will or her mother to help her. But if she could make her way unseen to the hidden castle, she was sure she could manage to live there for the time—a week? a month?—however long it took for Hamish Kilmahew to tire of waiting and pick another wife. Someone like Shona or Clara. She thought of her friend Clara and shuddered at the thought of the repulsive-looking offspring a union between two such malformed individuals might produce.

She left off thinking those thoughts and hurried to her room. The abandoned castle was her focus now. She could fix the broken bed, harvest the garden, cook her own meals. She was an excellent archer; surely she could take down a deer or at least a rabbit. She wasn't above stealing a lamb or a goat from her father's flocks either, if she became

25

desperate. She was quite happy she hadn't told a soul about the old castle. How fortunate. No one would know she'd escaped to dwell there.

Then she wondered if Jack might return. She laughed to herself; maybe he was still sitting there waiting for her. Then she thought no, he'd be too busy preparing for the Highland games. It'd bee weeks before he returned, if ever.

She bustled about her room, picking out things she'd need and then dismissing them as unnecessary. The more items she took, the harder it would be to carry them all. She wasn't a strong girl; she'd been pampered her whole life. She could sing and play the pianoforte and embroider and sew and read, but to saddle a horse or carry a bushel basket or lift a pail of water ... those were skills she'd never developed the muscles for.

A book! She definitely needed to bring a book with her. The library at the old castle—*Castle Falaichte* she was calling it in her head, because it was hidden—had but a dozen books, their pages yellowed and brittle. The only one she'd touched had threatened to crumble in her hands, the brown leather cover frayed and cracked, the pages within faded, unreadable.

She took the only book that was in her room, a translation of a Spanish tale of a knight, his horse, and his squire. Next she looked through her trunk for a comb, an old one, and laid it on the book. She'd leave her good brush and comb and hand mirror where they were. She didn't want to leave a clue that she had planned to leave. If she hoped to return without penalty or punishment, she needed to invent a story of abduction. Perhaps she should throw a few things about the room to look as if she struggled with an intruder.

Anabel's mind raced through the possibilities of what else to take. She put on a second dress over what she was wearing. That would be easier than carrying it in her arms.

What else? A book, a comb ...

On a whim she picked up a tiny vial of perfume, an expensive gift sent after Laird McKelvey visited her father last winter. She uncorked it, sniffed the heavenly scent, and dabbed her wrists. She flashed again on Jack McKelvey and tucked the perfume into a skirt pocket. There were several other bottles and vials on her dressing table; it wouldn't be missed.

A book, a comb, an extra dress … she required nothing more. Oh, perhaps a shawl and a bonnet. She threw her warmest one over her shoulders, pushed the comb into the thickest part of her hair where the maid this morning had crossed her red braids, and tied the bonnet under her chin. She snatched the book and tucked the heavy thing under her arm. She looked no different from any other morning, off to read a chapter or two under a tree in the garden.

She went down the stairs and into the kitchen. Cook was baking and offered Anabel a napkin full of hot biscuits to be her lunch. She eagerly accepted. She passed by the larder and remembered the time Keir and Logan had come for her brothers' help in searching for Princess Nora and her abductor. She had offered a hunk of cheese to Keir on the end of a knife, and though he hadn't touched her directly, she'd felt the terrible pain he was in when he took the cheese. She had dropped the knife. The memory served her now as a reminder of two things. First, she'd take a sharp knife from the many they had. She would of course need one for any food preparation she did on her own. And … it seemed most prudent to be prepared with something for defense. There were several knives in the larder; she hoped Cook didn't keep close count of every utensil. She slipped one between the pages of the book.

Second, after the men had found the princess, her brothers, Will and Alpin, had brought the abductor here. For many weeks now, the Englishman had been in the MacLeods' dungeon, as a prisoner. She'd almost forgotten about it. Will was in charge of seeing to his recovery and keeping the horrible man fed. They planned to release him eventually, winter perhaps, but Anabel wondered if unlocking his cell now and freeing the Sassenach, might not be to her advantage. Would the family not think that he'd abducted her and fled? She was, if not a princess, a noblewoman, a lady much admired and this Englishman—Captain Luxbury, was it?—might think he could insure his escape and passage through Scotland with a delicate woman such as Anabel at his side … at knife point. Yes, that would explain the missing knife.

Ah, she applauded her cleverness. She'd have to be quite careful, though, and not let this prisoner touch her. She could throw the key into his cell and hurry away up the secret stairs.

***

27

"WHAT?" JACK HAD never yelled at his father before, but he was stunned by the Laird's off-hand remark. "Father! Ye cannae be serious. Am I to only marry a betrothed cast-off of one of me brothers?"

"Aye, mayhaps," Laird McKelvey answered, his face serene and calm, Mary by his side at the long dining table. "'Tis good ye reminded me of the other. If the McDoon lass is nay to yer likin', then we'll ask MacLeod to reconsider. Anabel might be better suited to ye anyway."

"Megan McDoon or Anabel MacLeod? Those are me choices?" He had so recently seen them both that their red hair and freckled faces meshed into one memory, one woman, and he wasn't as upset as he made out to be. If only there was a woman with Megan's delightful humor and Anabel's gorgeous face, hmm, there'd be the wife for him.

"Would ye rather I speak with old Campbell? He has a daughter whose face would scare the chickens and the fox." The laird chuckled then sucked in his cheeks as Mary frowned. "Or I suppose ye think ye can marry at will as every other McKelvey." He sighed. "Och, dinnae fash. I'll let ye choose yer own bride. But let it be one with a dowry."

Jack gave Mary a thankful look. He hadn't expected his father to relent so easily or so quickly. Love was changing the laird as it had his brothers and sisters. He looked around the table. His brothers' wives, Eleanor and Hannah, were picking at the food like birds while Keir and Logan and Colin, too, were taking second helpings of the roasted lamb. Elspeth hovered near Hannah, holding a pitcher of warm goat's milk, something Hannah had requested.

The conversation turned to other subjects and Jack let his mind wander, his gaze resting on the maid. Elspeth was certainly a bonnie lass, with nary a freckle, a pert nose, and rosy lips. He could see a strand of dark hair escaping her cap and wondered why he'd never noticed the color of her hair before … or her eyes … they were brown.

There was a hush and he came to his senses, looked at the others, and realized he'd been staring and all eyes were on him now. Logan clicked his fork against his plate. "Brother, ye cannae choose jist anyone." He and Keir laughed, Elspeth's face reddened, and she set the pitcher down by Logan and hurried out of the dining room.

"The heart wants what the heart wants," Eleanor whispered.

Jack scowled. He had no idea what his heart wanted, but he knew what it didn't want: to lose to his brothers or anyone else at the Highland games. He needed to practice in private, far from his brothers' teasing. He knew exactly where he could go. He'd waited a full hour at the hidden castle, examining everything in the room Anabel had left him in, finally realizing she wasn't coming back.

And she probably never would; she'd promised not to, hadn't she? He'd take his axe, a pitchfork, the hammer, and a knapsack full of the new cook's delicious concoctions she called sandwiches.

"What are ye smirkin' aboot?" Logan's question brought him out of his deliberations.

"I shan't be practicin' alongside ye on the morrow." He glanced at his father. "I'll be huntin'. I haven't touched me bow in months and ... and ... I think I'll see if me aim is good enough fer the archery competition."

***

ANABEL RELEASED THE prisoner without thinking through her plan. She crept into the dungeon, tossed the ring of keys at the huddled body, and got out of sight an instant after he lifted his head. She panicked when she realized he'd seen her. She heard him begin trying the keys one by one. She scurried up, out, through the gates, and away from her home, heart pounding and breath heaving, until she reached the place where she always met Alpin. Had the man followed her? She hadn't looked back even once until she sat on her usual rock and listened for a pursuer. Once she was certain she was alone, she went on and made it to the castle unseen.

She pushed the massive door open with her shoulder, thankful that Logan had closed it after she left him waiting. There'd been no signs of animals nesting inside. It would have been frightful if she'd come all this way and found a critter like a squirrel or a badger, or heaven forbid, a wildcat inside. She pushed the door closed behind her and set her few things down. The door presented a different problem now that she'd decided to live here for a while. It was crucial she be wary of intruders ... and with that escaped Englishman on the loose, she felt vulnerable. She wished she hadn't liberated him. How could she secure this door? There wasn't a locking mechanism as on a treasure box or trunk—or a dungeon cell—with a keyhole and large iron key, however, by providence there was metal hardware on either side of the door to hold a bar. But where was the bar? She'd have to find a thick fallen branch to use as a bar, several, in fact, as there were various entrances.

"Candles!" she suddenly cried out. "I've forgotten candles and flint." She was furious with herself, but then she had a good reason for her forgetfulness. She'd acted much too quickly. She should have spent a few days, not minutes, planning this venture.

Oh well, she had the rest of the day to hunt through the store room, the larder, and the many places where the previous inhabitants had left things. She needed to stay calm. She could do that; there was no one to touch her and fill her with those uncomfortable feelings.

First things first. She wanted to thoroughly explore the castle, not just walk around idly daydreaming as she'd usually do. This time she kept her eyes wide, her curiosity on alert, and her steps purposeful. Her shoes echoed only slightly, her feet muted by fine dust. She entered the front room with its half circular expanse of windows, still all intact. There were several armchairs, each upholstered in faded fabrics with carvings along the arms, legs, and back. A wingback chair sat behind a rosewood desk. Two settees faced each other in front of the arched windows. She walked between them and over to the desk. She pulled out a drawer. Empty. Another drawer, however, held a stack of letters, the handwriting on them barely legible. She'd come back to those if ever she was bored. The last drawer held several oddities, artifacts from another time which were completely unfamiliar to her. Those she took out and set on top of the desk for later examination.

Anabel glanced around the room. The fireplace was grand with a mantel higher than her head. She went to it and ran a hand along it, feeling for a fire striker. She was rewarded at first with a handful of mouse droppings, but she struck a finger against something made of steel which tumbled to the hearth when she swept her fingers forward.

"Flint and steel," she said aloud, pleased with the find. She set it on the desk, then changed her mind and dropped it into a pocket in the apron dress that covered her day dress.

She moved on into the next room, the laird's room, she deemed it. It was full of decaying taxidermy, poorly preserved, and frightening. There were shields and weapons on the walls. She remembered coming in here the first time she'd discovered the castle, but she'd closed the door and never entered it again. This time she looked past the dead animals to seek out which of the weapons might be useful to her. There was a two-handled pole with an axe blade and a spike on the end. She'd seen her brothers with one; a halberd was what Alpin called it. There was also a crossbow and a quiver of bolts and quarrels, six in all; she was excited there was something here she could make use of. She reached up and lifted the crossbow down. She was familiar with its parts and she checked the lever, the rod, the nut, and the trigger. The string was miraculously still strong enough. Her adventure was starting with good luck and grand surprises.

Chapter 4

THE SITTING ROOM was silent as Megan McDoon nervously pulled needle and thread through the quilting material about to broach the subject foremost on her mind. She'd been thinking about having this conversation with her mother since she left Clara Campbell's home. Of course, she wouldn't say anything about Dylan's behavior. Her mother was devoted to Dylan and believed he could do no wrong. It was unfair, but her brothers always won their arguments over hers. she'd have to twist the facts a wee bit in order to explain how Jack McKelvey rescued her.

She pricked her finger, gasped, and stuck it in her mouth.

"Megan, dear, ye keep missin' stitches an' now ye've gone an' poked yerself. What's the matter? Pay attention to what ye're doin'." Her mother, Isobel McDoon, looked at her from under pale lashes and scowled, then continued sewing a fine running stitch to join two pieces. "Did somethin' come up at Clara's? Some news that upset ye?"

Megan's stomach doubled its knot, but she mustered the courage to speak. "By chance and happenstance, I saw ... I met ... er, I had occasion to speak with ... wi' the young McKelvey ... the lad ... er, the man Father meant to give me hand to."

Isobel lifted her head and left off stitching. "Nay, ye mustn't speak of him." She glanced at the closed door and then back at her daughter. "'Tis a great humiliation for us as how Laird McKelvey backed off. He claimed me precious Dylan took off with one of their maids and 'twould be an affront to Castle Caladh to join our houses after that." She lowered her voice to indicate the seriousness of the gossip. "An' I heard on market day that his other son, Logan, then took the same maid to wife." She shook her head in disgust and pointed at Megan with the end of her needle. "Ye'll nay be talkin' to a McKelvey, Megan, let alone marryin' one."

Megan swallowed hard and pressed on. "Mother, 'twasn't a maid, but an English maiden, companion to the princess. And ye doan understand about Dylan. Me brother was in the wrong, fer sure, but there be none so gallant and mannerly as Jack McKelvey. He ... he saved me after Dylan abandoned me ... on the way to Clara's."

"Abandoned ye? What's this? Why, Dylan was kind enough to hitch his own horse to the cart and drive ye there and back. I saw it with me own eyes."

Megan stared at her reddened finger and took another breath. She risked a slap or worse by claiming something her mother refused to believe, but she tried anyway. "Dylan did indeed unhitch his horse and gallop off when he saw a ... a stranger on the road. He left me at the mercy of the stranger." She widened her eyes and pleaded with her most honest expression. "'Twas beyond fortunate that the stranger was the kind and helpful Jack. He hitched his own horse and walked alongside it to take me all the way to Clara's. Most gentlemanly, he was." Her cheeks blushed with momentary shame as her own brazen behavior came to her—how she'd flirted with him and the thoughts she'd had.

Isobel was staring hard at her daughter. "Tell me the truth now, Megan. Did he have his way with you?"

Megan froze, the denial ready, but her lips trembled and she felt tears coming on instead. Was she about to let her mother believe a lie? Would such a lie result in disgrace or a quick marriage between her and ... oh, the tears couldn't help but spill onto the newly started quilt.

Her mother jumped to her feet spilling squares of fabric as well as needles and threads. Her jaw was set. "It'll cost us twice the amount Laird McKelvey asked for before, but elsewise ye'll be ruined. The lad'll boast of his conquest an' ye'll be worthless." She huffed and gave a final order before leaving the room. "Gather the pieces and take them with ye. Ye're confined to yer room 'til we settle this."

***

JACK MEANT TO go no further than over the hill and out of sight to practice the hammer throw or the axe, but he was thinking lonesome thoughts and let his horse, Soldier, have his head, oblivious to the fact they were heading in the general direction of the hidden castle.

His mind was on his brothers; they had acted differently all summer. First, Keir returned with his bride from their lengthy travels through England and he seemed relaxed, older somehow, happy with his new life and not particularly excited about the games. Second, Jack had been with Logan and Hannah at the beginning of summer on her quest for her real parents. That trip had culminated in a private wedding ceremony between the two with Jack as a witness, even though Logan and Hannah were already handfasted. He smiled to himself at the memory. Logan, too, had changed into a settled man, also acting older, but now with an anxious anticipation for the life growing in Hannah. No longer did Logan participate in Jack's fun: playing pranks, sneaking out, spying on village girls, racing horses, or any number of other types of mischief Jack came up with.

Soldier balked at something in the grass and Jack came out of his reverie. The horse bobbed his head, snorted, and began to back away from the movement. Soldier was clearly spooked, his nostrils flaring and his body shaking. Jack nudged his sides with his heels and clucked his tongue. Soldier dug his hooves into the ground and refused to go forward.

Jack patted the horse's shoulder and looked for the problem. The slithering movement of a snake caught his eye and he stopped fighting his horse's hesitation and turned him in another direction. They trotted off and past the turn-off that led to the loch and on to the hidden castle.

With the sun on his face and a mish-mash of birdsong in the air, he started to talk to his horse, as he was used to doing. Soldier snorted throaty answers to Jack's ruminations, but went silent and only twitched his ears when Jack began to sing. He made up his own tune to the few lines of a psalm he remembered his mother reciting.

"*I will praise the Lord,*" he sang, then repeated it changing the cadence. "*An' I will keep me eyes always on the Lord ... keep me eyes on the Lord.*" He reined Soldier to a halt. "Och, we've missed the trail to the loch."

"Which loch?" came the voice of young woman. "An' yer singin' voice is mighty fine, Master Jack."

Jack looked around, surprised to see a maid he knew off to his left. "Elspeth? What are ye doin' so far from Castle Caladh?"

Her maid's cap was not on her head and her long dark hair feathered out around her shoulders. She carried a basket in one hand and led an uncooperative lamb by a rope with the other.

"'Tis me day off an' I get to tend to me family. Did ye nay ken the Laird allows me to bring them a bit of yer bounty each season? A lamb, this summer. 'Twas a goat last spring. Most generous, he is." She smiled up at him and his heart gave an extra thump as he thought of something to say. His lack of words must have been from the surprise of seeing her in this setting, her hair down, her smile so easy, her skin flawless ... oof, he needed to mind his manners and his position. She was a servant. He was Master Jack.

"Aye," Jack finally made his tongue work, "me father is well-known for his charity. Do ye need help taking that rascal to yer farm? I can fling 'im across me saddle." He pushed the axe at his waist to the side.

"I thank ye, but we've only a few yards to go." She raised her brows and chin to use her face to point the direction out to him. Jack saw the trail leading to a modest cabin; he'd not come this way in quite a while, but he remembered now. Elspeth came from a poor family that lived between the McKelvey lands and the McDougal estate.

"Have a good visit, Elspeth. I'm off to find a place to practice me skills."

"Guid luck to ye, Master Jack. I'll be rootin' fer ye when the games begin."

She pulled the lamb harder and nearly lost her basket. Jack presumed she had some of the new cook's fresh bread in it as his nose detected the yeasty scent and his stomach responded with a growl.

"Oh, an' Master Jack, if ye were lookin' fer a loch ... the big one is on through here, but the smaller one ye passed a ways back, but I doan recommend ye swimmin' in it. Me mum says 'tis haunted as a whole family drowned in it long past ... before she was born."

Jack gave a nod and turned Soldier in that direction. He wondered if Elspeth knew of the castle hidden beyond the lake and the maze. He almost asked then bit his tongue and only looked back at her to smile. What a bonnie lass she was, always so prim and proper in the castle, bowing her head and curtsying, scampering in and out of rooms, serving them at supper, bringing fresh linens to his room and hurrying out with his dirty shirts. But out here, near her home, she was a different person. The tenseness was gone. She glowed. If his sisters put her in a fancy dress, she could pass for a young lady of their station. He could imagine her ... *nay, corral yer thoughts, ye idiot.*

He trotted on, found the deer trail to the loch, and started down the hill.

Soldier nickered.

"I hear ye. Ye're a smart horse an' ye're wonderin' why we're here as there's nay place to throw me hammer without hittin' a tree or losin' it in the water."

Soldier's head bobbed.

"Aye, 'twas in the back o' me mind all along to see if Anabel MacLeod's come back." He pulled the horse to a stop at the shore and let him drink his fill. "If I'm bein' honest wi' meself, I'd have to admit ... hmm, I'm nay better than any other fool. 'Tis her looks what be drawin' me to her as I ken she's a might pouty and too demandin' to be ... Och, where are these thoughts acomin' from, Soldier?" He pulled the horse's head up from the water and they followed the shore around to the secret trail by the rock, but this time, when they entered the maze, Jack hopped off and tied Soldier to a branch and whispered, "I'll be back fer ye. I only want to spy it out and ye might make a sound."

He walked the maze, but stopped to listen before the last turn that opened onto the bailey.

***

ANABEL WAS PLEASED with herself. She'd made progress. There were hefty logs, or rather limbs, strong and dry that she used to bar each door. She'd found a metal bar on the floor by the kitchen door; that would

36

be the door she'd make it her habit to use regularly and keep all the others barred. If she had to leave one unsecured when she went out, it would be best if it were this one, its entrance somewhat hidden by overgrown grape vines. She'd keep searching for iron keys, but as yet she hadn't found any.

Usually castles were bustling hives of activity, full of family and servants, and there'd be no need to bar any door until night fell. Anabel tried to imagine a time when these grounds might have been filled with people going about their daily lives. Perhaps merchants came with their wares, carts laden with trinkets and tools from another culture; she'd seen some strange items in the front room. Perhaps there'd been musicians employed here, their music echoing in the ballroom. It was disconcertingly quiet now.

She went out the kitchen door again, this time intent on checking the garden for carrots or potatoes. Once again outside she looked up at the tower and turrets. Might guards have patrolled the walls and kept an eye on the comings and goings of visitors or the laird's children or the laird himself? Oof, she caught a shiver. Why was it so quiet? Where were the birds this day?

She eyed the woods. She'd been there already to find the limbs she needed; she'd need to go back for firewood. The woods were dark and eerie … and too quiet. She'd rather spend time in the fields and meadows that also surrounded the castle. She looked in the other direction where horses, sheep, or cattle had once grazed. Strange, she thought, that she hadn't yet discovered a water source. Then it came to her Jack's horse had been wet yesterday. She assumed Jack had arrived through the maze; she reasoned out where the water must be.

She changed her mind about the garden and went back inside to find a bucket or pail. Somewhere beyond the maze was a creek or a loch or a stream and she meant to find it.

A heavy iron pot was hanging in the fireplace. She dirtied her hands getting the heavy thing off its hook. She wondered if she'd be able to carry it when it was full of water. Well, she'd have to.

She carried the pot to the maze and set it down, deciding she'd better master the path unencumbered first. She went in, turned right and then left and then turned around and got herself out. Puzzles were not appealing to her. She broke the silence with a groan and a mild curse.

"Ye best sit right there," she said to the pot. She walked the grounds and discovered what must have been a simpler path leading alongside the south edge of the maze and downward toward, she hoped, water. She ran down the path and quickly came to a stop at the shore of a pristine blue loch. "Well, that wasna verra much effort. I can do it ag'in." She liked how her voice sounded and repeated, "I can do it ag'in." A bird flew past, landed on a branch, and chirped. "Well, thank ye fer yer encouragement. I'll be back shortly." She turned and ran up the hill, grabbed the pot, and came back to the loch's shore.

"Hmm." She gave some thought to her dilemma. How did the servants in times past manage to dip for water and not get themselves wet or muddy?

The bird began to call out a shrill tune. "Well, if ye're the only one to see me …now doan tell a soul." She stripped down to her chemise and hiked it up to her thighs before she waded in. She had to catch the hem under her chin and hold it tight under her neck to keep it dry as she rinsed the pot several times. Then she dunked it under to fill it, caught the ends of her chemise in one hand, and hauled the pot out with the other.

She set the pot down on a flat rock and redressed, thinking ahead to the next few days and how she'd look for something to tie her clothes up out of the way before coming for water. She had a new and deeper respect for servants now and wished she'd been kinder to them … well, she would be in the future.

She huffed. By now her father might be worried about her and regretting his decision to betroth her to Hamish Kilmahew.

Nearly half of the water spilled out before Anabel made it to the castle's kitchen door. She was out of breath and sore, perspiring heavily, and too thirsty to wait another step. She dipped a cupped hand in and drank, then lugged the pot inside.

***

JACK WAS SATISFIED and rather disappointed that the silence meant no one was at the castle. He retraced his way through the maze, untied his horse and rode him along the shore. He wanted to see if there might be another path up toward the castle. He found what looked like footprints though they were so faint they might have been deer hooves. What was curious were the splotches of water that obliterated some of them. He urged his horse up the path to follow and realized what he was seeing was a trail of spilled liquid. When they reached sight of the castle, Jack noticed a round indentation where someone had rested a pail and then moved on. The ground was dry, and he saw no more prints, but he assumed there'd been a traveler or vagrant probably making use of the old castle. If Anabel had come upon such a person ... she'd be at the stranger's mercy. His heart skipped a beat as he thought of what could happen to a lass alone, especially a beautiful one like Anabel, and he kicked Soldier's sides to hurry forward.

"Hey-o! Anyone here?" He yelled it several times and circled the castle, stopping to peer at the windows and listen for a response. He noticed the garden had been dug into. *Probably a rabbit after wild carrots or a deer pawing at the roots.* He admonished himself for being concerned and confided in his horse, "I mustna worry aboot a MacLeod who can break a bed, make me laugh, and then leave me to wait fer nothin'. She'll nivver come back here, fer fear I did indeed wait."

Soldier had no answer. Jack walked him to the field, loosened the saddle, and let him graze. He paced off a distance he knew Keir could throw a hammer and then he commenced practicing until he succeeded, after fifteen tries, in making the hammer land a full pace further than he'd ever thrown it before.

He'd need a tree to aim at for his next endeavor. One of the doors into the castle might make a good target, but he'd been punished severely a few years ago, when he'd convinced Logan to throw axes with him at the thickest wooden door at Castle Caladh. It wasn't the memory of the punishment now that stopped him, but the remembrance of how disappointed his mother had been with him. She'd only lived another year after that, a year he spent bringing her flowers and feeding her whatever she could stomach.

"Och," he said aloud, "come on, Soldier. We'll go into the woods." He led the horse across the field, through the castle's bailey, and around the kitchen garden, and tied him to a moldering post. He continued on into the woods and found a rotting stump that would work well enough, wide and tall and soft. He paced off somewhat crookedly the distance he needed to practice, but that put him back near the garden. That was not a problem, except that he saw then the small footprints in the dirt and also that a square patch of the garden had been weeded. *An industrious rabbit, indeed.*

He glanced over his shoulder at the castle and felt a shiver go up his spine. Was someone watching him? He shook off the feeling, took a stance, and hurled the axe at the stump. It hit dead center.

"What did ye think o' that, Soldier?" he yelled. If anyone else heard him, there was no answer. He walked back and forth between stump and garden and threw the axe a great number of times, until he'd worked up a sheen and his muscles started cramping, especially his back. He removed his shirt and stretched, worked out the cramps, and threw the axe some more.

"Ah, Soldier, should we take a swim, ye think?" he said after his last throw. He twirled suddenly as he thought he heard a voice, but it was nothing … *just a squirrel, methinks, chattering at a bird.* He dried his face with his shirt and put it back on.

Jack went to Soldier, tightened the saddle, and mounted, forgetting the axe was still lodged in the bark of the old stump. They trotted past the maze and took the path instead. Down at the loch, he decided not to swim; a quick splash in his face was good enough. He wondered if he'd meet up with Elspeth on the ride back. He'd certainly get down and walk alongside her if she should appear. Or … should he stay upon the horse? The height would lend authority and he was one of the Laird's heirs after all. He mustn't get overly friendly with the servants, or he'd be accused of … well, he'd gotten himself into a lot of different kinds of mischief, but a dalliance with a maid had never crossed his mind. Before.

***

ANABEL LET OUT a relieved sigh once she saw Jack ride away. He'd almost caught her. When he'd yelled if anyone was there, she'd been about to light a fire under the pot of water. She ran to the kitchen door and barred it. *Oh no*, she thought, her hidden castle, *Castle Falaichte*, though isolated, was not so private with this persistent McKelvey dropping by again.

She stood by the barred door, her heart racing. *Would it be so bad if Jack found me here? Would he keep my whereabouts secret?*

She took the servants' stairs up and found a room that faced the back. She peeked out and saw him riding into the nearest field. While his back was toward the window, she dragged an old chair over, sat down and watched him practice his hammer throw. He was good, better than her brothers. Once she even jumped up and clapped her hands, a single sharp, crisp sound that echoed in the castle, but Jack didn't hear it. When he finished his practice, she raced from room to room to spot him from different windows as he made his way through the bailey. She let out an exasperated grunt when he stood in the garden, *her garden,* she thought of it now. She then ducked when he turned to face the window where she was. She waiting out of sight until she heard a grunt followed immediately by a thump. She spied on him; he'd begun a new exercise.

His axe-throwing was impressive and she smiled. She wouldn't be able to cheer him on at the real games; she had to support Will and Alpin, but …

Oh … a terrible thought came to her. *What if I have to root for a new husband? Can scrawny Hamish Kilmahew even lift an axe?*

When Jack removed his shirt, extended his arms, and expanded his chest, she shuddered. This man was far from scrawny. She watched as he threw a few more times, his arm muscles rippling. Her eyes followed him as he walked away, toward the tree, and then she enjoyed watching him come back, his chest glistening, his face proud. He threw one last time before speaking rather loudly to his horse.

"Don't forget yer axe," she murmured.

When his eyes darted toward the upper floor, she froze, but he grabbed his shirt, wiped his face, and slipped it over his head. He mounted his horse.

Her eyes flicked back to the axe in the tree stump. He was indeed going to forget it … or … maybe he intended to make this his own personal practice place. She'd have to make sure her fire was out in the morning. She couldn't have any telltale smoke alerting him, or anyone, to her presence here.

She turned away from the window as he rode out of sight. She was in the second-floor room with the portraits and the collapsed bed, and now that she'd been spying on Jack and had seen him shirtless, she felt a wee bit vindicated from the embarrassment she'd endured in this room. She studied the portrait of Jack's ancestor. Yes, he certainly had those eyes. What a handsome man he was—a masculine counterpoint to Hamish Kilmahew's lily-livered persona.

She sighed and went to the broken bed. She rolled back the top blanket and revealed a fairly dust-free quilt beneath it. The handiwork was remarkable and though the colors weren't as vibrant as they must have been at first, the intricate pattern was unique and the design harmonious. Some long-ago woman had taken much care to fit the pieces into a beautiful patchwork, adding embroidery along the edges. Anabel lifted it off the bed and carried it to the next room. She set it on a chair while she stripped this bed of its top layer, then tested the strength of the ropes. As long she didn't jump on the bed or fall on it as she had on the other one, she was confident she could sleep tonight without incident.

She checked under the bed for a chamber pot.

***

JACK WOKE TO insistent knocking on his door and a polite, but firm voice asking him to wake up and … *something* … to go … *something, something* … right away.

"I can't understand ye. What do you want? Open the door." He lifted his head and waited to see who was ordering him around this early.

The door inched open and Elspeth's cute face frowned in at him. "Sir, yer father sent me. There be an entire clan of McDoons in the courtyard and an angry father, Patrick McDoon, in the library makin' demands of the Laird."

Jack wiped his hand over his eyes and squinted at her. "Och, 'tis old news. There was a match to be made and then Dylan McDoon offended us. Remember when we were searchin' fer Hannah, and Logan brought her back all feverish? The McDoon was at fault and all plans to marry his wee sister into our clan were postponed." He flopped back onto his pillow, his brain paralyzed for a moment by how familiarly he was speaking to a servant.

"Sir?" Elspeth still spoke through the narrow gap, respecting Jack's privacy, but persisting in rousing him. "Ye must come down at once. I'm to sound the alarm and bring more McKelveys to the castle if the need arises."

Jack sat up again. "What? The alarm? How serious can this be?" He threw back the coverlet exposing bare legs and Elspeth instantly closed the door. Jack dressed as fast as he could, and adding dirk, axe, and sword to his outfit. His head was clearing fast. He thought back a couple days to when he'd helped Megan get to her friend's home. Was he in trouble for that? Perhaps they were again negotiating their nuptials. But why would Patrick McDoon be angry? It was his understanding that Megan wouldn't be of age until next summer so what was the sudden rush?

42

He tore down the stairs and slid to a stop outside the library door. He listened a moment before entering. It was suspiciously quiet. He opened the door slowly and it was as if he'd added oxygen to a fire. Both fathers shouted his name and called him forth. Laird McKelvey was standing behind his massive oak desk and Patrick had been pacing in front of it, now taking long strides toward Jack.

Jack held one hand up and the other went to rest on his sword hilt. "Greetings, Laird McDoon. What be the problem, Father?"

"Leave 'im be, McDoon. Let 'im explain. Jack, he's come with his whole clan to demand ye marry wee Megan. He claims ye had yer way with her."

Jack's eyes went wide. He stumbled through several sentence starts before getting his tongue to cooperate. "I ... we ... she ... she needed me help. I nivver touched the lass ... well ... except to help her down from the wagon." He took a step toward McDoon, one hand turned palm up to plead, but the other still close to his weapons. "She's a bonnie lass and she was alone ... on the cart path to the Campbells—"

"Aye," McDoon shouted, "so ye admit it, do ye?" He twirled to face the elder McKelvey. "As I expect ye'll have the vicar at the games to unite in matrimony as many as have been awaitin' for that occasion. We'll have Megan prepared for that day and the second bag of gold ... as agreed." He scowled at Laird McKelvey then pushed past Jack, a sharp shoulder to Jack's tense one along with a look as mean as a snarling wildcat.

Patrick McDoon marched out and Jack's eyes followed him, then he looked at his father who was now emptying a before unnoticed bag of coins, half the dowry promised. Jack sucked in air, but it wasn't enough. The games were a week away ... and he was to marry Megan McDoon on the final celebration day? His head spun.

"Father ..."

"Doan say a thing, son. We've twice what I bargained fer last spring. Megan'll make ye a fine wife and we'll have more bairns than this castle can hold. I only wish yer mother was alive to see it." He started lining up the coins in columns.

Megan ... Megan McDoon.

"Ye could do worse, ye ken," the Laird spoke softly. "I had an inquiry from Ian Campbell aboot his daughter, Clara, but I've seen the poor lass once or twice and had to look away both times. I wouldna bind ye to such a face." He looked up at Jack who stood as still as a scared rabbit. "I ken I said I wouldna force ye, but ..." He shook his head. "I saw ye sittin' wi' Megan at the weddin' feast. Ye seemed to admire the lass, and as ye've nay spoken of lovin' any other ..."

Jack's hands fell limp to his sides. "Admirin' a bonnie lass is one thing, but marryin' her is ... is ..." His mind flashed on her face and he shook his head. He took a seat and put his head in his hands. More faces flitted through his mind's eye. He'd admired lots of pretty faces. Eleanor. Hannah. Megan. Elspeth. Even Orla and Shona. And, of course, Anabel.

Anabel.

Why couldn't his father make a deal with the MacLeods instead?

Was that what he wanted? Everyone said Anabel was surly and disagreeable, but ...

"Son, 'twill be all right ... and ... if ye hadn't guessed ... yer ole father will be gettin' wedded to Mary Macfarlane on the last day of the games, too. Same as ye." His lips tilted upward, but Jack barely noticed. The Laird wiped his brow and made to stand. "Off with ye now. Ye should be practicin' yer sheaf tossin', aye?"

Jack barely nodded, but he managed to stand and walk slowly toward the door. He went out and through the bailey until he got to the gate. He could see a lion's pride of McDoon men riding away through the field where the caber lay. He threw the gate open, ignored his growling stomach, and stomped through the field, reaching the caber about the same time as the McDoon group went out of sight down the hill.

Jack grunted, worked on raising the pole by himself, sword and axe dangling inconveniently against his kilt, and balanced it against his shoulder. He threw it up and out and made it flip end over end as it should, his first time ever, and then he fell onto his backside with a howl that caught in his throat.

If he had to, he'd win every event, every purse, and replace that dowry ... and then ...

What? Ride away? Hide?

He knew the perfect place. He'd take a few things to the abandoned castle each day this week. By the time the games began, he'd have his claim on the mansion by right of adverse possession, something he'd learned of during his recent stay in England.

44

He spent the rest of the day wearing himself out with the caber toss, avoided eating supper with the others, and went to bed early.

Chapter 5

CLARA, ORLA, AND Shona sat in Megan's spacious drawing room, faces blank, hiding their disappointment that another Mc-Kelvey brother was now unavailable, but also trying to understand Megan's glum demeanor.

"Ye're actin' a wee bit silly, lookin' all sad aboot it," Orla said, her fingers tracing the top of a tea cup.

"I'd be dancin' if I were in yer shoes." Clara stood up to tap her feet and twirl. "I was hopin' me father would arrange me betrothal wi' Jack McKelvey. The fairies have blessed ye, sure enough. Ye've won the prize, Megan."

"Aye, an' we must celebrate." Shona jumped up and grabbed Megan's hand and Clara's, too, and once Orla set her cup down and stood, they danced in circles in a clumsy attempt at spontaneous joy.

Megan was first to stop and turn away. "But it's a lie," she mumbled. She lowered herself onto the divan and covered her face with her hands.

The others looked on, confused.

"What's a lie, Meg?" Clara's puckered brow made her eyes seem more beady than they already were.

"It's nay an honorable match. I let me mother think he'd … he'd deflowered me." She shook her head as the others exchanged glances and covered their own mouths with hands flung forth in shock. "'Tisn't true and Jack … he kens the truth, but Father says he admitted to it."

46

Orla gasped loudly. "Those McKelveys! And I believed them to be a noble clan. How …? Oh, it must be fer the dowry?"

"Aye." Megan chanced to meet her gaze. "'Tis doubled as me father wants us wed soon … at the games."

"But that's but days away," Shona cried out with great disappointment. "We'll have scant time to make yer dress. The games start in a week and …"

"I'm so ashamed." Megan twisted the bow on the front of her dress and kept her eyes down. "I liked Jack, but he must think me a senseless puddin' head now."

The ladies were quick with denials and gave Megan as much encouragement as they could until she stopped her fussing with her dress and relaxed her hands. "Thank ye. Ye're guid friends, ye are, but … I'm utterly mortified … I cannae wed him in front of all the clans … I'd rather die." She paused. "If ye doan see me at the games it'll be fer a desperate reason. I'll have run away."

"But where would ye go?" Clara frowned.

Orla glanced at Shona before she said, "We ken a place. There's a hidden bothan ye can spend a while in, but what of the dowry? Ye cannae lose all yer family's coin fer fear of lookin' like a fallen woman."

Megan grunted. "I must speak wi' Jack. Can ye think of a way I can properly meet him?"

***

IT WAS THE first time Anabel had ever emptied a chamber pot. She didn't exactly know what to do, where to empty it, if she should rinse it in the loch or scrub it some other way. Oh, how she missed her servants.

Finished with that disgusting chore, she spent a few moments digging in the garden for something to eat. She'd finished cook's biscuits the first day, had nothing but two small carrots and some berries yesterday, and was on the verge of giving up and returning home for want of something, anything, to fill her gnawing hunger. She'd already hunted through the store room, the larder, and the many places where the previous inhabitants had left things, but other than a pot of honey, which still tasted all right but wasn't enough to satisfy her, she hadn't found anything useful or edible.

She had no idea how to make bread. She knew it involved sacks of flour and adding water and some other mystery ingredients and then putting it all into an oven, but … ugh, why was something so simple suddenly so difficult?

She continued digging in the old garden, the scent of fresh-turned dirt filling her nose with its subtle appeal, and awakening a desire for something she couldn't quite define.

Ah! A potato! She pulled it out of the earth and brushed as much dirt off it as she could with her bare hands. She was so hungry she almost bit into it then, but stopped herself when she remembered the potato soup their cook would make. Wouldn't it be better to have a whole bowl of food instead of one measly potato? She could chop this up. She had the knife she brought. But her eye went toward the woods and she spotted Jack's axe there, just begging her to use it. She chuckled to herself and dug around the garden some more. She found another potato, a couple of carrots, and another root she wasn't sure she could identify. No matter. These seemed more than enough for a breakfast stew.

She brushed the dirt off her skirts, then went and pulled the axe off the stump. She made her way back into the castle, forgetting to bar the door behind herself, and stepped into the kitchen where yesterday's pot of water hung over a mound of tinder and broken branches. She'd tried several times the day before to light a fire and failed repeatedly.

"I gave up too soon," she said to the empty space beneath the pot. She'd begun talking aloud from lack of contact. She missed her mother, her brothers, and maybe even her father and, she hadn't realized it before, but she also missed her friends, Orla and Megan and the others. Even Clara, that wretchedly homely lass.

She looked around trying to remember where she'd seen different items. She set the vegetables on what once must have been a preparation table and searched out a ladle and some small bowls. She dipped the ladle in the loch water and poured it into a bowl. "Oh." She frowned at the color of it, then ignored her revulsion and swished the carrots and then the potato around in the water, cleaning her own fingers at the same time. Then she laid the vegetables out and took the axe in hand. "Ye probably need a wee bath, too," she talked directly to the weapon and then gave the blade a dousing.

"Now what?" She went to the fireplace and stared a moment at the wood and sticks all ready for lighting. The flint and steel weren't on the mantel, then she remembered she'd put them in her pocket last night.

"Here ye are." She pulled them out and squatted down as she'd seen her maid do many times in front of her bedroom fireplace. She closed her eyes a moment and tried to picture exactly how the gal had gone about it. She needed something else. Her eyes popped open when she thought of what was missing: dried grasses or dead leaves. Or wait! Pages from her book! She'd read at least the first twenty. Who would miss them? Now where had she left that novel?

***

JACK LOOKED EVERYWHERE for his axe before deciding he must have either dropped it along the trail or left it stuck in the tree stump at the hidden castle. He ignored the sounds of his brothers practicing behind the stable, saddled Soldier himself, and rode out quietly.

He kept an eye pealed for a dropped axe and also touched his hammer often to be sure it didn't also slip away from him. The ride to the hidden castle seemed shorter this time as Soldier learned the way and chose the easier path, avoiding the maze entirely. Soldier was intent on reaching that delicious field where his master threw the hammer and he was left free to munch and enjoy the long seedy stems of late summer grasses. But Jack pulled the reins the other way when he noticed a wisp of smoke from one of the many chimneys.

Seeing that hint of human habitation jogged Jack's memory. That last throw of the axe ... he'd thought he'd heard a voice. He'd been distracted and left without retrieving the axe.

Soldier picked his way around the garden, straining his head down, trying to nibble some greens until Jack pulled his head up with the reins. Jack could see what was so attractive to his horse. He also saw how the ground was turned over in spots; it was definitely human rather than animal involvement. He stopped Soldier, tied him to a tree and walked to the stump. The axe wasn't there; it hadn't fallen to the ground. There was only one other explanation ... easy to come to with the the clues he'd had. He stared at the castle, watched the plumes of smoke dissipate, and knew for sure. There was a squatter. Someone had beaten him out of his plan to take possession. Well, this new resident wasn't going to keep his axe.

He strode toward the castle and tried to open the door he'd come through before, but it would not succumb to his pushing. He tried another door and another. He circled the entire castle, taking what must have been twenty or thirty minutes to try to get in. He ended up back near the garden, puzzled by how locked up the castle had become.

Soldier whinnied at him and he looked over to see him nibbling at the grasses where he'd tied him. Then Jack spotted the footprints. They led to an almost-hidden entrance … and a way in … through the kitchen.

"Hey-o!" he yelled as he entered. Then, in a softer voice, barely audible he said in a sing-song tone, "Here be a friendly neighbor what left his axe in yon tree stump."

There was no answer to either his shout or his warbled clarification. He continued on into the kitchen, saw his axe on the table, and a pot bubbling over a fire. Then he heard a sound in the larder. He picked up his axe and moved to the larder door.

"I mean ye nay harm." He expected a poor peasant or a traveling trader, though now that he thought about it, there'd been no sign of horse or cart so it must be a peasant lad or perhaps a runaway. "Hello?" He pulled the door out. "Anabel?" His heart caught in his throat. The poor lass was curled on the floor, weeping, and shaking. "'Tis me. 'Tis Jack. Are ye hurt, lass?"

He hurried forth, knelt and gently gripped both shoulders.

***

ANABEL HAD HEARD the noise of someone coming in the kitchen door and panicked. She ran into the larder, huddled into the corner, certain she was breathing her last breaths. Surely the intruder would find her and slit her throat … or worse. How helpless she felt; how stupid not to have grabbed the knife, or the axe. Could she hide further? Pull this raggedy rug up over her head and disappear? She had a moment's hope that it was her father or brother coming to find her and haul her home, but they would have called her name.

There was a male voice yelling a cryptic greeting followed by what she could only describe as an evil taunt, like when she played hide-and-seek as a child and her brothers would sing out how they'd torture her when they found her.

The relief that flooded her veins when she heard Jack identify himself put her into a different state, a cross between discomfiture and exasperation. She did not want him to see her like this. Her dress was filthy, her braids undone, her face undoubtedly smudged with dirt. She flung her palms to her cheeks, covering her nose and mouth, and peeked through the tips of her fingers, hoping he wouldn't look in here. She started to sob silently, her whole body quaking. He was just behind the door; it swung open slowly and she shuddered all the more. This would be the second time he found her cowering like a poor animal, afraid of its own shadow. How dreadful.

Suddenly he was right there, down on the floor with her, grabbing her shoulders. She braced herself for the inevitable rush of feelings that skin contact would evoke. What would she sense this time? She couldn't bear any arrogance or self-importance … and if he was the least bit ill, she'd suffer such anguish and misery. It always happened.

"Did ye hear me? What's wrong?" He looked back over his shoulder then peered at her face and said, "Was it the fire? Did ye burn yerself?" His hands went down her arms and held her palms. He studied her hands, her fingers. "Ye seem fine."

She stared at her hands, now in his, and was stunned by the sensations. "I was … I was scared. Ye startled me, is all." Her tears stopped on their own, replaced by a calmed heart and several completely new feelings. Jack's touch hadn't made her feel sick or sad. She felt gentle relief, sympathy, concern … and a fluttery attraction, something more than simple charm or appeal. There was a magnetism, a pull much like temptation.

Nevertheless, she pulled her fingers out of his grasp, wiped her cheeks dry, and tried to speak. "Oh, my. I've lost me bonnet." She patted her hair down. "I must look a fright."

Jack reached for her hands again and rose, bringing her to her feet with him. It was dim, hard to see him in the empty larder. "Come," he said, but he didn't move. She hesitated to look up at him, but the tingling she got through his fingers convinced her it was safe. She lifted her chin and stared into his eyes. "Ye're right to hide," he said. "I mighta been a highwayman or … or that rascal Dylan McDoon. But ye've guid fortune today … 'tis only me, again, to continue waitin' on yer order to me … 'wait' ye said and then ye disappeared." He chuckled. "Och, dinnae fash. I've come to practice throwin' me axe." He smiled down at her, still in possession of one of her hands. "I spied it on the table. Have ye been chopping wood fer yer fire?"

Anabel let a tinkling laugh escape her lips, out with the breath she didn't know she was holding. "Aye, and I've made a stew out o' the vegetables growin' wild in yer great-grandmother's garden."

She returned the smile and realized she was doing so without any of her usual artificial cheer. She was genuinely elated. Was this what he was feeling toward her? Even while she must be looking ordinary? He dropped her hand and pushed the door wider so she could walk out first. Even without the physical contact her senses still remained full with some sort of novel expectation. Were Jack's feelings hers now? This pleasant mood? This convivial temperament?

She liked it. She liked Jack. She could be at ease around him, no fear of accidentally touching and being overwhelmed with unreasonable anger, or jealousy, or suspicion, or any of a hundred other bad humours that she had to endure when her father or Clara or the maid or a stranger chanced to touch her.

They moved to stand between the table and the fire.

"And what was that sigh fer?" Jack said, picking up his axe and inspecting the blade.

"Oh, 'tis only that I'm a might uneasy to ask ye ... to offer ye to share a meal, if ye're willin'. To ... beg forgiveness fer me bad manners afore. A peace offerin' between us, aye? Ye'll nay be poisoned, as I've only added God's own ingredients, scant though they be."

Jack eyed the pot. "I am a might hungry." He stuck the axe in his belt and picked up a bowl.

Anabel nodded, took the ladle, and dipped it in, tilted it until she'd gotten broth and vegetables, and filled Jack's bowl. Then she did another for herself and frowned. "Oh, I only found the one spoon."

"Och, dinnae fash. 'Tis a poor, unprepared Scot what doesna carry a spoon in his sporran." He opened the flap of the bag at his waist and pulled out an old silver spoon, wiggled it in his fingers, then grew solemn as he stared at it. "'Twas one o' me mum's special possessions." His eyes darted around the ancient kitchen. "There be a good chance it came from here." He held it out, moved closer to Anabel, and set it on the old table next to the spoon she found. "The design's a match, aye?"

Chapter 6

ANABEL WAS NERVOUS that a meal shared with Jack would once again show her devoid of proper manners and decorum. With coy timidity she suggested they take their bowls and spoons to another room where there was furniture to sit upon. They walked up the stone steps from the kitchen to the dining room, but passed it in favor of the sitting room that looked out onto the maze. They sat in two wooden armchairs, a short table between them, and dirty windows in front of them though the room was certainly brighter than the kitchen.

Jack held his bowl to his nose and sniffed loudly. "Och, ye've added a secret ingredient. I smell ... mm ... is it mint?"

Anabel's face fell. "Oh, my heavens, I hope I dinnae spoil it. I ken a wee bit aboot herbs and spices. I thought I was pickin' basil." She dipped her spoon in and sipped the broth. Her face puckered. "'Tis mint, indeed. I've ruined it."

Jack laughed and took a spoonful, then another, humming an approval after each swallow. "The carrots are improved by it ... mm ... most tender. The potatoes too." He continued to eat, his eyes sparkling. Anabel wished the table wasn't between them so she could touch him and know the truth of his opinion. Was he lying to save her feelings or did he mean it? She could discern a lie; her brothers had learnt that about her. If they didn't like the stew they would have spit it out and called her stupid for trying.

She tried another bite and grunted. The broth was bland when she'd tested it an hour ago; she had no salt and she'd hoped the small leaves, chopped finely with her knife, might make it better.

"I'm so sorry. You mustn't eat it." Her tongue agreed, but her stomach argued to continue.

"I'll eat it all and ye must, too." He balanced his bowl on his knees and studied her. "Have ye run away from home, Anabel?"

She froze for the moment it took to wonder if Jack had been sent to find her or if he had powers of perception that had eluded every other man she knew. She pretended to take longer to chew and swallow another spoonful of the dreadful stew.

Jack kept speaking. "Because 'twouldn't be the first time a lass has fled a command to marry. I was too young to understand at the time, but me oldest sister, Elsie, hid in the barn for a week when she thought me father was intendin' to send her off to wed the son of a laird in a northern clan."

Anabel widened her eyes. "And did it work? Did she have to marry him anyway?"

"Hah, runnin' away did indeed work. Later she chose a farmer named Charles, and they were handfasted 'til a new vicar was employed." He took another spoonful, ate it, and asked again, "So ... ye ran away, did ye?"

Anabel nodded. "Do ye ken Hamish Kilmahew?"

Jack gave her a look she couldn't decipher. If only she could touch him, she'd know his true feelings about Hamish.

"Och," he finally made a sound and set his finished stew down on the little table and twisted a bit in the chair to face her, "I ken a wee bit about the lad's clan. He ... well ... I think ye've done the right thing to run away. Ye can live here ... I'll help ye get along ... and bring ye things ye might need." His face scrunched into a more peculiar set, a small smirk forming. "I ... I have me own reasons fer keepin' this castle hidden from everyone else."

Anabel kept her voice steady. "I thank ye, Jack McKelvey. I call it *Castle Falaichte* because—"

"Aye, because 'tis hidden. I ken the old words." He grinned at her.

Anabel hadn't finished her meal, but suddenly it felt awkward to eat in front of him. *Oh. How is this even proper? Alone, unchaperoned.*

"Ye've thought of somethin' disagreeable, aye?" Jack's smile wilted into a frown. "Are ye thinkin' I should go? I've intruded long enough. I beg yer pardon, Anabel." He reached down and picked up the bowl. "I can at least wash yer bowls. I'll fetch ye more water from the loch, too."

Anabel would have clapped her hands in glee if she hadn't been cradling the bowl. How nice of him to do her this favor. "Thank ye, Jack." She stood and dared to reach one hand toward his arm, to touch him in what might be perceived as too intimate a gesture, but there was an inch of skin showing where his sleeve had fallen back. She had to know all she could about him.

Her fingers brushed his wrist and she gasped. "Oh, Jack!" She pulled her hand back. "Ye've a problem of yer own, I fear."

"Nay, 'tis nothin. A bit of family obligations, ye ken. And, o' course I'm needin' more practice at me hammer an' axe throwin'. The games are but six days away."

"Oh, I'll miss them."

***

THE LOOK ON Anabel's face when she said she'd miss the games, sent Jack's heart into a tumble. Here he was, alone, with the bonniest lass in the land, a maiden who others thought was aloof and difficult and pouty, but he saw none of that. She was brave and vulnerable and sweet and here she stood inches from him, disheveled and forlorn, hungry and no doubt embarrassed, and she'd just touched his wrist. Anabel MacLeod never touched anyone, he'd heard. The rumor was she thought herself so far above every other lass that—

"Jack? Ye're starin' at me. Have I got a rash? Am I breakin' out from the mint in the stew?"

He had the same problem she did: he'd intended to run away from an arranged marriage with Megan McDoon. Had Anabel heard of it before she herself fled from home?

"Jack?"

Her face scrunched into a curious frown, her loveliness replaced with concern.

"Och, I … nay, ye've nay got a rash." For half a second he thought to reveal his own haphazard plan to hide out here at his mother's family's castle and avoid his fate, but he held his tongue. "Allow me to carry that fer ye." He took her bowl and started out of the room. "If ye doan mind,

55

I'd like to look aboot the castle some and gaze a wee bit at me great-grandmother's portrait." He was afraid if he said anything more, she'd discern his truth. Was the lass clairvoyant?

"Ye're most welcome to. Jack, ye won't tell anyone where I am, will ye? I'm thinkin' if I can stay here past the last day of the games ... when the vicar weds all the couples ... then, maybe I can go home again."

Jack looked back at her as they took the stairs back to the kitchen. "I promise ye. I willna tell and I'll come here on the last day and stay with ye whilst all the ceremonies take place." They reached the kitchen and he set the bowls down.

"Oh, ye cannae miss the awards. I've seen ye throw the hammer and ye'll surely win. The axe as well."

"Nay, me father will collect me prizes should I win. Och. What's that burnin' stink?"

Anabel rushed to the fireplace and peered into the pot. "Oh, 'tis scorched. I dinnae think the coals would do that."

Jack watched her shudder. She was disappointed in herself, but she was not to blame. How could a lady be expected to know things best left to a cook or a maid?

"Do ye have a cloth to cover the handle? 'Twill be too hot to touch."

She shook her head. "Will me apron do?" She untied what was meant to be a fashionable skirt, folded it in two, and handed it to Jack.

He protected his hand with it and pushed the iron arm until the pot no longer hung over the heat. "Is there anythin' else I can carry water in?"

"I looked everywhere and dinnae find another pot or pail." She glanced at him with a wry smile. "'Cept fer chamber pots."

Jack didn't expect her to be funny. He laughed and they shared a moment of awkward humor.

"I've heard," Jack kept smiling, "that in the old days people would hide their things before they were routed from their palaces or castles so they could run away unhindered and return some day to all their treasures."

Anabel glanced about the room. "But where? I've looked in every cupboard."

"But have ye looked in every room? At Castle Caladh we have ... secrets ... secret passageways and secret rooms and even ..." he thought

56

better of saying it, but then he remembered how Logan had shared with Hannah the most forbidden secret about the second keep and tower, "... even a hidden tower. Perhaps we need to take a better look around."

***

JACK SUGGESTED THEY start with the room where his great-grandmother's portrait was.

"Me mum took me to that room especially. I remember it well." He glanced at Anabel as they headed upstairs. "O' course the bed was a wee might sturdier then." He was pleased to see how Anabel took his reference to her mishap. She smiled and pushed some hair out of her eyes. The lass was still quite lovely even in her present untidy and rumpled state.

They walked into the room and both stopped. At this time of day there were beams of sun rays crossing the floor and illuminating the room. Both looked toward the portraits.

"Ye have her eyes," Anabel said.

Jack nodded. "I thought I might take the old beauty back with me, hang her in me own room, but 'twould raise some questions we doan want to answer yet."

"This must've been her bedroom."

"Mayhaps. But I've been thinkin' on it and I believe this was later me mum's room as a child. It pleases me to think she had a fine childhood, raised here ... sleepin' there," he wiggled an eyebrow at Anabel, "and warmin' herself there ... and bathin' there." He walked toward the old copper tub that sat under the window. "Saints be praised. There are two water buckets ahidin' behind this tub." He picked them up to show Anabel. "I can use these to fetch ye what ye need to boil fer ... cookin' and, uh, if ye want to clean yerself." He carried the pails to the door and set them there. "Now, let us look fer a secret door."

They patted the walls that were paneled, looked under rugs that were shabby and threadbare, and pulled rickety furniture out from the walls. They found nothing and moved on to the next room. They searched every room on the first two floors. Jack grunted when he moved something large and Anabel giggled when he was startled by a trembling mouse. They discovered some well-preserved clothing items in trunks and plenty of oil lamps still full of oil, all things Anabel had come across on her

57

earlier explorations. When Anabel showed him the weapons room, he went straight for the crossbow she'd taken off the wall and left on a chair.

He spotted right away where it had hung and said, "Looks like they left in a hurry, started to take this, and then forgot it."

"Nay, 'twas I who took it from its hooks. The bolts and quarrels are still here, too." She picked up the quiver. "I thought I might shoot a deer fer supper as the lever still works."

Jack looked at her with new respect. "Ye ken the parts of a crossbow? Me sisters have no idea which is the nut and which is the trigger."

Anabel lifted a finger to point and name each part.

"Ye're a smart lass. I'm glad to get to ken ye a wee bit better, Mistress Anabel MacLeod." He acknowledged her with a formal bow, bending at the waist and sweeping an imaginary hat off his head. He noted the shy smile she gave him before she looked away to stare out the window.

Jack set the weapon down, crossed his arms, and stared out the window, too. "Ye'll nay have need to kill a deer. I see ye intend to stay here a while and I'll see to yer food supplies. I'll swipe a sack o' flour. Can ye bake bread?" Her nod was slow in coming. "Och, 'twould be a chore fer ye. We have a second cook, an English servant, once Hannah's nanny, and she'll nay refuse me a loaf each day."

"Ye'd come each day?" Her eyes showed her surprise and he was certain he saw pleasure there too.

"Aye. I need to practice me skills and I …" He almost told her of his own troubles and that he might need to hide here himself. He'd told her before that he'd come visit on the awards day when all the couples wedded. He almost told her now that he wanted to run away for the same reason she did. "Let's go outside and look around."

Anabel was willing to continue the search. It pleased him that she had a rather adventurous side to her. He unbarred the front entryway and they stepped out. There had obviously been an extensive garden surrounding the castle at one time, now overgrown and weedy, and Jack had to use his axe a few times to clear branches out of the way. Again they found no secret entrances, no hidden doors, no extra towers unaccounted for.

Jack was flummoxed. "I thought there'd at least be a dungeon or an attic."

"I have all I need. A bed, a blanket, and now some lamps. I'll be fine. I have a book to read and a garden to tend." She held out a hand to indicate she would bid him farewell.

Jack cocked his head. "Are ye dismissin' me, m'lady?" He caught her sudden intake of breath as he took her hand and bent to kiss it.

Anabel breathed loudly. "Ye've got other things to do, I'm sure. I'm most grateful fer yer help today. I doan ken how I'll repay ye."

He kept hold of her delicate hand a moment more. "A smile will do. And then I'll fetch ye that water before I go."

***

ANABEL CRADLED HER kissed hand while Jack lugged two buckets of water from the lake. She rubbed her tingling hand with the other, trying to sort her thoughts. Again she'd had an unexpected surge of feeling when he touched her and a precise impression of his very soul when his lips touched her skin. Now she wondered what it would be like if his lips kissed hers. Her heart fluttered at the thought.

Perhaps she should return home now and beg her father to reconsider a union with the McKelvey clan. She had thought herself fortunate when she'd learned of her engagement to Keir McKelvey, but a single physical connection to the man when he was hunting down the stolen princess … well, that had settled it in her mind: she had discerned Keir's love for Eleanor, resented it for a moment, then grieved not a bit for her broken engagement. While her friends commiserated over the breached promise, she considered it providential not to be betrothed to a man who loved another.

What was she thinking now? That she wanted to marry Jack? Had she lost her mind? Did a few moments with him and a mystical connection, skin on skin, mean something so significant?

She thanked him for bringing her the water and nodded when he insisted she boil it before drinking any. He promised to bring her many things on the morrow, told her to bar the doors again, and rode off smiling back at her. She'd managed to act as normally as possible, but her mind was reeling with plans. Before he returned tomorrow, she needed to bathe in the lake, do something with her hair, clean her clothes, and figure out how to scour that pot of horrible stew.

She was busy all evening, but at least she now had lamps to see her way around the dreary *Castle Falaichte*.

***

MEGAN GAPED AT the letter Orla sent her. It was a hand-drawn map, labeled with directions, but confusing nevertheless. Orla had drawn arrows and sketched trees and roads and homes, but the whole thing looked like a mesh of out-of-proportion landmarks winding past x's that represented places they knew, such as 'where the road flooded last year' or 'where the pine trees are bent.'

She'd already stuffed a sack full of things she thought she'd need in order to hide in the bothan for a while. She was anxious and excited, but she didn't want her mother to worry. She turned her attention from Orla's letter to writing one of her own. She penned a missive that made it clear she was still a virgin, that she did not wish to marry Jack under false pretenses, and that she would return, safe and sound, when the Highland games were over. She hoped she could last that long on her own.

Once she was sure everyone, family and servants, were asleep, she sneaked out and began her trek down the road to the first turn-off the map indicated. She never doubted that Orla's depiction might be off by miles, or mis-remembered, or even that the bothan might be non-existent now. She didn't question why Orla and Shona even knew of the old bothan; she simply trusted that she needed to run from her problem and all would be well in the end.

She was tired within an hour, but she trudged on. The moonlight dimmed and she started to guess at the images drawn on the map. When she came to a small loch, she set her sack down and sat with her back against it, waiting for dawn and better light to interpret the drawings.

She awoke to something crawling across her face. She brushed a spider off and leaped to her feet. The morning light bounced off the loch, tiny ripples multiplied the diamond-like reflections, and she glimpsed a deer drinking then bolting into the woods on the other side.

Megan checked the map, holding it up, and trying to make sense of what now looked to her like a child's scribblings. A sudden breeze ripped it from her fingers and sent it flying toward the water. She splashed in after it and fished it out as it sank. The ink on the sodden paper leached and spread and no matter which way she held it, it no longer made any sense. The only thing she clearly remembered was to look for a boulder, a solitary boulder near a creek. Well, this was a loch, not a stream, but perhaps Orla's drawing distorted the land. She picked up the sack and walked around the shore, her shoes wet and her spirits dampened as well.

***

ANABEL WOKE TO the sound of weeping, faint but real. It wasn't a dream. She'd managed to open the window last night, its hinges rusty but still working, to let in the fresh night air. The castle had few sounds to inspire thoughts of ghosts or intruders; this weeping must be some night creature. She imagined a rodent or rabbit nabbed by a night owl and dropped, now injured and crying.

She slipped on her shoes and wound her way through the castle, down to the kitchen, and out that way, grabbing the knife off the table for a weapon. If only Jack had left her his axe; she'd ask him today if he'd mind leaving it with her.

She stopped in the garden and listened. The crying continued, interspersed with words. Laments, they were. Real words, so it wasn't an animal. The voice was shrill. *'Tis a lass,* she thought, *perhaps a lost child.* She made her way to the maze and stood at the entrance.

"Who's there?" she called out.

"Megan McDoon," came the answer. "I'm lost and cannae find me way out."

"Come toward me voice. I'll keep callin'." Anabel walked in a short ways, afraid she, too, might get lost. She continued to call out and after quite a while Megan crept around the last bush and then ran to Anabel.

"Anabel!" She almost grabbed her into a hug, then pulled back when she saw the look on Anabel's face. Megan knew how much Anabel abhorred affection. "Where are we? What are ye doin' here?"

Anabel sighed. "Ye've found me out. I've run away from home. I swore I wouldst nivver marry Hamish Kilmahew and so I'm hidin' here 'til me father relents."

Megan laughed. "'Tis the same predicament fer me. Though I would indeed marry the handsome man me father has promised me hand to. I'll nay burden ye wi' the name of the poor lad, but I cannae bind him to me under falsity. Me father believes I've come undone at his hands, but 'tisn't true. I'm still pure as I was at birth."

Anabel frowned. "Then why are ye runnin' away?"

"Fer me honor. And fer his. He's a worthy Highlander, deservin' of choosin' his bride himself."

61

"Well, ye're welcome to stay as long as ye need. This be *Castle Falaichte*. I named the abandoned dwellin' so because 'tis hidden."

Megan looked up at the tower and turrets. Anabel followed her gaze. From out here she could see the tower that led to a spire, something not visible when she and Jack had walked closely around the perimeter. She'd have to show him. There had to be a way up that they'd missed— *oh! what would he think of Megan being here?* Another thought came to mind: perhaps she should find that tower with Megan and have her hide there when Jack came. What reason should she give Megan? She needed to think about that.

"What do ye have in yer sack?"

Megan hauled it back onto her shoulder. "Clothes and food."

"Ye have food? Praise be. I was going to have to break me fast with a raw carrot."

She helped Megan with the sack and took her into the castle.

"I've been explorin' the place. There be places to hide ourselves should someone come alookin' fer us. How did ye find it?"

Megan glanced around the first room they entered, the kitchen. "Orla sent me a map. I was lookin' fer a bothan, but I stumbled upon the maze. Who did this castle belong to?"

Anabel opened her mouth to tell of Jack's ancestors then bit her tongue. "I've found no names."

"Nothin' engraved in the mortar?"

Anabel shook her head.

Megan pointed toward the other door in the kitchen, the one to the food storage room. "Is that the larder? Someone will have left a clue there, scratched a name or a date." She dropped her sack and strode to the door, swung it open, and looked in. "'Tis too dark to see. Have ye a candle?"

Anabel thought of where Jack had set the oil lamps upstairs. She could run up and get one; she knew how to produce a spark to ignite them using a piece of flint and a steel striker, but for some reason she felt ambivalent about letting Megan take over the search of the castle. It was something she'd enjoyed doing with Jack. She simply said, "Nay, I dinnae think to bring candles."

Megan backed out of the larder. "Perhaps when the sun is higher 'twill be bright enough to have a peek."

62

Megan had more questions: how long had Anabel been here, what was this Hamish Kilmahew like, when did she think she could return? And on and on. And wasn't it awful that they'd have to miss the Highland games?

Anabel did her best to answer, but it was beginning to feel like one of the gatherings with Orla, Clara, Shona, and Megan, which she dreaded, though if she had to be isolated with one of them, she was glad it was Megan.

She kept an ear listening for Jack's return and growing more and more nervous, wondering how she'd keep Megan from learning she'd been keeping unchaperoned company with a Highlander.

Chapter 7

JACK COULD NOT think of a way to refuse. Keir and Logan insisted he come with them. They meant to gather all the clansmen to choose the team for the final contest on the last day of the games: the tug of war. The thick anchor rope had at last been brought from the coast and Keir thought it best that they have a go at working together.

Jack had several excuses, but Keir dismissed each one. "Ye're comin' with us and that's the end of it, brother. Ye can have yer secret practices in yer secret meadow this afternoon."

There were fourteen men eager to be on the McKelvey team, but they could only have seven. Keir divided them up and they competed seven against seven, rotating men, until they had a team of the strongest seven. Keir wanted all the men to plant their feet and pull together and listen to his instructions. By the time the men had finished pulling, straining muscles, and working up a sweat, Jack was exhausted. The other men rode off and his brothers went back into the castle anxious, as usual, to see their wives. Jack would have called a teasing word or two after them, but he realized he was as eager as they to see someone special. He cooled off in the pond, collected the items he promised Anabel, gathered the food stuff the new cook prepared for him, and saddled Soldier.

"Can I come and watch yer secret practice?" Colin asked as Jack led his horse out of the stable. "I've learned to ride these last few days. The Laird taught me."

64

"Then I'm sure ye're a fine horseman. He taught me, too." He stopped outside the stable door and mounted Soldier. "But … I'm nay goin' out to practice … I've … I've other business to tend to."

"Ye mean with yer intended? Me mum told me of yer betrothal … to mend relations between the clans."

Jack looked down at the lad and considered which lie would work then thought perhaps he should turn things around. He resolved in that moment that he should, indeed, go meet with his intended's father. Old Patrick McDoon wouldn't like what he had to say, but it was the honorable thing to do. His own father might disown him, but he'd also be proud he didn't just run away as he wanted to. And besides, his plan to hole up at the hidden castle could not be accomplished with a lady staying there.

"Aye, lad, I'll be off to McDoon Tower. I need to have some words with Laird McDoon and with wee Megan."

"I ken her. She was at me half-sister's weddin'. Ye sat with her." He grinned at Jack as if he knew some delicious secret. "When ye return, I'll help ye wi' the caber toss, if ye want."

Jack nodded at Colin. "Aye, 'tis a fine idea. I can make it turn end over end now, but doan tell me brothers."

Colin waved as Jack trotted off. The smile he had on his face for Colin's benefit dissolved as he reined Soldier in a new direction and headed toward the McDoon lands. He only hoped he didn't run into Dylan McDoon or he'd have a few words to say to the man. It still angered him that he let his sister, Megan, sit unattended and helpless on the road, not to mention the trouble the McKelveys had with him concerning Hannah. He tried to hang on to that feeling as he worked out a speech in his head. It wouldn't be the best plan to arrive without the backing of his brothers and at least another ten men. It was a brave thing he was doing and he knew it. The McDoon ire would be matched by his father's. There was a good chance his father would be done with him, ban him from the games, or worse, send him off to England.

He came to a fork in the road and stopped to consider again what he was doing. His courage was evaporating fast. He could go left and take his chances with ole McDoon or rein Soldier to the right and circle back toward Anabel. A deep breath and a little more fortitude and he clucked at Soldier, urging him on to the left. It would be the right and proper thing to do, to see Megan face to face.

He hadn't gone much farther before he heard the pounding of horses' hooves. Two riders were galloping toward him and one was Dylan McDoon. Jack braced himself for the encounter.

"Och," Dylan finished the shout with an epithet claiming an abominable character trait and attaching it to Jack and his entire family. "'Tis yer fault our sister has fled. Ye've a lot of nerve to show yer ugly face on our land. What? Are ye bringin' weddin' gifts?" He eyed the sack behind Jack.

"She's fled?" Jack backed Soldier up until he was standing in the weeds. Dylan and his brother, Benjamin, held the road. "What mean ye? She ran away?"

"Aye, she left a note absolvin' ye of yer carnal intent, but ye're to blame anyway. Ye McKelveys are a bad lot and we'll show ye all yer weaknesses at the games … if nay before."

The threat was reinforced by Dylan drawing a sword. For a split second Jack wondered if Soldier could outrun these McDoons. He had his dirk, his hammer, and his axe, but not his sword or his pistol. There was a sackful of things lashed onto Soldier's rump that might slow them down. *Nay, I can neither fight nor run.*

He thought back on how angry and frantic he and Logan had felt when Hannah went missing—by Dylan's ill treatment. "McDoon, we could waste our time arguin', but 'tis better spent in search of the wee lass. Put yer sword away. I'll help ye look."

It seemed his offer was suspect as Dylan scowled and raged on. "We've nay need of yer help. 'Twould be best if ye turned around and stayed away from us. Whatever gifts ye thought to bring yer bride are nay welcomed."

"Aye," his brother added. "Go on. Git!"

Jack took but an instant to evaluate the order. He squeezed his heels against Soldier's sides and turned. It didn't matter what Dylan wanted; he'd search for the lass despite his order not to. Then he had another thought: *perhaps Anabel, being a lass herself and friend to Megan, might ken where the girl would hide.*

"Come on, Soldier." He went down the right fork and on toward another path that would lead him where he wanted to be anyway.

***

MEGAN THOUGHT ANABEL was hiding something. There was more to the story than running away to avoid marriage to a stranger. That was why Megan was here, after all, so she was sure there was another secret Anabel was keeping since Anabel's behavior was off. She'd even touched Megan voluntarily once as she showed her a room Megan could sleep in.

"'Tis almost bigger than me room at home, though the floor needs scrubbin' and the furniture a good dustin'. Wouldn't Orla and the others be appalled to think we're stayin' here and without a single servant?"

"Aye." Anabel moved to the window and looked out. The long grasses, fading from their vivid green to pale yellow, were swaying in the breeze.

"What do ye see?" Megan moved to her side and Anabel grabbed her hand and pulled her away. Megan looked anyway. She noticed the field had some trampled areas as if someone had paced back and forth a few times.

"Come. The next room has a better view. Ye'll like it." Anabel led her out and into an even larger bedroom. Megan was impressed.

"Ah, it musta been lovely in its day. I did like the one with the broken bed, but this'll do." She took the quilt off the bed and gave it a shake. A shower of dust rose and settled. Both women sneezed and coughed. Megan laughed. "I shan't do that again." She expected Anabel to laugh and agree, but her friend quickly moved to the window in this room, leaned close and looked down.

"Anabel, arc ye worried aboot somethin'? Ye doan seem yerself."

"Um ... I keep a watch fer highwaymen ... and now we must be vigilant if yer brothers be followin' after ye." She frowned at Megan.

"And? There be somethin' else ye're nay tellin' me."

"Oh ... I guess I should tell ye ... I let a prisoner go ... an English soldier. I did it to hide me own escape. To make me father think he stole me." The corners of her mouth quirked upward.

"That was a canny plan," Megan said. "Ye're a shrewd one, Anabel. So ye've been keepin' watch alone. Ye musta been mighty scared, I see. 'Tis one thing to fear yer family, but quite another to worry that a Sassenach might catch ye."

67

"Aye," Anabel moved away from the window. "'Tis best if we stay away from the glass. Use yer ears. Most folks announce themselves and yell a greetin'. Then we hide."

"Where?"

Anabel shrugged her shoulders. "Under a bed. In the larder. Down into the maze."

"Oh, nay. I'll nivver set foot in that labyrinth ag'in." Megan bent to peer under the bed. "Nor will I hide in that filth. I've a mind to sneak home and bring me maid here."

"Oh, Megan, doan suggest such a thing. I'll sweep it out fer ye. And should anyone show up, I'll bar ye in the larder and then I'll hide in a cupboard."

Megan nodded. This was a different Anabel than she knew before, but then the poor thing had been alone here for a few days, it was no wonder that she acted differently. But to offer to do a servant's chore? Unthinkable. The nights must have been terrifying; she's lost her mind. And as for releasing a prisoner from the MacLeod dungeon, well, that was the bravest thing she'd ever heard of a lass doing, but also quite unlike faint-hearted Anabel. Megan did, however, have more respect for Anabel now, especially since she'd touched her in a friendly manner, been so hospitable, and dropped the arrogant manner she was famous for.

"Shall we have a lunch? I'm happy to share what I brought." Megan smiled at Anabel.

***

"HEY-OH!" JACK YELLED as he came up the back path. He was watchful for signs that anyone else had been here since he left. He remembered a time several years past when Logan and Keir bragged to him that they were old enough and brave enough to spend the night alone in the ruins of Strathnaver Castle. They dared him to come along, claiming that at eleven he was old enough, too. It was a dare he accepted and regretted when, as soon as he dismounted, Logan grabbed the reins and the two older brothers trotted off with his horse and left him alone. A night by himself in an undoubtedly haunted castle loomed before him and, once the sun set, he staved off anger and tears by singing songs his mother taught him. Logan and Keir did come back for him a mere hour past dark. All three received lashings from the Laird upon returning home so late.

He chuckled to himself now remembering that time as he rode up to this abandoned castle, haunted now by none other than the exquisite Anabel MacLeod. Anabel was certainly braver than a young lad to stay here alone. He tethered Soldier to a tree near the garden and untied the sack of food. It was early afternoon. He hoped Anabel hadn't fainted from hunger having to wait this long for his return.

"Hey-oh!" he yelled again.

He started toward the kitchen doorway, knowing she'd have all the others barred, and gave a third holler. He cradled the sack in one arm and ran his fingers through his hair, then touched his beard—*och, I must remember to shave meself before the morrow's visit.*

Before he reached it, the door opened and Anabel appeared. Her cheeks were rosy, as if she'd scurried down from on high, but her dress looked clean, and her hair was properly styled though she wore no cap or bonnet.

"Greetings, Mistress MacLeod." Jack grinned. "I've brought ye what I promised. Ye shan't starve. I'm only sorry I took so long. Me brothers—"

"'Tis all right, Jack." She hurried forth, touched his free arm, and turned him back toward the garden.

"Why be ye whisperin'?"

"Oh, Jack, ye'll nivver guess." Her voice was still low and she glanced back at the castle. "I've a visitor."

"Megan McDoon?"

"However did ye guess?" She stopped a few feet from Soldier. "She's runnin' away, as I am, from an arranged marriage she cannae abide."

"I ken. I came upon her brothers on the way. I ... uh ... I said I'd help look fer the lass as it's ..." he was about to say it was his responsibility, but it seemed Megan hadn't revealed the groom to be Jack himself, "as it's dangerous fer a lass to wander these parts." He breathed out, searching her face, and wondering what she'd think if she knew his part in the story. "Anabel ... I've somethin' I must tell ye."

69

She looked up at him, her eyes wide and questioning, her face like a jewel, her whole countenance sparkling. "Yes, Jack, what is it?" Her fingers, still on his arm, slipped toward the skin on the back of his hand.

He sighed. "'Tis I."

"I doan understand."

"Did Megan nay tell ye who her betrothed is?" She shook her head. "'Tis I."

He watched her face fall and then she said, "Is she daft? Why wouldn't she want ye?"

He tried his hardest to read her expression; she still had a finger on his knuckle. "There was a misunderstandin' I suppose. She's a bonnie lass, but I ..." he looked deeper into her eyes "and you ..." *Och, 'tis the wrong moment, but...* He dropped the sack and put his hands on Anabel's shoulders, bent his head to hers, and found her lips. His eyes closed, but he could see her lovely face in his mind, see those enchanting lips now pressed so perfectly against his own. So soft and warm and willing. He pulled her more tightly to him, careful not to crush her. He felt her fingers on the back of his neck, moving up into his hair then back down to the skin at his nape.

***

ANABEL HAD NEVER been kissed before, of course, though she had caught her brothers kissing the maids and wondered what it would be like.

She never imagined this. It was doubly pleasant as she not only thrilled to the special warmth and excitement in Jack's lips upon hers, but felt as well his pleasure and desire. Jack McKelvey held her firmly, but with a gentle suggestion of something more complicated than plain adoration. Her senses sored. His hands felt so powerful and yet he held her as if she were quite fragile. She pushed her fingers up into his thick hair, felt the curls, but lost that extra sense she had of how he perceived her. She closed her eyes tighter and concentrated on their lips. She slid her fingers back to his neck and knew what he was thinking. This was heavenly bliss. She delighted in all her senses and his too.

And then he broke it off; he let go of her and she of him.

"I'm most sorry, Anabel. I doan ken what came over me. Ye must think me a horrible rake to take advantage of ye thus."

She held his gaze and smiled. "Nay. I feel the same as ye do, Jack." Then she dropped her eyes and shook her head. "I cannae believe we did that, both betrothed to others, and yer intended nay thirty feet away." She looked over her shoulder. "And locked in the larder."

Jack raised his brows and Anabel went on to explain. "'Twas our plan. If anyone showed up, she was to hide in the larder, and I in a cupboard, but I kent 'twas ye who hollered and so I barred her in as well. I dinnae want her to see ye."

Jack picked up the sack. "Well, ye cannae keep her locked up like a prisoner. We best let her out and I must take her home."

***

ANABEL WATCHED JACK pull the log away from where she'd wedged the larder shut. He pulled the door open and Anabel stood close and said, "It's all right, Megan, it's —" but then she gasped. The larder was empty.

"There!" Jack exclaimed. "She found what we missed." The threadbare rug on the floor was crumpled back a bit. Jack lifted an edge with the toe of his boot and pushed it back all the way. "See? A trap door. She must have gone down far enough to grab the edge of the rug and throw it forward. Me brothers taught me how to do it. We've a secret passage at Castle Caladh, covered by a fine rug."

Anabel stared. "I should have thought of it. We've a second way to our dungeon, too. I used it when I released Captain Luxbury." She felt Jack's eyes on her and knew she'd have to explain that later. "Go ahead, Jack, open it."

He raised the boards and peered down the steps. "'Tis dark as a mink's back. She dinnae have a candle?"

"She took the oil lamp I'd just shown her how to light. I thought she'd put it out once I closed the door."

"She musta looked under the rug and thought it a better choice to escape and leave ye to the stranger." He smiled at her. "I'm honored to be the stranger."

Anabel blushed. "I'll get another lamp. Who kens how far this tunnel goes."

Once lit, Jack took it and started down the steps. He reached back to take Anabel's hand.

Cool, dank air enveloped Anabel, first at her ankles, then, as she reached the bottom step the chill reached her cheeks, relieving the heat the recent kiss put there. She called out for Megan and was met with an echo of her own voice and then a faint reply from Megan.

"It sounded like she said she's hurt." Anabel peered around the space obviously used as cold storage for food. Jack lifted the lantern and walked forward toward two dark openings.

"There are two tunnels. Which one might she ataken?" Jack said. He motioned to Anabel to join him. They took the left one and found a room full of the treasures they'd been hunting for: several barrels of very old whiskey, a stack of leather-bound tomes, a trunk of fine silks, dozens of silver spoons and candlesticks, and a box of jewels.

Anabel wondered if the sparkle in Jack's eye was lust for wealth. He seemed to have forgotten about Megan for a moment. He could certainly claim the treasure all for himself. By rights, it was his and his brothers'. She put her hand on his wrist as if to help him lower the lantern to see better, but her intention was to discern his heart. She felt no covetous greed on his part, only incredulity.

"Be ye amazed, Jack? Did ye ken yer ancestors were so wealthy?" She kept her hand on his.

He shook his head and whispered, "They shoulda hidden it better. They musta believed they'd return soon enough and not be gone fer decades. Well, 'tis yers now. Ye're the one who lives here." He glanced at her. "Come now. Holler again fer Megan. I doan want to scare her with me deep voice and put more fear in her heart."

Anabel called out and they left the treasure room to follow Megan's cries down the other passageway. Jack had to crouch a bit as the tunnel ceiling was low and narrow too; he could have touched both sides at once. The passage wound back and forth much like the maze behind the castle; Anabel deduced they were heading downward and toward to loch. Mostly the ground was damp, but not muddy, and there was a considerable number of stones crushed into the earth. Then, at one turn, their lamp shone on bits of broken lamp and darker smudges of ash before revealing Megan leaning against the rock wall.

"Careful," Megan warned, "I tripped on the pebbles and dropped the lamp. It broke and the oil flamed up and burned out. I was in a black hell of blindness 'til ye came." She wiped her eyes and exclaimed, "Oh, 'tis

Jack. How … why …?" She stared as they stepped over the mess and came to her.

Jack handed the lamp to Anabel and bent to Megan. "Can ye stand, lass?" He held a hand out and Megan promptly took it, but fell back as she tried to stand.

"I twisted me ankle when I fell."

"Here." Jack scooped her up, leaned forward, and awkwardly carried her in a back-straining effort to keep from scraping his head.

"I thought," Megan spoke to Anabel's back as she led them out, "that there might be a way out and if I followed the tunnel to its end I could escape and get ye help, Anabel. I wasn't leavin' ye."

"Och," Jack grunted, "ye did right, wee Megan. I'm sure the tunnel was me family's route to safety. I ken jist the rock they musta pushed to cover the entrance at the loch's shore. Ye wouldn't've been able to move it though."

"Yer family?" Megan's voice had a whine to it. No doubt, Anabel thought, she's holding back her cries of pain.

"I'll explain once we get ye up the steps." Jack straightened as they came into the cold storage room.

They were met with the sounds of male voices in the castle rooms above.

Jack whispered, "I'll see who's here. Ye may have to blow out the flame if ye hear me stompin' above."

He set Megan carefully on the second step.

"If it's me father and brothers, please doan tell them I'm here," Megan begged.

Jack nodded and went up. Anabel watched him close the trap door and heard the soft thump of an old rug dropping across it. She looked at Megan and frowned in sympathy at the painful expression on Megan's face.

Megan rubbed her ankle and scrunched her face further. "Anabel, why were ye with Jack McKelvey?"

***

JACK DROPPED THE rug in place as louder shouts echoed through the castle and reached his ears.

"We've seen yer horse, McKelvey. We followed yer prints here. Where be ye hidin'?"

Jack recognized the voice. He stepped out of the larder the same moment Dylan McDoon appeared in the kitchen.

"Aha! Hidin' in the larder, were ye? Like a lad of three."

Jack huffed a laugh and responded. "Me fine upbringin' means I'm honor bound to help ye in the search fer yer sister."

"Search, be it?" Dylan drew his sword. "Are ye keepin' her here ag'inst her will? We found ladies' things on a bed upstairs. A verra messy bed. And long red hairs!" His lips went white as he pressed them together and his face countered with scarlet rage.

Jack didn't have his sword, but the axe was in his hand before he thought it out, a scene from his past jumped through his thoughts: an axe fight in a Scottish pub with his brother, Logan, and friend Dougal. Dougal had his arm slashed. Jack resolved not to inflict such a wound on a McDoon, no matter how unreasonable either one was.

"I'll nay fight ye, McDoon, but I'll defend meself and ye may get more than a scratch."

Another man came stumbling down the back stairs and into the room. He joined the argument. "Our sister's honor … ye stole it, no matter what she may say." It was the other brother, Benjamin, and he drew his sword as well. Jack backed up against the hearth.

"Benjamin," Jack began, "yer sister's well-bein' is the most important thing. Show me the room ye found her things in." Jack scanned the kitchen for another weapon, but there nothing but the stew pot behind him. It gave him an idea though. Swinging the iron pot might knock the sword from at least one of the brothers.

"Ye ken which room. Why, it looks like ye have a harem hidden here. Smells like women. Combs and bonnets." Dylan eyed the sack on the table and swiped his sword along its edge. Sugar and flour spilled out from the tears and several baked goods. Dylan stabbed a bun. "Aha! And I thought ye were bringin' dear Meg betrothal gifts. Ye've enough here to feed her fer a week."

"Ye're mistaken, McDoon. The food is … this castle belonged to me great-grandparents. I'm takin' back possession of it and I brought provisions to establish meself here."

Dylan glanced at his brother.

"If we find Megan here, we best find that ye've been handfasted to her or there'll be hell to pay. Megan! Come out, lass!"

All three men stood still, listening, two swords quivering, one axe steady.

Dylan tried again. "Come out and we'll nay tell our father of yer sordid indiscretion. Do ye hear me? Megan!"

There was a thump and all eyes went to the larder.

Anabel appeared.

Jack immediately stepped to her side. "Lass," he said, "ye should've stayed in the larder."

Anabel pulled a face at Jack, then turned to the McDoons and flashed them a most contrite expression. "Gentlemen, please. Ye'll nay find Megan in the castle. The comb, the hairs, the mess … are all mine."

Dylan stared. "Anabel. Mistress MacLeod, I mean. How did ye come to be here? Did this rogue kidnap ye?"

Jack cursed. "Ye ken I wouldna do that. I thought wee Megan might be here or that Anabel might think of where to look."

"Of course he dinnae do such a contemptible thing. Jack McKelvey is an honorable man." Anabel looked down at her feet for a moment then searched the McDoons' faces. "Please, I beg ye to keep me secret. McKelvey here has been aidin' me. I've run away to forestall a match between me and Hamish Kilmahew. Do ye ken the rude dog?"

Benjamin's face crumpled with sympathy. "'Tis a travesty, m'lady, that a pimple-faced skeleton of a lad be wed to a magnificent beauty such as ye. Aye, I'll keep yer secret." He sheathed his sword.

Dylan glared at him and they exchanged a silent argument. Dylan lowered his weapon and spoke. "Mistress MacLeod, would ye be open to a pledge with a McDoon? I'd fight me own brother here fer yer hand."

"Aye," Benjamin chimed in, "I accept the challenge." He put his hand back on the hilt.

"Gentlemen," Anabel smiled at them while Jack held his breath, "I'm most flattered. A duel willna be necessary. I'll make me choice after the games, if that be to yer likin'." She fluttered her lashes and held a hand out to each of them. Dylan took the right and Benjamin the left, each bending to bow and kiss her knuckles and promise aloud that they'd neither tell of her whereabouts nor speak of the hidden castle and Jack's presence.

"All right then," Anabel withdrew her hands and looked up at Jack, "I think we can trust them to nay tell a soul about this hidden castle. Now,

75

off with ye … all. Ye must find me good friend Megan afore that awful English soldier finds her. Did ye hear? The captain, that me brothers Will and Alpin captured and imprisoned, has escaped."

Jack slipped his axe back into his belt and restrained himself from smiling at the tale Anabel was spinning. The lass was a wonder. He was enjoying her even at this tense and worried stand-off with the McDoons.

Dylan's growl was less threatening, directed again at Jack, as he said, "I'll expect ye to bring our Megan home if ye cross paths with her. Yer brother Logan stole me horse and I willna have ye stealin' me sister. I'm goin' to insist me father break the pledge he made with ye."

Jack nodded and resisted saying that Logan won the horse fairly; he was much too thankful for Dylan's word to end his betrothal. He smothered his grateful smile with a more somber and regretful frown, to let Dylan think he'd upset and wounded him.

"I'll ride with ye now and search to the north. Did the lass take a horse or is she walkin'?"

Chapter 8

O H, YE'RE BACK so soon." Anabel beamed at Jack over the head of a weeping Megan, then her face resumed a sympathetic frown as she rested a hand on Megan's shoulder. "She had to lean on me to hop up the hidden steps. I dragged a chair over and ... oh, the poor thing."

"I beg yer forgiveness, but I had to get them away. I led them out in such a way they'll nivver find their way back. Then the McDoons split off south and west and I circled back here." He paced around the table grinding his teeth and avoiding looking at Megan. "Arguin' and cussin' and spittin' vile oaths, they were. Tryin' to get me to fight them. Well, to fight Dylan. He's a nasty lad. I'm sorry to say it, Megan," he stopped and looked at her, "but he is." He looked at Anabel and said, " 'Twas marvelous all ye said to them. Charmed them, ye did."

"Are ye sure they willna find the way back?" Anabel scowled. "I doan need either brother acomin' courtin'."

"Aye, there be dark clouds promisin' to turn prints to puddles."

Megan had stopped her mewling as he spoke and now asked for an explanation. They recited the words they'd had with Benjamin and Dylan while she was beneath the larder and couldn't hear, and told her why Jack went with them to pretend to search for her.

"Yer brother vowed to have our betrothal broken," Jack said. "So I think ye can return home, if ye wish. Ye can think on it a day or so."

77

Anabel shook her head. "How can she go back? She cannae stand or walk."

Jack knelt and asked, "Megan, may I touch yer leg? I have some skill with the horses. I might ken if it be broken or jist sprained."

She lifted her skirt a couple inches. Jack slipped off her shoe and ran his fingers around the ankle bone. He touched and tapped and as she made no screams nor jerked her foot out of his grasp, he pronounced it a sprain. "Ye must stay off it fer a few days. But I'm certain 'tisn't broken. Ye'll be fine."

"Thank ye, Jack," Megan squeaked out. "Can ye help me to me room? I can hop a bit."

Jack glanced at Anabel then rose. "Nay, I shan't make ye hop. I'll carry ye. Ye're a light load."

Once installed in the dusty room, Anabel promised to come right back with food and drink.

"I'm afraid some of it is ruined. Yer brother slit the sacks with his sword," Jack said.

"Oh, we have some of Megan's food left. I'll bring her that." Anabel glanced between Jack and Megan and caught a slight hand movement from Megan, signaling her to come closer. Anabel told Jack she'd join him downstairs in a moment and moved to Megan's side as he left the room. "What is it? Did ye need the chamber pot?"

"Nay, I only wanted to learn yer feelin's."

"Me feelin's?"

"Would ye really wed one o' me brothers?"

Anabel laughed. "I dinnae mean to deceive them, I only said I'd make me choice after the games. Me choice may be to run farther away."

"Me brother Benjamin would make ye a fine husband. Far better than Hamish Kilmahew."

Anabel stared at Megan a moment, debating what else she should say. The kiss she'd shared with Jack was high on her mind and she was anxious to be near him, alone with him, again.

"Doan ye think he'd be better than Hamish?" Megan prodded again.

"Surely." Anabel focused on Megan instead of her amorous thoughts. "As would any Scot, I fear. And what about ye, Megan? Now that I ken ye ran away from weddin' a McKelvey I'm flummoxed as to why. There's nary a man in the land Jack's equal." She bit her lip and held her breath, moved closer yet and sat on the bed near Megan's side. She took Megan's hand in hers hoping to read her thoughts.

Megan squeezed her fingers and spoke in a whisper, as if Jack might be listening outside the door.

"I get all dizzy around him. He carried me here and I wished we had farther to go. It awakened somethin' in me." She sighed and stared at her ankle. "I'm glad of the sprain. He touched me and though it hurt, I would've borne worse pain to have his fingers on me flesh." She sighed and wriggled her fingers free of Anabel's. "Am I a fallen woman to speak so?"

Anabel gulped and shook her head.

Megan went on. "'Tisn't fair that ye're betrothed to Hamish and I to Jack. Ye're the fairer one. I ken what folks say o' me ... that I'm—"

"Nay, Megan, ye mustn't think such things. Ye're a bonnie lass. That's what everyone says." Anabel slipped off the bed and stood.

"But ... I'm verra confused now." Megan clenched her jaw. "I doan ken the right thing to do. If what ye told me is true, me brother will convince me father to break the pledge ... and then perhaps I shall go to a nunnery."

There was a moment of silence and Anabel went to the window. "Ye cannae see Jack practice from this room. I've watched him from the other windows. As I told ye under the larder, he comes to practice here. He'll surely win at several contests."

"And he nivver kent ye were hidin' here and watchin'?"

Anabel turned from the window and clasped both hands in front of her. "Megan. I must tell ye somethin'."

There was a longer pause as Megan twisted to see her and winced when her foot moved.

"He ... Jack ... he kissed me."

***

MEGAN PONDERED THINGS while Anabel went to fetch her some water and food. She was stunned at first, had held her tongue and stared at Anabel until she turned and left. Then the anger welled up. To learn that her betrothed—she'd think of Jack that way for as long as it was still true—had kissed another woman, made her want to tear out every red hair on Anabel's head. The woman was a harlot, always so haughty and arrogant while all the men in the county adored her for her beauty and wealth. Anabel had never fit in with Shona and Clara and Orla and her. She proved it every time she missed one of their gatherings and now Megan knew why: the lusty sinner had come here to hide from them and probably meet other admirers besides Jack.

She hit the mattress with a fist and made her leg jiggle. A sting shot up from her ankle and her anger was replaced by pain. As the discomfort faded so did her ire. She wasn't being reasonable. A single kiss didn't make Anabel a harlot. She should direct her resentment at Jack instead. Anabel had helped her and been nothing but kind and considerate yesterday and today. The fact that Anabel had hidden here and spied on Jack's practices didn't make her a Jezebel. And besides, Anabel had confessed the trespass. Had said it was Jack who kissed her.

Megan breathed in and blew air out through parted lips and clenched teeth.

She might forgive Anabel. But not Jack, no matter what.

Oh, this pain. Her ankle kept throbbing.

Uh. It was taking Anabel quite a while to fetch the food. Megan imagined Anabel down in the kitchen with Jack. What might they be doing? Making plans to run off together? It wasn't inconceivable. The mere thought was getting her dander up again ... and relieving the pain.

Earlier, when Megan and Anabel were hiding alone under the larder, she had asked Anabel why Jack McKelvey was there. Anabel had answered quite briefly that Jack came to practice his axe throwing and then she'd changed the subject, gone on at length to describe the treasures they'd found while searching for Megan.

Treasure. They had treasure enough to buy passage to America if they wanted to.

Uh. She laid her head back down and closed her eyes. She wasn't being fair vacillating between opinions, but the pain definitely lessened when she focused her anger on them.

***

ANABEL TOOK A deep breath as she stopped on the last step. She could hear Jack down in the kitchen, whistling. Why was he whistling? Men only whistled when they were happy; women not at all.

She straightened her spine and pulled a cap out of her skirt pocket. She hoped covering her head would make her seem more ... more what? Dignified? Untouchable?

She started for the back stairs and tried to keep from thinking about Jack's lips.

"What are ye doin'?" she said when she saw him squatting down by the table and scooping flour into his hands.

"Tryin' to salvage some of this mess, if ye wanted to bake bread." He rose and added another two handfuls of flour to a large bowl he'd brought. "That McDoon spoiled a little of what I brought ye, but I can replace it on the morrow. I pilfered some bowls and things from Caladh." He opened the sack the rest of the way and pulled out several things.

Anabel took a step closer and picked up a wooden plate. She looked at the buns and muffins and picked two to place on the plate. "I'll take these up to Megan."

"Wait."

"Ye must go, Jack. Go do yer practicin' and then get yerself back to Castle Caladh."

Jack looked at his hands, clapped the white dust off them, and held them out palms up. "Please wait."

"I told her, Jack. I told Megan that ye kissed me. She deserves to ken the truth. She's still yer betrothed."

She felt his eyes on her; she felt her cheeks growing hot; she felt that prickly emotion dividing her thoughts. Right. Wrong. She wasn't sure she knew the difference right now.

She raised her eyes.

They locked with his.

"I understand," he whispered. "I'll practice me throwin' and then be off. Is it all right if I come back tonight? I feel as though someone should guard ye lasses."

"Ye said ye confused the McDoons when ye led them away and they would nivver find their way here again ..."

"Aye, but I cannae promise it ... and there are twice the searchers out now, lookin' fer ye and Megan. One could stumble upon it. See yer smoke. Or yer lamps."

Anabel looked at the cold hearth and then the table with the flour and then at the plate in her hands. A hint of the bun's flavor reached her nose. "All right, Jack McKelvey. 'Tis neither proper if ye stay nor proper if we be alone here. I would feel safer with ye here, now that I've been so close to the McDoon brothers." She thought of the feelings that passed through

81

their hands to hers when she tested their intent. One had seemed honest enough in promising to keep her whereabouts secret, but the other had a duplicitous spirit. "Ye may come back, but ye'll need to camp by the garden. I'll nay have Megan believin' there be somethin' untoward between us."

She turned to go up, then looked back at him. "I heard ye tell the brothers ye were takin' back possession of this castle as it belonged to yer great-grandparents. I doan think ye can trust them to hold onto that secret, if secret ye want it to be."

Jack nodded. "I would like to keep *Castle Falaichte* a secret place as long as I can."

"Ye've decided to name it thus?"

"Aye, yer name fer it stuck with me. 'Tis perfect fer many reasons."

She went up one step, pleased with his response, then stopped again. "Because the castle is hidden? And the treasure too?"

He pressed a still floury hand to his chest and patted his heart. "And other things as well."

***

DYLAN MCDOON ARRIVED home at dark. Benjamin was already there, mucking out the stall their stable hand hadn't done, since he too was enlisted in the search for young Megan.

"The lass has nay been found. Most of the searchers have returned, and," Benjamin grumbled as Dylan dismounted, "and we need to talk."

"Aye, poor Meg may be gone fer guid, I fear. I rode to the Campbells and that unsightly Clara swore she dinnae ken where Meg might be." Dylan unsaddled his horse and let him out into the pasture. "And what do we need to talk about?"

"Anabel MacLeod, o' course. Ye said ye'd fight me fer her hand." Benjamin stood, stance wide, hands on his hips just below the sporran that was tied to his kilt's green belt. "I say fight me here and now as I plan to go back to that abandoned castle and—"

Dylan swung his fist hard and fast. He connected with his brother's jaw, sending Benjamin back and down. The stable was dark, but not so dark that Dylan didn't see his brother's eyes rolling to their whites and then closing. He stood over Benjamin until he woke, then said, "There. We fought. I won. Ye can have the hideous Clara Campbell, but Anabel MacLeod will be mine if I have to end Hamish Kilmahew's life meself."

82

"Nay." Benjamin raised himself onto one elbow and rubbed his chin. "'Twasn't a fair fight. Nevertheless, I feel obliged to help ye destroy Hamish—" He raised an arm for Dylan to help him up. Dylan clasped his hand and pulled. "We'll do away with the scraggy pup and then," he held onto Dylan longer than he needed to, "we'll finish this fight and *I'll* win the lass."

"Doan count on it unless ye get some help from the fairies ... but ... I was thinkin' as I searched ... loser should get somethin' too. I'm nay sayin' I'll be the loser, but ... I was thinkin' on that castle. McKelvey claimed it belonged to his ancestors," Dylan crossed his arms, "but I jist might find a parchment that says otherwise." He raised his brows and snickered. "I ken how to swirl a quill in the ink as well as any scribe."

The sound of hoof beats drew their attention and the stable boy came into the barn leading a horse that looked to have been ridden hard.

"Masters," he said as soon as he saw them, "I've news. There be another lass missin'. I crossed paths with Alpin MacLeod. He claims his sister was abducted by an Englishman, a captain what escaped from their dungeon." He tied the horse to an iron ring and started to unsaddle it.

Dylan smirked at Benjamin who returned the look.

"Be they offerin' a reward?" Dylan reached a hand up to stroke the horse's muzzle.

"Aye, 'tis a good sum. But mayhaps the soldier stole Mistress Megan, too. With yer permission, I'll rub down this mount and saddle up a new one and search all night. Ye must be sick with worry for yer sister."

Benjamin nudged Dylan, their fight forgotten, and then answered the lad. "Aye, we be frightfully worried fer the lass. The Englishman should be headed south." He lifted a hand to point in that direction. "Ye be sure to keep yer mount's nose headed toward England, aye? And if ye earn the reward, we'll be takin' a fair cut."

"Aye, o' course, sir."

The brothers walked out of the stable in step and headed to a spot where they could speak more privately.

"A reward fer findin' Mistress Anabel, is it?" Benjamin chuckled. "And we ken where she be. I'll ... we'll fetch her tomorrow, collect the gold, and insist on a union between clans. Let the lass choose between us. Hamish Kilmahew be damned."

Dylan shook his head. "Nay, 'tis too soon. Ole Bram MacLeod'll raise the reward the longer she's missin'. I say we let her stay in her hidey-hole. You did promise her ye'd keep her secret."

Benjamin frowned. "Aye, I did. But what aboot McKelvey? He could claim the reward."

Dylan grunted. "Hmph. Did ye see how he protected her? He'll nay say a word 'til after the games. And besides ... I think a well-aimed axe might eliminate him from the contests ... permanently."

Chapter 9

"ANABEL! ANABEL!" MEGAN'S urgent whisper was hoarse and growing louder as she put her good foot on the floor and then hopped to the door, keeping her sprained ankle up.

Anabel came rushing to the doorway and Megan grabbed her to stay upright.

"What's wrong?"

"There's someone or something outside, walking around the bushes. I could hear him ... or it."

"It's probably jist Jack. He promised to come back and guard us all night."

"He did? Are ye sure 'tis him. Can ye see?"

Anabel helped her back to bed and assured her, "I'll look from every window, but the doors are barred. No one can get in." She handed her the quilt that had crumpled to the floor and left the room.

Anabel went to her window first then the others on the second floor. She saw and heard nothing. From the first-floor library window she could see a horse tied, but wasn't certain if it was Jack's or not. Then she heard a thump from below in the lower area where the kitchen was. She descended the stairs cautiously, glad to make out the shape of Jack's axe on the table. There was only a faint bit of light coming in the upper window there, but it was enough to find her way quietly to the door, retrieving the axe on the way.

She stood a few feet from the barred entrance. She couldn't very well offer a clue to her presence by calling his name, for it may not be Jack. But how was she to know if he was there or not?

She heard the horse nicker, but that was no help at all, for all horses sounded the same to her. She crept toward the door and listened. If he would only cough or clear his throat or say *"och,"* then she would know.

"Jack?" she whispered. Then louder, "Jack."

"Aye, 'tis only me, Anabel."

She dropped the axe and lifted the metal bar from its ancient holders on either side and set it down. She pulled the door open and there stood the figure of a substantial man. His shoulders looked broader in the shadows, his arms thick and strong, his legs firmly planted on the ground in a stance that signaled he was ready for any surprise that might present itself.

He made a sweeping bow and smiled, his teeth catching a momentary glint from the moonlight before a cloud rushed by, and then he said, "M'lady, yer servant has found nay evidence that there be any intruders aboot."

"Thank ye."

"Ye're most welcome. Ye may retire in peace, Anabel. I'll sleep aside me horse."

She peered past him to Soldier. "I'll nay allow it, Jack. Ye must stay inside." She thought of the only place suitable and lowered her gaze. "A broken bed would be better than the ground where yer horse might trample ye or the comin' rain might drown ye."

"I accept." Jack was almost too hasty in his reply. He stepped forward and came through the entrance. "Did ye mean the empty larder? It wouldna be the first time I spent more than an hour in such a space."

Anabel gasped as he brushed past her. "Did yer father lock ye there fer yer impish behavior?"

"Nay, 'twere me brothers who held me prisoner there once when the cook had a day off." He laughed. "But e'en in the dark, I could find the tray of cookies she'd left fer after our dinner … and I ate them all."

"Oh, Jack."

She touched the end of the bar, intending to lift the heavy thing into its brackets, but Jack took the bar from her hands and said, "Allow me, m'lady."

It was completely dark with the door closed. There was scant light as Anabel looked up at Jack, a form indistinguishable from any other. Her breath caught in her throat as she felt warmth radiating off his skin. Then she felt his skin itself, as his fingers ran up from her elbows to her shoulders and back down again. Grasping, pulling her in. Her ear against his chest. His heart beats racing. Hers as well. She gave her hands permission to find their way over his shoulders and around his neck.

It wasn't but a second before she learned the deliciousness of a kiss shared in the blackness of night. Her knees went weak.

Jack kissed her several more times and then apologized. "I ken we mustna repeat this ... and yet 'tis all I think on. Anabel ... I love ye, lass."

The words were unexpected and yet seemed perfectly timed. Besides her ears, she had only one other of her senses to register the truth: that unexplained divining through touching his skin. Her lips appraised his words as true and her hands on the skin of his neck measured the depth of the judgment.

"I ... I love ye as well, Jack."

***

MEGAN WOULD HAVE paced about the room if her ankle allowed it, but instead she lay nervous and afraid on the straw mattress, clutching one end of the quilt and not at all liking this predicament she got herself into. Why did she run away? She could have stayed home, could have accepted the betrothal to Jack, and looked forward to a future full of children. Everyone said she'd have an easy time of it, what with her wide hips and sturdy frame, ample bosom, and patient disposition.

Patience was not her talent now. She was quite impatient, waiting for Anabel to return and give her the reassurance that all was well. She couldn't believe that Jack was coming back to guard them. Why hadn't Anabel told her? What other secrets did those two have?

Maybe she could walk a little bit. She put her good foot on the floor and then her other toe. No, it wasn't going to work.

But ... if she got down onto her hands and knees ... *oof ... this might work.* She could keep the discomfort at a minimum and crawl to the door. Slowly at first, hand, knee, other hand, other knee. Repeat.

The stairs were a different problem. She swung herself around and went down step by step on her hands and bottom. Her shift was going to be ruined, but now she could hear two voices whispering far below.

The perspiration on her hands collected more than dust from the floor and steps, bits of mouse turds and animal fur, and other filth that had come in on the bottoms of their shoes now stuck to her palms and fingers.

Once on the first floor, she needed to cross to the servants' staircase to get to the kitchen.

Well, she certainly wasn't scared anymore. Those voices were definitely Jack and Anabel. There was no highwayman come to rob them, or evil woman-ravisher bent on taking their purity, nor were her brothers back to woo Anabel as she knew they eventually would be. She got back on her hands and knees again without clapping the grime off her hands.

She made it to the stairs and peered down, listening hard. Jack's laugh floated up along with a word or two. She caught the word 'cookies' and then there was a metallic thump as the kitchen door's bar was dropped into place.

Whispers. *My oh my, he was still inside.*

She strained to hear and threw a hand to her mouth when she heard the words of love. *Oh no! What a fool she was. There was no trusting Anabel ... or Jack.*

She had to get back to her room. She rose, one hand on the wall for support, and hopped, then she took a panicked step, screeched from the pain, and dropped to the floor. Before she could try to stand again, Anabel and Jack—her own betrothed!—came running to her side.

"I'll carry her back." Jack barely looked at her. "Megan, however did ye get this far? Ye must be mad with pain."

She burst into a fit of crying and smeared her dirtied hands on her shift, suddenly aware of her immodesty. "Please doan touch me. Ye must leave me, Jack." She glared at Anabel. "And ye, Anabel MacLeod, ye should be ashamed o' yerself, lettin' Jack come in whilst we're abed." She waved them both off and struggled up onto one foot. She started to limp off, then raised her injured foot and hopped. "Ye must make him leave, Anabel. Now," she said over her shoulder.

***

JACK WOKE STIFF and sore from sleeping on the grass near the garden, wrapped in the saddle blanket. He'd watched Megan hop across the hallway last night after she must have overheard them. Anabel tried to help her but Megan shoved her away. Anabel came back to Jack and the two of them stood helplessly watching and then listening as Megan grunted and whimpered her way to her room, berating Anabel and ordering Jack to leave.

They did not exchange another word until they went down to the kitchen. Jack unbarred the door and said, "I'll be close by." He went out and listened for the clunk of metal on metal to be sure the castle was again impenetrable before making a spot for himself to bed down.

Now, in the bright and rather warm morning, he sloughed off the blanket and rose. Soldier whinnied and he untied the horse from where he stood. All the grass the horse could reach was now nibbled down to the ground.

"Come on, we'll get ye some water at the loch and I'll wash up a bit." He decided to go by way of the maze and was proud of himself for leading Soldier through every turn correctly. They came out by the rock and went to the shore. The horse drank his fill while Jack splashed his face and then looked around for any evidence that others might have come looking this far. Soldier wandered toward a patch of wild clover and Jack climbed upon the rock to sit and have a moment's contemplation.

The start of the Highland games was two days away. He wanted nothing more than to have Anabel watch him compete. He needed to fix things with Megan, though. The lass was not deserving of all this misery, physical and emotional. He wasn't unaware that the lass had feelings for him, and though he'd been enraged that his father had brokered an arranged marriage between them, he'd never been completely averse to it as the lass was not insufferable. But now ... now that he'd spent time with Anabel ... he could not entertain a single thought about any other woman.

"I'm sorry fer her feelin's, Soldier, but what can I do?"

His horse kept his opinion to himself.

"Should I ride ye to the McDoons' place and tell them she's all right and I ken where she be? They could fetch her with the wagon." Soldier huffed a snort at that. "Or should I go to me father and explain me

89

feelin's?" Soldier snorted again. "Aye, ye're right. Me father will take me axe, me sword, and me name. He'll have me whipped and banned. I'll nay get to compete and I'll let down me brothers." Soldier made no comment, simply moved on to another patch of green.

Jack bit his lip and stared at the ripples on the loch. A fish jumped and made more ripples. Jack climbed off the rock and stood at the shoreline, remembering. There was a story his mother told him, a story from the Bible he now realized. She had paraphrased and repeated it to her children, emphasizing that they never needed to fear God. He was kind and loving and just. He gave good gifts. He was their Heavenly Father, and their earthly father was a good representation of those qualities. Would the Laird of Castle Caladh take Jack's things, leave him penniless, and banish him for loving Anabel MacLeod?

He asked the question of Soldier as he walked to him, grabbed the trailing reins, and patted his neck. The horse tossed his head and that was answer enough for Jack.

"Right, then. I'll see to the lasses, do me practice throwin', and pay a formal visit to me father. All will work out. Ye're a smart horse, Soldier. Ye ken that the Laird has allowed me three sisters and two brothers to wed who they wished. O' course he'll do the same fer me."

He led Soldier back through the maze mumbling his thoughts aloud.

"I remember when me father told me of the betrothal to Megan ... me father said ... he said 'as ye've nay spoken of lovin' any other' and then he dinnae finish." He thought further back on that day that Patrick McDoon came to Caladh and demanded he wed wee Megan. Hah! His own father had named his choices: among them Megan and Anabel and Clara Campbell. There was the dowry to consider, but what did that really matter? Wasn't there a doubling of the dowry when Keir was betrothed to Anabel and yet his father did not seem displeased when Keir defied the contract and wed Eleanor. His father had no reservation either when Logan chose Hannah, whose station appeared to be far below Logan's.

"Och, Soldier, I've figured out the secret of me father's words." They stopped in the middle of the maze for Jack to make his revelation. "Me father was awaitin' fer me to find love. As he has. As me brothers and sisters have." He gave Soldier a long stroke down his neck. "And now I have. 'Tis Anabel I want ... and she wants me."

90

The horse bobbed his head and nipped a bunch of leaves from a bordering bush. Jack led him out the rest of the way. "Och," he scolded himself, "I should've strung the buckets across yer back and brought some water up fer the lasses. And here's another thing I should have done," he said to himself as he spotted a fallen limb the right length and thickness to make into a cane for Megan. "She'll nay have to hop around if I take me axe to it."

***

ANABEL CHECKED ON Megan first thing in the morning. Megan wouldn't speak to her, but she reluctantly allowed her to help her tend to things of a personal nature and to get dressed. Then Megan refused to leave the room.

Anabel sighed and tried to get Megan to speak. "Ye must tell me what to do. First ye ran away to avoid weddin' Jack and now ye're angry that he wishes the same ... well, what are we to do?"

Megan folded her arms across her chest and huffed. "I cannae walk home. I cannae ask ye or Jack to fetch a wagon and take me home."

"I'm sure Jack would do that fer ye." Anabel risked touching the back of Megan's hand in a show of comfort and friendship. When she sensed the entirety of Megan's feelings, she let her own tears flow in empathy. "Oh, Megan, I'm so verra sorry fer ye. The pain in yer ankle is far less than the pain in yer heart." She tried to wrap her in an embrace, but Megan pushed her away.

"Ye best get down to the door. I hear him poundin' on it now. Go on."

Anabel didn't hear a thing, but she left the room anyway. She went to different windows and looked out. She did hear a far-away sound now, much like pounding, but not on their door. She rushed down the main staircase and took the spot by the front door where once a footman would have stood. She opened the small metal door that allowed for an eye-level peek at the front courtyard as well as a chance to listen. She did hear the pounding Megan mentioned, but realized it was the sound of horses' hooves and wagon wheels. There must be a caravan of Scotsmen coming early to the games and passing near enough to the hidden castle that she could hear them.

She closed and latched the little door and rushed to the servants' stairs to the kitchen. She nearly tripped on her skirts as she hurried down

91

and over to the barred door. She lifted off the heavy bar and stepped out into the bright morning.

"Jack?" There was no sign of horse or man, but the saddle and blanket lay near the garden. She lifted the saddle and nearly fell backwards from the weight. She had no idea it would be so heavy. She lugged it to the kitchen and ran back for the blanket, just as Jack and the horse came into view.

"Jack, hurry." Her voice was low, but urgent. "Bring the horse and come inside. There be folks travelin' on the road yonder. We mustn't let them see I've been livin' here."

"Ye needna fash, Anabel. They'll nay find the front path. And besides, Soldier would nivver fit through the kitchen door." He laughed gently and tied his horse to the nearest tree. The sounds beyond began to fade. "See? They've rounded the bend and are headin' fer me home. 'Twill be the McGowans as they live the furthest away and always come early to sell their things before the peddler arrives." He handed her the stick he carried and took the blanket and laid it on Soldier's back, then he collected the saddle from the kitchen's stone floor and chuckled some more.

Anabel got her emotions under control, propped the stick against the wall, and followed him to the horse. "Jack, Megan's in a pitiful state of anguish and pain. I think she wishes she could ask ye to take her home. Might she ride upon Soldier? Ye could lead her there."

"Aye. I'd be willin'. Look, I made her a cane." They both turned their heads to the castle wall.

"'Twas most thoughtful of ye, Jack. I'll take it up to her now. Come break yer fast with us."

"'Twill be a pleasure, but first I mean to fill those buckets with fresh water fer ye."

Chapter 10

BETWEEN ANABEL'S SHOULDER to lean on and the cane Jack made to balance her, Megan had all the help she needed to manage two flights of stairs and limp out to the garden. She had refused to eat anything and insisted she'd be fine; she wanted to go home immediately. She was emphatic about it and would not meet their eyes or listen to arguments against leaving.

Jack helped her up onto the saddle, apologizing repeatedly that it wasn't a side saddle, but assuring her there was nothing immodest about riding astride. He'd gone riding with his sisters and with Logan's wife, Hannah, and he'd not found it offensive. He tipped his hat at Anabel, gave her a wink, and cautioned her to stay inside until he returned. He started off carrying the cane and leading Soldier. He stopped often to listen for passersby, then, once away from the castle and on well-traveled lanes, he walked briskly toward McDoon Tower. The tension stretched between them. It was a long, quiet journey.

"Are ye nay goin' to say a word to me?" Megan finally asked.

"I thought ye meant to punish me with yer silence."

"Do ye need punishin'? Have ye done somethin' wrong, Jack?" Her voice was tight, her meaning evident.

He stopped walking, rubbed Soldier's nose, and looked up at Megan. "Aye, I suppose ye believe I have. I'm terrible sorry, Meg, but I've lost me heart to Anabel. Have ye nay heard that things always work out fer

93

the best? I'm sure ye'll find a match more to yer likin' than bein' hitched to a mischievous rascal such as me."

He held her gaze. "Can ye forgive me, Megan?"

She sighed and dropped her eyes. "I suppose I must, but I cannae promise ye me father or me brothers will let ye leave without a proper punishment."

Jack started walking again. "Aye, I expected as much."

Soldier suddenly stumbled and then seemed to limp. Jack stopped them again and rubbed a hand down his front leg. "Ye can stay aboard. I think he musta caught a rock. Whoa, let me take a look." Jack lifted the hoof and held it between his knees as he examined it. He drew out his dirk and picked away at something lodged there. "A bit of dried sheep dung, is all." He resheathed the dirk and tested Soldier's gait.

"He seems fine now." He glanced at Megan, but she looked off.

They went on without any further conversation until they were in view of McDoon Tower and its tree-lined entrance.

It was mid-morning and the smells from the sheep herds the McDoons were so proud of, reached their noses. Jack crinkled his nose, but Megan breathed in deeply. They stopped in the front courtyard and Jack addressed Megan as formally as possible, hoping his actions were being observed from one of the windows. He bowed and said, "May I help ye down, Mistress Megan?"

She nodded and held her arms out. Jack dropped the cane and reached for her. As gently as he could he got her down onto one foot. "Steady yerself against Soldier and I'll get the cane." He bent to retrieve it, handed it to her, and stepped back.

Still, no one had come out of the great house.

"Will ye keep certain things to yerself? Anabel sought refuge as ye did in the hidden castle. I hope ye'll honor her request to tell nary a person where she be."

Megan nodded slowly. "Let our tale be that ye found me wandering. I lost me sack of things, and hurt meself climbin' aboot those rocks we passed a ways back."

"I found ye wanderin', hurt, aye. 'Tis nay enough truth to keep me face from twitchin' at the lie, but I'll give it a go." He offered her the faintest of smiles.

She looked toward the doors. "They musta sent every servant out in search o' me." Megan's frown slanted toward wonder.

"'Tis like the Prodigal Son. Perhaps they'll have a feast to celebrate yer return."

The door flew open then and Megan's mother bustled out, crying and uttering nonsensical words. The poor woman seemed more upset to have been left alone without a single servant than that her daughter was back.

"Oh my," she wept into Megan's neck, her arms around her and her face buried in her hair, "even the lasses are combin' the fields. I've had no one to fetch me a cup o' cider or braid me hair." She released Megan, who wobbled and made quick use of the cane to steady herself. "Oh, are ye hurt?"

Megan recited the agreed upon explanation and her mother at last took notice of Jack standing there.

"Saints be praised, 'twill be a blessin' to have ye in the household, Master McKelvey. 'Twas fate that brought ye to me daughter's rescue. Tie yer beast there and come inside. I'll ring the tower bell and hope Ginny comes in from the field to fetch some refreshments." She hugged Megan again. "They've been lookin' fer yer body in the gullies. I've been sick with worry. I prayed every promise to get ye home."

"Mother … did ye read me note? I wasna goin' to return until after the games, but this misfortune came upon me. Still … " she glanced briefly at Jack "I'll nay marry Jack. Ye cannae make me or I'll run away again."

"Are ye nay fond of 'im? He's rescued ye twice now. Ye cannae ignore such providence." She put a gentling hand to Megan's head and tucked stray hairs into place. Megan stared at her feet. Her mother looked at Jack. "And ye, sir, are ye nay anxious to wed me daughter? The Laird of Castle Caladh approved the union."

"Lady McDoon, me father accepted on me behalf under the false impression that something untoward had taken place between us."

Megan whispered, "I'm so sorry."

"But Megan doesna wish to marry me, nor am I so inclined, though any Highlander would be most fortunate to have her as a wife. Me heart is set on another lass, one ye may well ken … Anabel MacLeod."

Lady McDoon covered her gasp with a hand. "But she's been abducted by an Englishman. We had word of it last night. There's a reward for her return." Her face puckered and she touched Megan's face and whispered, "Yer father was trustin' ye'd come home on yer own."

Jack and Megan exchanged quick glances.

Jack managed to cover another falsehood by bobbing his head and saying, "Anabel's abduction was why I was out searchin'. I hoped to come across them, but I found Megan instead. And now that she's safely home, I'll resume me search, if 'tis all the same to ye." He continued nodding, his hand on his sword hilt as an indication of his imminent leave-taking.

The sound of hoof beats distracted the three and Soldier whinnied. Benjamin and Dylan galloped up and produced a nasty cloud of dust as they reined in their horses.

"She's been found!" Lady McDoon called out.

Dylan jumped down and came face to face with Jack. "So off with ye then. We doan want the likes of ye at McDoon Tower." He clenched his jaw and butted his chest against Jack's, making him take several steps backward; Soldier followed.

"Son, ye should be thankin' 'im and then wishin' 'im luck findin' the MacLeod lass."

Dylan's head jerked toward his mother and back at Jack. "Ye ken of the reward?"

"Aye."

From his horse Benjamin shouted at Dylan, "Help our sister inside, while I have a few words with this McKelvey. Mount up, sir. I'll see ye to the road."

Dylan gave a growl but put an arm around his sister, nodded at his mother, and started helping them toward the door. Jack hurried to mount Soldier and urged him toward the road.

"Hold up, man. I've a warnin' to give ye," Benjamin's voice was stern.

Jack looked back to see Megan, Dylan, and Lady McDoon enter their home and then his eyes went to Benjamin who had trotted up beside him, pistol out, aimed at Jack.

"Ye'll turn left ahead and go down the path at a walk or I'll shoot yer horse first and ye second."

"Whoa, Soldier. What's this aboot, McDoon? Are ye as crazy as yer brother?"

"Nay, but that reward'll be ours."

"Ye promised—"

"Shut yer mouth, McKelvey. We'll nay bother the lass until after the games. Games that ye'll miss." He kept his eyes on Jack and said, "See that whippin' tree yonder?"

Jack caught sight of a monstrous old oak and he knew what Benjamin had in mind, but he wasn't about to let him tie him up and take leather straps to his back. He reined Soldier to a halt and stared at Benjamin. "Why doan we come to a deal? I ken ye want that reward and fear I'll win it first, but what if I promise to pay ye the full amount and double it with me own coin?"

Benjamin's horse turned on its own to face Jack's left knee and give his master a clearer shot at Jack.

"'Tis a handsome offer, McKelvey, but I prefer to give ye a whippin' fer touchin' me sister."

"I found her and brought her back safe and sound. I'd nivver touch her, though she be me betrothed yet." He pleaded with his free hand and on his last word dropped it to his side, where he fingered the sheath his dirk was in.

"Ye're wrong there, Jack. Dylan convinced our father to negate the agreement ... and furthermore," his lips parted in an evil grin, "we've found a deed to that old ruined castle ... and it'll be ours." He gave a short laugh. "Now git off yer horse and walk to the tree. Ye're goin' to be too sore to throw yer hammer or lift a caber. The McDoons'll take the prizes."

Jack moved slightly forward in the saddle and simultaneously drew his dirk. With but an instant to aim, he threw the knife and hit Benjamin in the right shoulder. Benjamin dropped the pistol and the reins in surprise and pain, clutched his shoulder, roared and cussed, and fell from the saddle when his horse bolted. Jack didn't wait to see if his help was needed. The vulgar boor could bleed to death on the ground and there'd be no mourning from this McKelvey. Soldier must have agreed for he smoothly took off at a canter toward the only road that led to Castle Caladh.

***

ANABEL MOPED ABOUT the castle waiting for Jack's return. She spent a fair amount of time trying to make bread, but it wouldn't rise.

She dusted some of the rooms, but had nothing to mop the floors with. She used to come to this abandoned castle and sit staring at the pictures or out the windows, making up stories of things that might have happened here, sometimes whispering them aloud. She knew a lot more now, from what Jack told her and the treasures they'd found in the cellars. She tested her voice in the empty room. There was no echo, only a stillness after each word.

"Once a grand family lived here."

She had no names for them except for the one she'd read on the back of the portrait: Nella.

"They had to leave suddenly, but they stored their favorite and most precious things in a hidden cellar under the larder." Now she had that to add that to one of her tales.

Ah, but the most precious things were the children. She imagined the woman in the portrait taking a daughter, Jack's grandmother perhaps, and layering her dresses on her for their journey. They would have carried what they could and left trunks and furniture behind. She remembered then the letters she'd previously discovered in the desk drawers. She hadn't read them, but now seemed like a good time.

She made her way to the front room with its half circular expanse of windows, the wingback chair behind the rosewood desk, and the two settees that faced each other. She walked between them and over to the desk where all the small metal devices she found before in one of the drawers still sat, now gathering dust. She put them back in the drawer, and used her apron to clean the top of the desk. She opened the second drawer and withdrew a stack of old letters, sat down in the wingback chair, and spread them in front of her.

The date on the first was from sixty-five years ago. Anabel reasoned that by then Nella would have been nearing thirty, probably married and the mother of at least one child, Jack's grandmother or perhaps it was Jack's mother.

Dearest Nella, the oldest letter began, *I write to you today with heavy heart, for I am ever so far away from the warmth of your embrace. I have ventured to England on a mission of political ambition, and though I have accomplished much here, I find myself longing for the comfort of your loving arms. My days are spent in the midst of politicians and powerful men, and though I am gaining much favor, I cannot help but feel isolated and alone. I have found myself in a difficult position, as I must stay in England to further my ambitions, yet my heart longs to return to our dear Scotland and to you. My love for you is as strong now as it ever was, and I am filled with sorrow knowing I cannot be with you. I hope that soon I will be able to return and bring you the fruits of my labor. Until that time, I remain ever devoted to you, my dearest. With love, Your husband, Finnias*

Anabel smiled at the lovely words, yet her brow creased in a sad frown at the thought that such well-spoken sentiments were lost forever in time and death. She wondered what Nella had written in reply and how she'd gotten along alone here. Did she wait for Finnias? Or did she pack up what she could and join him, never to return? Or did he come back and collect her, the children, the servants?

She read the next letter and the one after that, but there were no clues as to what might have occurred. She raised her head and daydreamed, looking out the window. There was a mystery here. Jack had that spoon that matched the only one she'd found in the kitchen ... did it mean something that one was left behind to be found by her so many years later?

She liked the thought that she and Jack were meant to be together ... like the matching spoons.

When would he return? It had been hours. Not that she was afraid. The doors were all barred, but she'd like to go outside, dig in the garden, maybe go down to the loch and wash up.

She rose from the desk and went to the room Megan had stayed in. Her sack was still there, left behind on purpose. She looked inside and found a clean day dress, but it was unusual in that it was a drab color and of a fashion only a poor peasant would wear. Perhaps Megan got it from a servant or stole it from a washline intending to disguise herself by wearing the ugly thing. There were also in the sack some stockings, a comb, and a napkin wrapped around something squishy. She carefully unwrapped it and found a crumbling mess of fruited bread—something Megan had served to her friends before. Anabel was pleased to find it. She devoured the treat at once and picked away any crumbs stuck to the napkin, leaving nothing for a scavenging mouse. She shook it out and considered that it might be useful as a drying towel. She took it and the clothing with her downstairs, and unbarred the front entrance. It was closer to the path to the loch and she was determined to clean herself and her dress and then don Megan's clean things while her clothes dried.

She got maybe twenty feet away from the door before she heard a rustling sound. Her imagination got the better of her and she rushed back inside, barred the door, and didn't move for several minutes.

She absolutely hated being alone here now. It was no longer a peaceful retreat for her, not now that four other people had been here. She was sure Megan would never return; she hoped Jack would … and soon … but she feared the McDoon brothers could arrive at any moment … maybe that was one of them in the bushes … and then what would she do? Might they force their way in knowing she was inside? Could she hide under the larder and leave no clue of where she went? Would a crumpled rug give away her hidey-hole? She had no way of testing it, but she thought she should at least give it a try. She did a stealth-walk through the manse and down to the larder. She set the clothing down and got the oil lamp ready—she'd need it in the cellar. She felt her pocket for the striker, took it out and lit the lamp. The acrid smell of the old oil didn't surprise her this time. She set the lamp down on the floor of the larder, lifted the rug, and studied the trap door. It was not an obvious door; anyone might miss it. Perhaps she needn't worry about the rug at all. She rolled it up and pushed it to the back of the room.

She lifted the trap door and peered down the steps. All right, she might be able to go down far enough to close the door and huddle on the upper-most steps until they were gone, but the thought of descending all the way down in the dark was unacceptable. She couldn't bring the lamp for it would give away by scent and maybe smoke her whereabouts.

Another thought occurred to her: a disguise. Of course. She could wear the peasant's rough frock, wrap her hair in her dirty apron as a field worker might do, and pretend to be a poor young lass with a wish to see the Highland games before returning to labor in the McKelveys' fields.

She laughed aloud. "I'll do it," she said to the empty room. She closed the trap door and blew out the oil lamp. She told herself not to worry, that Jack would return, she would be safe here, and the day after tomorrow she'd walk the distance to Castle Caladh, and witness the first contests. She couldn't wait to tell Jack her plan. In the meantime, if the McDoons came back, she'd hide under the bed upstairs.

Later, after a bored afternoon, she thought about her family. Her brothers looked forward to the games and they'd probably be obligated by her father to keep hunting for her and miss the games. They might even be halfway to England by now. They might even have recaptured that poor English captain if he didn't get far.

Hmm, when would Jack get back here? Now she could imagine Nella's letters back to Finnias: full of despair and loneliness, begging him to return soon. The hidden castle was a forlorn and isolated fortress for a solitary female.

***

JACK LEFT HIS panting horse with the stable lad and ran into Castle Caladh hollering for his brother, Logan. He paced back and forth in the entry hallway, wringing his hands together. He didn't want to ask his brother for help, and he knew he would get a less than enthusiastic response, but he needed to try.

Logan appeared, coming out of the dining room, grinning ear to ear. "What's yer hollerin', little brother? Did ye drop yer hammer on yer foot?"

Jack shook his head and signaled for him to follow him into the portrait room where the McKelvey coat of arms hung. "I need yer counsel. I ken what Father and Keir'll say, but I want to hear yer advice." Jack closed the door and strode toward the tapestry. "Generosity, loyalty, courage … and grief. All parts of our … our heritage."

"Aye, and faith, strength, and valor." Logan eyed the tapestry, his gaze wandering down to where someone had replaced the red cords he'd cut when he'd used them to handfast himself to Hannah.

"I need yer help," Jack said, his voice quavering slightly. "I found our great-grandparents' castle … hidden beyond the loch you cannae see from the path to Elspeth's home."

"Elspeth? Have ye been courtin' the maid, Jack?"

"Nay. Listen. The castle. It exists. It's hidden and abandoned and there are portraits of our ancestors that I get me eye color from." He gave an exasperated sigh as Logan plopped onto the divan and thrummed the table next to him.

"Our mother's secret castle, aye?"

"Ye ken of it?"

"Aye. She took me there once. We collected candle holders and brought them here. Like that one." He pointed to a single silver candlestick.

"And ye nivver went back?"

"I doan remember the way. And if ye think ye'll find it again, I'll bet ye the horse I won from McDoon that ye won't."

Jack sat across from him and shook his head. "I should take that bet. I've been back every day for the last week or so. I've been practicin' there with me hammer and me axe."

"Och, so that's where ye've been."

"Ye jist mentioned McDoon and he's been there, too."

Logan sat up straighter and scowled. "What's that scoundrel doin' creepin' around our ancestors' place. We've graves there, ye ken."

Jack didn't know, but he dismissed the thought, and said, "Anabel MacLeod is hidin' in the castle. I must guard her there, but I cannae do it alone."

"Guard her? Jack, what have ye done, lad? There's a reward the MacLeods be offerin' fer her return. That Captain Luxbury got loose and stole off with her. Are ye sayin' ye're in league with him?"

"Nay. She's been promised to Hamish Kilmahew and cannae abide it. She released the captain to hide the fact that she's run away. And she wasn't the only one to run away." He spent a few minutes to explain about Megan and then how she got hurt, how Anabel fooled the McDoons, how he took Megan home, and finally—and still talking faster than his sisters—that he threw his dirk at Benjamin McDoon and wounded him in order to get away.

Logan crossed his arms and thought a moment. "Ye cannae bring Anabel here," he warned, "if that was what ye were plannin'."

Jack shook his head. "Logan ... I ken what ye feel fer Hannah ... and I feel that way about Anabel. I've kissed the lass and she's kissed me back. I'll nay wed Megan."

Logan huffed. "O' course ye willna do any such thing. I'm sure the McDoons would rather see ye dead now than take ye in as a brother. Are ye sure ye dinnae kill the lad? Benji isna nearly as bad as Dylan, but I wouldna want a blood feud with that clan." He shook his head and mumbled a few Gaelic words.

"I aim to ask Anabel tonight to wed me on the last day of the games. She'll stay hidden until then, but I'm afraid the McDoons might find their way back there. I thought … I thought we might install ourselves there … and protect her as well as lay claim to the land."

Logan bit hit his cheek and thought a moment. "Did our father agree to the match with Megan McDoon?"

"Aye, but she willna have me and Benjamin said her father annulled it."

"'Tis a twisted problem. An' now ye want the MacLeod lass that once was betrothed to our brother, Keir. Och, 'tis a knotted cord indeed. I see why ye're more interested in me opinion than in Keir's."

Jack rose. "Well, I cannae stay 'til dark to argue out a solution. I'll gather some supplies and stay there campin' in the garden."

"Ye'll nay be at yer best fer the games. I have another idea so ye'll get yer proper rest and keep Anabel safe as well."

Jack leaned in to listen.

***

WELL AFTER DARK Jack pounded on the hidden castle's kitchen door. "'Tis I, Anabel. Open up."

He waited a moment then pounded again and repeated his greeting. It had taken him longer to come back as he'd brought the wagon, pulled by one of the carriage horses with Soldier tied to the back and he had to travel farther, skirting the loch and searching out the front way in.

The muffled sound of the bar hitting the floor and then being scraped to the side by Anabel's pretty little foot made him smile. He glanced at the person beside him and then back to the door. Slowly it opened and there stood Anabel, holding the oil lamp, its faint light illuminating a tear-streaked face.

"Oh." She looked from Jack to the unexpected person with him. "Who's this?"

"'Tis yer personal maid fer the duration of yer stay here. And our chaperone." He chuckled. "Meet Elspeth. Elspeth, this is Mistress Anabel MacLeod."

Elspeth climbed off the wagon, curtsied, pushed the hood of her cape back, and said, "Most pleased to meet ye, Mistress." She curtsied a second time then nodded at Jack. "I'll bring in the food stuffs and start on the bread right away, sir."

"Thank ye, Elspeth. I'll get the other things."

Anabel stood to the side and watched as Jack and Elspeth made several trips back and forth to the wagon.

Elspeth lit some candles they'd brought and set them about the kitchen. Anabel blew out her lamp which had begun to smoke and stink.

She stepped outside as Jack went to unhitch the horse. "Are ye stayin' here, too, Jack?"

"'Tis the best way to keep ye safe." He turned to face her. He touched her cheeks. "Ye've been cryin', aye? I told ye I'd return."

"I heard sounds. I was afraid Megan's brothers had come back." She put her hand on his, the one still touching her skin.

"I'm afraid they will try to find me first and when they doan find me at Caladh, they'll come here." He cleared his throat. "I took Megan all the way home. Her mother was most pleased, but then her brothers came. Benjamin meant to whip me. I stopped him with me dirk."

Anabel gasped. "Ye killt him? Oh, Jack!"

"He'll nay be in the grave. I'm sure I only nicked his shoulder, but …"

Anabel let her breath out and threw her arms around him. She cried into his neck, "They'll hang ye fer it."

"Nay, dinnae fash. He had a pistol on me. I was in me rights." He lifted her arms from his neck and looked her in the eyes. "Are ye fearin' fer me life, Anabel?" He kept hold of both her hands.

"I am. In these last hours alone, I pondered on many things and one thing in particular … Jack, will ye marry me?"

"Anabel MacLeod. 'Tis why I'm here, lass. I meant to ask ye that verra question. Aye, I'll marry ye. Will ye have me?"

"Aye."

The light from a candlestick flickered at the doorway then disappeared, but their eyes were closed and neither of them knew Elspeth had caught them in a long embrace.

Chapter 11

A
NABEL HAD A second helping of the porridge Elspeth made and insisted the maid sit and eat with her in the dining room.

"Oh, Mistress Anabel, I couldna. I ken me place." She curtsied and bowed her head.

"Please, please." She waved Elspeth into one of the seats she herself had dusted the day before. "And ye must tell me how ye baked this bread. I was at such a loss as to what to do here by meself."

Elspeth lowered her backside tentatively onto the front edge of the chair as if she'd be ready to jump into service or at the least to quickly stand and curtsy in deference to anything this high-born woman said. She took a nervous breath. "I used to help in the kitchen, but now that there are two cooks, I only have to do the cleanin' and the washin'. I 'spect they'll notice me absence tomorrow when the hordes flock in to the games and they'll need help servin' food and ale."

Anabel smiled at the easy way the girl talked to her. Her own family's servants kept their distance and their tongues. "Have some bread, Elspeth."

Elspeth took a piece of the warm bread from the plate on the table. She'd sliced it before carrying it and the porridge up from the kitchen. Plates and knives and mugs were a few of the many things she and Jack and Logan had loaded onto the wagon last night, hastily gathered from

Caladh along with blankets, buckets, and Logan's last-minute suggestion: soap.

She chewed quickly and swallowed. "'Tisn't as good as the new cook's." She nodded at her own assessment and took another bite.

"Tell me about Castle Caladh," Anabel urged as she took a spoonful of porridge.

"'Tis a most welcomin' place to be. The Laird is kind and just. His new wife-to-be is gentle and undemanding. Her lad is a lively one, flittin' in and out of the castle, eatin' six or seven times a day, and growin' this summer like a marsh-side cattail. Young Colin willna be strong enough to enter the games this year, but I can see him competin' in a year or two." There was a noise down in the kitchen and Elspeth bolted out of her seat.

Anabel reached over and took her hand and pulled her back into her seat. "'Tis all right. Jack willna mind if ye're sittin' with me." She experienced something vague from her moment of skin contact with Elspeth. It wasn't off-putting as usually happened when one of her servants touched her. Her impression from Elspeth was like the taste of something sweet, as if the girl held no deception in her soul.

Elspeth shrank back into the chair. "He'll be fetchin' water fer yer bath."

"Oh no, that'll take too many trips to the lake. He'll be too worn out to practice."

"Nay, Mistress, Logan described fer him where the well be. Hidden, it was, but we uncovered it early this morn."

"Ye found the well?"

"Aye, 'tis jist inside the maze, so 'tis a short jaunt. Master Jack built a fire, too, so we can heat the water in the cookin' pot."

Anabel frowned. "I must look a fright."

"Nay, Mistress, ye're most beautiful. Jist … jist a smudge or two on yer face, is all. And I can help ye with yer hair. I used to do Mistress Rory's hair when she'd let me and now I help Hannah and Eleanor and Mary, too."

"Tell me more about the ladies at Castle Caladh."

Elspeth started speaking even faster and rattled on first about elegant Eleanor and how generous she was to all the servants and then about Hannah, whose former nanny was the new cook and would, next spring when Hannah and Logan's baby came, be a nanny again. And then about Jack's sisters and what she knew of their lives. She had stories and tales that Anabel gobbled up as eagerly as she did the porridge.

"I ken ye were once betrothed to Keir," Elspeth slowed her speech, "and I ken that Jack is besotted with ye … ye're a most fortunate one, ye are, for … of the three brothers … Jack be me favorite."

Anabel smiled. "And why is that? Tell me."

***

MEGAN MCDOON CRIED softly as her friend Clara Campbell patted her shoulder and tucked a loose strand of fiery red hair back under Megan's bonnet.

"Ye poor little bird," Clara stopped patting and fussing and took hold of Megan's hand instead. They were seated together on a bench in the garden behind the lookout tower from which McDoon Tower got its name. No one else was around. Megan's father and Dylan were out recruiting a substitute from among their cousins to replace the injured Benjamin in tomorrow's games.

Megan peeked at Clara from under wet lashes and murmured, "I nivver found the bothan Orla promised me." Her gaze went back to darting between her aching ankle and the cane on the ground.

"Did ye sleep outside?" Clara frowned deeply and let her eyes wander to a stretch of dirt beneath a recently trimmed bush. Little green berries hung off its limbs.

Meekly Megan answered, making up lies as she spoke, "Aye … 'twas most dreadful … and dirty … and, and I had nary a thing to eat or drink."

Clara shook her head. "Orla should be ashamed of herself for sendin' ye that letter. Well, ye're home safe now." She released Megan's hand and raised both of hers to emphasise what she said next. "Did ye ken? They cannae find dear Anabel. Whisked away by that English soldier. Her brothers, Will and Alpin, may miss the games asearchin' fer them." She sighed. "I did so want to see Alpin." She looked to the sky and closed her eyes. The sun hit her face and cast a sharp shadow of her crooked nose onto her cheek.

Megan sniffed the last of her phony tears and stared at Clara. "Alpin? Are ye pinnin' yer hopes of marriage on him now?"

107

Clara's small eyes popped open. "Mayhaps. There be other choices. Now that ye've let the young McKelvey off the hook. Oh, pardon me slip of the tongue." She tipped her face away from the light. "And then there's Hamish Kilmahew ... if they cannae find Anabel, he'll be the next one me father approaches."

Megan bit her lip and thought of what Jack had said to her. "Jack loves her." She didn't mean to say it aloud.

"What?" Clara shielded her face with her hand.

"Oh ... I'm ... I'm still all bothered by me ordeal. I dinnae mean a thing." She fanned herself with opened fingers and made a hasty decision to unburden herself. "Oh ... oh, Clara ... ye mustna tell a soul ... but," she glanced around the garden, "but Anabel is safe an' sound, hidin' in a place that's ... well, she's found good shelter ... and ... Jack is with her."

She couldn't have said a more shocking thing to Clara whose face now likened itself more to that of a mal-formed owl than a human. She rose from the bench and looked down at Megan. "Were ye there with them? All alone, ye three?"

"Who three? What?" It was Benjamin's voice. He strode up the path and stopped where Megan's cane lay. He put his good arm on his hip, the other was wrapped up tightly, well-bandaged by his mother who had thought his wound, by the amount of blood on his shirt, was far worse than it was. "Sister, ye best tell me the truth. I was at the ruined castle. I saw, as did Dylan, that scoundrel McKelvey and Mistress MacLeod. Are ye sayin' ye were there with them?" He roughly jerked her up and she screeched more from the tight grasp he had on her as she kept her swollen ankle off the ground.

"Let me go, Benji. Ow! Mother!"

Clara stepped back and kept her eyes down and her hands clasped at her bosom.

"Answer me, Meg. Were ye there? Do ye ken the way back?" He gave a shake to her arm.

"Nay, nay, 'tis well-hidden and ... and ... Jack made me close me eyes."

Benjamin let go of her and she dropped back onto the bench. Clara slipped in next to her and put her arm around her. She glared at Benjamin who quickly averted his eyes.

"Och," he growled, "me arm'll be healed by the last day of the games and I'll murder that McKelvey, I will." He turned on his heel and mumbled something about Anabel, but Megan had started to cry again and didn't hear it.

***

THE HIGHLAND GAMES in Scotland were a time-honored tradition and the McDoons and the McKelveys had been competing against one another for as long as any of the elders could remember, along with the Campbells, the MacLeods, the Kilmahews, the McDougals, and many more. Jack's mind jumped between thoughts of Anabel and thoughts of winning the caber toss or any of the other events he'd been practicing for.

He glanced up at *Castle Falaichte* as he carried the last two buckets of water from the well. He felt pretty good about his chances at each event and he definitely felt good about his pledge to Anabel. They'd talked in the parlor last night until the candle burned down and Elspeth ushered Anabel upstairs. He'd spent the night bedded down in that parlor—a more appropriate distance from the lady, according to Elspeth—and had awakened often to various night sounds. He didn't expect the McDoons or a lost traveler to come upon the castle in the dark of night, but now that it was morning, he was as alert as a cat at a mouse hole.

He brought the water into the kitchen, set the buckets near the hearth, and listened at the bottom of the stairs. Up in the dining room, the lady and the maid were chattering away like hens. He smiled and thought how wise Logan had been to suggest this solution. As long as no one came upon the castle, Anabel and Elspeth would be safe. He needn't worry about her while he was away. And if someone, a stranger or Dylan, got through the maze or found the front entrance, Elspeth was there to hold the rifle he'd leave her while Anabel hid in the cellars. He'd made that plan clear to them both.

It was going to be an exhausting week as he rode back and forth to Caladh, competing by day, guarding by night, but the exhilaration he felt even now gave him the confidence that he could do both things. And on the last day of the games, when all the couples waiting to be joined in the final ceremony were amassed, Elspeth was to bring Anabel in the wagon, hooded or veiled in some way. They'd sneak her in and he'd marry the lass before everyone and then reveal her face.

That pleasant thought fled his mind when he heard his name spoken above. He started up the stairs, making extra loud sounds and a clearing of his throat to announce his presence.

"Ladies," he said as he entered the room, nodding first to Anabel, stunned by her early morning beauty, her hair cascading in red waves over her shoulders. Then he laughed as Elspeth sprang from her chair and began curtsying. "Good morning to you again. I must be off. There's grain and grass enough fer the wagon horse." He looked specifically at Elspeth. "He's hobbled in the pasture where I've been throwin' me hammer. If ye need to leave, I showed ye how to hitch him to the wagon. It'll take the two o' ye to move the log that lies across the way in. And then brush away yer tracks." Elspeth nodded at every word. "But I doan expect ye to need to leave. I'll be back by dark. 'Twill be a long day fer me at Castle Caladh. There's much to do in the final preparations." He looked to Anabel, his heart thumping anew at the sight of her face framed by such luscious hair. "I wish ye could be there on the morrow. The namin' of the clans, the first feast, the villagers all singin' and drinkin' and laughin'."

Anabel blushed. "I wish there was some way I could see ye beat the McDoons … and the others … but I've seen ye throw yer axe and yer hammer and I ken ye'll be the champion."

"I'll have a story or two to tell ye, to tell ye both, tonight." He gave a rather formal bow toward Anabel and nodded at Elspeth. "I'll bring a leg o' lamb or some such roasted meat for supper and hope the aroma willna mean a pack o' dogs be followin' me back." He raised his brows and smiled a last time at Anabel. They said their soft farewells.

He went out and saddled Soldier, took the maze down to the loch, and made his way to Caladh at a fast trot. All the way back he prayed that Logan had smoothed things with Keir and with Laird McKelvey himself. His father wouldn't care that he'd diverted the servant from her duties, but the news about having hidden Anabel at the old castle and intending to marry her … well, Jack was glad Logan was breaking that bit of truth and not him. The Laird's response would be favorable, but Keir's reaction was harder to predict, though he'd been a different, calmer brother since his marriage to Eleanor; perhaps he'd wish Jack all the best.

***

DYLAN MCDOON LEFT his father and their newest member of the tug-of-war, a cousin from the poorer side of the family, to search out the way back to that hidden castle. He kept urging his horse to enter the woods where he was certain he and his brother had exited with Jack. Had that clever McKelvey come back and erased their tracks? He could not find a sign anywhere.

"These woods be too thick, methinks." He swatted his horse's rump with a branch he broke off, but the horse refused to pick his hoof up to step over downed trees. Dylan calmed enough to realize he was asking too much of the animal. He dismounted and tied it to a tree. "I'll go in on me own two feet."

He was on the hunt for that ancient castle and the delicious Anabel MacLeod. Surely Jack wouldn't be guarding her now. There were too many indispensable things the McKelveys had to do on this day before the opening of the games. He, on the other hand, had nothing to do but eat a huge meal and get to sleep at dark. Both things could wait while he pursued the perfect prey.

The woods were eerily silent as he stepped further in, stumbling over rotting logs and slipping on wet moss. It wouldn't do to break a leg now. Who would find him? Further in the land was drier and his boots crunched against the brown leaves and twigs, still though the forest was thick and difficult to maneuver. He used his axe several times to whack away vines.

Suddenly he came to an abrupt stop. In his way sat a large boulder. It should be a simple task to walk around it, but thorny bushes flanked both sides. It was an odd thing that such a rock would be stationed here like a sentry. There were pock marks on the boulder good enough for handholds. He decided to chance climbing the thing since when he looked up, there seemed to be a thinning of trees beyond it.

Atop the boulder he had a disappointing view of nothing else but woods. Surely this was not the way to the hidden castle, though he was sure it was in this area, somewhere. It may be a mile away or a mere few feet.

111

"Aha!" He nearly fell from the rock when he noticed something peculiar about the thinning of trees: there were small headstones sprouting at cockeyed angles between them, pushed up by strong roots. This was a burial site like no other, decorated long ago with flowering plants that still thrived.

He slid down the boulder and took a closer look. Only one stone was etched well enough to still be read and then only eight letters were visible, but the last letter was easy to guess. The stone bore no name he'd ever heard of before.

Curious. Most curious. He walked about, almost fell once, and then discovered something else: a very old, very rotting gate, fallen over and half covered by dirt and moss, but clearly on the side a resident of the castle would come from. He noticed again the small berries beneath the flowers and grabbed a few to chew on.

"If this be the ancient graveyard of McKelvey's kin, then the castle must be," he pointed a red-stained finger east, "that way."

Chapter 12

JACK HELPED HIS brothers move the cabers to the field they'd prepared for the games, having shepherded a flock of sheep through days ago to nibble the grasses down to nubs. They pounded poles into the ground and ran ribbons between them to mark successively farther distances. They would use this meadow for the sheaf toss first and then the hammer throw and finally the caber toss. A large target would be set up for the axe throw. This was the field for all the events, concluding with several competitions for the tug-of-war, until a champion clan emerged.

"Och!" Keir grunted as he dug a huge stone out of the earth. "This should do it for the stone put. 'Tis heavier than a full-grown goat and nearly as big as me sister's belly."

"Which sister?" Logan laughed.

Jack laughed along with him. "He means Rory, though Fenella may be bigger as it be her second."

"Aye," Logan took a stick to wedge under the stone and help Keir get it out, "there'll be plenty of cousins fer me bairn to play with. What about Eleanor, Keir? A brother can ask ye, aye? Will there be another McKelvey born before next year's games?"

Keir grunted as he lifted the stone out and rolled it away from the hole. He straightened and gave a funny look to Logan before answering. "Eleanor has been feeling a wee bit peely-wally the last two days. Her

113

mother, Mary, has been smilin' and twitterin' on about somethin' and then gettin' all quiet when I appear."

"Congratulations, brother." Logan slapped him on the shoulder. "The McKelvey clan will be full of warriors."

Jack nodded. "Even if they be lasses." He looked beyond to the next field where already a number of camps had been set up for those coming from distances too far to travel daily. "Look there. The flag of Kilmahew is set and also the McDougals'."

"I'll bring the McKelvey coat of arms out first thing in the morning," Keir said. "Jack, can ye be back at dawn?"

"Aye. Will ye be soundin' the gong or blowin' the horn?"

Keir brushed the dirt off his hands and then off his kilt. "Logan gets the gong, I'll have the horn, and ye, little brother, can beat the drum."

"And proudly I'll do so. 'Tis been a dream of mine since I was a lad."

Keir gave him a shove. "And ye're still a lad. At least until ye get a bride. Did I hear right that a betrothal with the McDoon lass was brokered by her father and ours?"

Jack and Logan exchanged awkward looks. "'Twas," Jack spoke slowly, "and 'twasn't."

Logan moved to Jack's side and addressed Keir. "There's a wee bit of a tale we need to tell ye, Keir."

***

DYLAN SAW THE roof of the old castle, but couldn't go straight for it through the tangle of overgrowth. He zigged and zagged until he finally came out onto a field. The castle stood wide and tall and grey and, in his opinion, beckoning for a McDoon to come to the massive doors and take possession.

The grin on his face was crooked. He was known for his mean streak and he felt a malicious mood gaining strength, starting in his belly and rising.

"I'm comin' fer ye now, Anabel MacLeod. Ye'll be mine afore night-fall." He glanced at the sky. The clouds were a fluffy white; he wished they were dark and full of rain. It would serve that Jack right to have the games flooded and his precious Anabel gone.

He did a little more imagining while he caught his breath; he hadn't realized how much energy he'd been expending in this endeavor. It didn't cross his mind that he should have been stronger from preparing for the games. He was, even this minute, feeling a feverish heat building and a pounding in his head.

A sudden motion to his left caught his eye. A horse. A horse was grazing close to the castle. Hobbled and left probably for an extended amount of time. It didn't look like Jack's horse, but the McKelveys had many fine animals. He had to proceed expecting to encounter Jack. A short oath escaped his lips and he wiped the sweat from his brow. His hand went to his dirk and his lip curled. No doubt Jack had replaced the one he'd thrown at Benjamin, but knife-throwing was one of Dylan's best skills as was axe-throwing. He pulled out his axe again as he began to creep toward the castle.

The main doors were impenetrable, but he tested them anyway. He could have broken a window, but each window, though tall, was too narrow for his body to fit through. He continued to skulk his way around the massive structure, using his ears as much as his eyes, and continually mopping his brow with his sleeve. He stopped and remained as still as a rabbit when he heard the hesitant voice of a lass, trying to sing a ballad, but inserting nonsensical syllables where the words should have been.

Ah, 'tis the beauty, keepin' up wi' her musical skills. 'Twill be a pleasure to hear that bird each mornin'.

He took a step and stopped. Took another and frowned. Took another and put a hand out on the nearest thing, a branch, to steady himself. A drip of sweat fell from his nose. He squinted at the sky, but there were no rain clouds.

The voice seemed louder now. He was closer. Another step and he'd be at the corner and this side of the castle would no longer conceal him. He went down onto his knees and pushed his kilt out of the way. He crawled around a bush and wondered for an instant if the pounding in his head meant he was dying and the voice he heard was that of an angel calling him to heaven. A crazy thought … but the earth was near at his hands now, the fingers of one hand clutched around the shaft of the axe, the other hand spread against the dirt, his breath coming in heaves. What was the matter with him? Was this a new excitement, far more thrilling than letting an arrow find the heart of a buck? Did his own heart beat so loudly because Anabel was close and she was going to be his? Forever?

He peeked around the bush and saw double. There were two of Anabel … two … but … dressed differently. Kneeling in a garden. Singing. Now two voices. What was this dream?

Poor Dylan tried to rise to claim her, but he couldn't. The axe he'd held in his hand now escaped on its own from his fingers. His head was suddenly too heavy to hold up. What sickness was this that came upon him so suddenly? He flashed on the graveyard and uttered a curse.

He lost his breakfast in an irrepressible vomiting. An unholy groan preceded his fainting, his face falling into his own filth.

***

ANABEL STARTLED AT the strange sound and then, as she whipped her head around to look, she screamed at the sight of a man collapsing onto the ground. Both she and Elspeth jumped to their feet, their hands clasping each other's arms, locked together in panic.

"Who is that?" Anabel trembled.

Elspeth pulled her toward the kitchen door, herself spewing peasant oaths and hollering curses at the fallen figure.

But when there was no movement from the intruder, they halted their retreat.

"Who …?" Anabel squinted at the man. "Is that …" She released her hold on Elspeth. "Is he dead?" She looked back at the garden, spied the tools they were using, and took the sharp knife from the bowl that held freshly dug carrots. She waved the weapon in front of herself and took a few tentative steps toward the body.

"Oh, Mistress, ye mustna go near him. Quick, come into the castle. We'll bar the door and wait for Master Jack." Elspeth knew not to touch the lady again. She was sorely ashamed that she had, from sudden alarm, grabbed Anabel. "Please, Mistress. 'Tis a beggar, mayhaps, a sickly man on his way to the games to beg for food and coin. Ye mustna touch 'im."

Anabel glanced at Elspeth's worried face. She didn't need to touch her again to feel the fear; she could see it in her eyes. But there was something about the man's clothing. This was not a beggar in rags. That kilt, she was certain, was made of cloth woven in the tartan colors of the McDoon clan.

"I think 'tis Dylan or Benjamin McDoon." She took a few more steps in his direction, knife out, eyes darting around for signs of the brother. This was a terrible risk she was taking, but with Elspeth nearby, now also

116

holding a knife, she felt more confident. The sound the McDoon had made before collapsing was a sound she was not unfamiliar with. The man had heaved out the contents of his stomach. Surely he was too ill to molest them. "McDoon?" She took another step and called his name again. "Dylan? Is that you?" She was close enough now to see the cleaner side of his face and though bearded she was certain it was Dylan. He groaned.

The smell hit Anabel's nose then and she gagged.

"Mistress, please. No closer. He'll catch ye."

"Elspeth, fetch a bowl of water. 'Tis Dylan McDoon and he appears to have been felled by the ague. Go." She waved the maid off, her hand motion not to be denied.

Elspeth disappeared into the kitchen and returned a moment later with the bowl. She slowed her pace the nearer she got to Dylan. She whispered to Anabel, "He be a mean one, Mistress. He stole Mistress Hannah once and left her to wander in the woods. She had a terrible illness after … was a fever … and now the devil be doin' the same to him." She spit on the ground and mumbled a hex.

Anabel took the bowl and knelt by Dylan. She put her fingers behind his head and lifted it from the ground. She poured half the water over his face and he came to, rolling himself onto his back and away from the filth and from her. Anabel rose and went to his other side. She knelt again and spoke softly to him.

"Dylan, ye're ill. It's nay the pox unless … unless there be spots where I cannae see'em." She touched the neck of his shirt and peered at his throat. His hand moved to hers before she could react. She gasped and Elspeth screamed. He held her fingers tightly at first, then he dropped his hand back to his chest and groaned. His eyes closed. She set the bowl down and got to her feet.

"I doan see how we can move him, but we cannae leave him here."

"Aye, Mistress, we can. Master Jack will return and he'll ken what to do. We can nurse him back to health … tied to a bed … and then young Jack can send fer his kinfolk."

"He'll nay want to bring them here. Do ye think we could get him in the wagon and take him to McDoon Tower ourselves? I'm sure I could find the way."

Elspeth's eyes went wide.

***

ANABEL LOOKED AT Elspeth's back as they bumped along the road. The maid was amazing. She'd rounded up the horse, hitched it to the wagon, and now was driving the wagon as well as any stable hand could. Elspeth had reluctantly admitted she could do it, having been raised on a small farm not far beyond the loch, and she was right.

It had been a struggle to hoist Dylan into the wagon bed, but he came to again and added to the effort under the ladies' promptings. Anabel dreaded coming in contact with his skin, but whatever illness was infecting him was also giving him hallucinations. The unfortunate McDoon believed his own sister and mother were helping him into his bed, and he therefore neither resisted nor expelled through his flesh any repulsive sensations.

Elspeth had taken watch of him then for the several minutes it took for Anabel to change. With a bit of bold attitude, the maid had stubbornly urged Anabel to wear the drab grey peasant dress that Megan had left behind—the better to hide her identity, Elspeth had warned. The clever maid also lent her her own hooded cape to assist in the disguise, should they meet any travelers along the road.

Anabel looked at Dylan's face, now serene, his head cradled on her lap. She tried not to breathe in the scent of his recent illness. She ran her fingers along his hair line and pushed back any damp strands that stuck to his forehead. She felt a burr in his hair and wondered where he'd been to pick up such an annoyance. All traces of sickness and dirt that had been on his face and beard Elspeth must have cleaned away while Anabel changed. Oh … almost all … besides the burr she noticed a spot of filth had been transferred to her skirt.

Another bump jostled them and Dylan's head jounced; he groaned and flung one of his hands back toward her face. His fingers touched her chin for a moment, then traced their way down her neck, but before touching her bosom, his whole arm went limp onto the wagon bed. He mumbled something that ended with *Mother*.

Anabel looked down at him with growing pity. His face was contorted by some invisible pain and she'd gotten a sense of it when he touched her chin. She whispered to him, "It'll be all right, Dylan. Ye'll be home soon," she added, "son," so in his delirium he would continue to mistake her for Lady McDoon.

She looked again at Elspeth. "Jist stay to the left when ye come to a fork."

"Aye, Mistress." Elspeth flicked the reins to urge the horse to speed up. She glanced back at the passengers and frowned at Anabel. "Best ye pull the hood up, Mistress, I see a horse up along the side of the road."

They trotted on, passed a loose but saddled horse that turned from its grazing to start trotting after the wagon, its single rein snaking up and down.

Elspeth stopped the wagon and asked Anabel, "Mistress, what shall we do? It looks as if the horse has pulled away and broken its leathers. We've nay gone far. Perhaps this be the McDoon's own gelding. Should we bring him too?"

Anabel scanned the sides of the road. There'd be no reason to leave a horse tied along this lane unless someone, someone like Dylan, as she suspected, meant to find his way on foot to the secret castle.

The horse, which had stopped when the wagon did, nickered softly and hung its head over the side of the wagon and brushed its muzzle against Dylan's chest. Anabel put a hand up to shoo him away, then changed her mind and grabbed the rein.

"Whether 'tis a horse of the McDoons or someone else's, we shall let him decide if he trails along." She stroked its long face then let go of the leather when Dylan gave a loud groan. The horse snorted and Elspeth slapped the reins on the back of the wagon horse to get it going again. Dylan's horse trailed after them. Anabel absently stroked Dylan's head and face as they juddered along. The touching of his skin was not at all abhorrent to her now that his eyes were closed and he seemed to be more deeply asleep.

***

JACK WAS STUNNED to arrive at *Castle Falaichte* and find it empty, the wagon and horse gone, and no sign of the women. His heart was in his throat as he called their names and searched about a second time. He wasted more time going down into the cellars on the off chance that they had hidden there, perhaps hiding from the thieves who took the wagon. He finally admitted to himself that the lasses were undoubtedly on the wagon. He hoped there was a good reason.

He looked around for tracks and found wheel marks leading north. He was confounded at first, then a sudden realization came to him.

119

Elspeth! If she were driving the wagon she very well might have gone in this direction, having lived nearby all her life. She must know of another way in and out. Of course. The lass had not been the least bit surprised when he brought her here. Could Elspeth have known all along about this old castle?

No sense in thinking about it now. He followed the tracks until they disappeared where soft earth was replaced by flat slate. Soldier clopped across the broken expanse of hard stone, obviously laid a century ago and now with edges outlined by green weeds forcing their way between the stones. Jack assumed a formal drive had once been a grand entrance. It wouldn't have been hard for the wagon to roll across here and join the road ahead leaving no indication that they'd come from the castle.

Jack studied the road dirt, but there were many tracks. What worried him was that there was no reason to go west and two reasons to go east: McDoon Tower and Castle Caladh. He pressed Soldier into a gallop.

Chapter 13

ANABEL'S HEART WAS pounding as Elspeth turned the horse into the lane leading up to McDoon Tower. She'd been here several times to visit Megan, accompanied by Clara, Shona, and Orla. It was always an uncomfortable gathering with Megan's mother flitting in and out of the parlor and the sounds of Megan's brothers arguing in another room. Anabel had missed several of these get-togethers to spend a quieter time at her secret place, the castle.

"Uugh," Dylan groaned and Anabel pulled the hood further over her head and gave him no sympathetic answer. She rubbed her nose as she got a whiff of the distinctive odor of sheep nearby.

Twenty old oaks lined the drive, giving shade to the wagon's occupants as they rolled on, and leaving no room on either side for a carriage or coach to pass. It was impossible to turn back now; they'd have to go all the way to the courtyard. The loose horse whinnied and cut around the wagon, the empty saddle's stirrups knocking against its sides and encouraging him to hurry to the barn.

Elspeth slowed the wagon. "Mistress," she whispered, "his horse has trotted off to the stable. Someone will be alerted to our arrival soon enough. I'll turn the wagon up ahead and … we should pull him out and leave him there for them to find."

Anabel's tongue stuck to the roof of her mouth. All she wanted to do was get back to the hidden castle and wait for Jack. Elspeth turned the wagon around when she could and whispered back to Anabel, "Now, Mistress. Push 'im out. Do ye need me help?"

Anabel shook her head and tried to slip out from under Dylan's weight. Carefully she eased him off her, at last finding her tongue and whispering words of comfort. She hoped she sounded like his mother, whom she knew to be a rather critical woman, complaining to Megan in front of the other ladies and quibbling over little things.

She whispered her commands, "Get up, ye wee monster. Ye can walk now, surely ye can. Get on now." She pushed on his arms and managed to wake him enough that he pulled his legs up under himself and turned onto his hands and knees in the wagon. Anabel scrambled over the side and motioned to Elspeth that now she needed her help. The two of them grappled with him, tried to keep him upright, but in the end, he fell to the ground.

"'Tis where he belongs. Come along, Mistress, we must leave quickly."

Elspeth took Anabel's arm and started to help her back into the wagon when a tall figure came storming out of the house.

Anabel's eyes widened in alarm and recognition. It was Dylan's brother, Benjamin, one arm raised in anger and the other tight against his side, a stain of blood seeping from his shoulder.

"What did ye do to 'im?" he snarled, advancing on the two women.

Before Anabel could react, Benjamin seized her by the arm and dragged her away from the wagon.

"Let me go!"

Elspeth grabbed the halter of the startled wagon horse and joined Anabel in hollering, "Let her go!"

Anabel's hood fell back revealing her face to Benjamin.

Benjamin cursed, then cursed again at Elspeth, loosened his grip on Anabel for an instant, then tightened it. He ordered Elspeth to leave and continued to drag Anabel away.

Anabel scratched at the fingers that were cutting the blood off in her arm and tried to dig in her heels, but it was useless. The man was angry and much stronger with one hand than she was with two. A chill of real fear ran up her belly to her bosom as she realized he wasn't going to let her go until he had exacted his revenge. She never should have let him see her face. She was well aware, by the sense flowing from his fingers into her being, that McDoon revenge included something completely reprehensible.

Elspeth left the horse and hurried around the wagon. She shook Dylan and pleaded with him to wake up and aid the lady. Foam dribbled from his mouth. Elspeth screamed at the top of her lungs, "He's dying!"

Benjamin barely eased his pulling. Through gritted teeth he yelled back, "Let 'im die." He yanked Anabel forward, but next came the moment his mother rushed out of the door, took in the spectacle, heard Elspeth holler another warning about poor Dylan, and raised the cane she had in her hand.

"Benjamin! Let the woman go. See to yer brother." She didn't use the cane as she hurried forth, but as she came close to Benjamin, she swung it hard at the back of his knees. "Let her go, I said."

Benjamin crumpled only slightly at the pain from the blow, but did release Anabel by throwing her to the ground. "Ye best sit right there, ye brazen hoor."

"Shut yer mouth, Benjamin. 'Tisna the way to speak to a lady. Can't ye see? Mistress MacLeod has rescued our Dylan." She helped Anabel to her feet. "Oh, ye poor dear, ye musta escaped yerself from that English captain, aye? 'Tis too much to fathom." Lady McDoon shook her head and rushed on to Dylan. She went down on her knees, ran her hands over Dylan's body feeling for broken bones, and finally, with the edge of her skirt, she wiped away the froth at his lips. "Dylan, me son, what be wrong with ye?" She looked at Elspeth and then back at Anabel. "Anabel MacLeod, what can ye tell me?"

Anabel rubbed her arm and tried to bring a more confident look to her face as she built the lie in her head. Benjamin was glaring at her, both fists opening and closing, his top lip twitching. She mustn't reveal too much; it was imperative she get herself and Elspeth away from here.

The words began to form in her head. "We found him aside the road … his horse, too … it musta thrown him."

Lady McDoon looked back at Dylan's face and laid a hand on his forehead. "He's nay injured. But he's burnin' wi' the fever."

Benjamin stepped closer. "She be lyin' to ye, mother. The wench has been keepin' secret meetin's with Jack McKelvey and Dylan musta found 'em. They've poisoned him. We best get her back to her father and collect the reward." He snorted. "And then have her hanged as a witch."

Lady McDoon glowered at Benjamin, then looked at Anabel and shook her head. "I cannae be worryin' aboot two things at one time. Benjamin, carry yer brother inside. Take him to his room." She gave her son another forceful gaze and Benjamin did as she requested, but with a certain amount of grumbling as it hurt his injured shoulder even more to lift Dylan to his feet.

"Ye there." He scowled at Elspeth. "Ye stand at his other side and help me."

Elspeth obeyed.

Anabel wrung her hands and tried to think of what to say to Lady McDoon to change this situation in her favor. She turned to the woman, opened her mouth, and just as quickly closed it. The mother was weeping, leaning on the cane, and trying to form words.

"That damnable Jack McKelvey. 'Tis all his fault." She raised the cane off the ground. "'Tis Megan's walkin' stick. Ye were nay the only one missin'. Megan ran off and Jack rescued her. Brought her back." She fanned herself with a hand. "Ah, the lad said he loves ye and ... oh! The rascal then stabbed me Benjamin." She shook her head and pounded the end of the cane on the earth. "I doan ken why I grabbed this from Megan. I suppose I meant to hobble her, keep her inside ... safe." She transferred the cane to her other hand and put an arm around Anabel. "Ye poor wee thing, wearin' rags and ..." She sighed. "I'm all a'flustered. Tell me, did this wagon lass rescue ye? Yer folks'll be mightily glad to see ye."

Anabel merely nodded and kept her mouth closed. Her red hair, released by a breeze that stank of sheep, fell against her cheek.

"Well, 'twill all be right with ye. Bad things come in threes. All me children are hurt. Megan's lame, Benjamin's wounded, and now Dylan's ill. I'm thinkin' Jack had a hand in this. Poisoned him, mayhaps, like Benji said."

"Oh, nay. 'Twasn't Jack. Ye mustna blame him. Lady McDoon ..." she took a steadying breath, "I must confess somethin' to ye. Yer sons believe me to be a hoor ... ye heard Benjamin ... but 'tisn't like that. Megan can tell ye."

"Megan?"

"Aye. May I see her?"

***

124

MEGAN'S JAW DROPPED when she saw Anabel, looking for all the world like her very own handmaiden who was the rightful owner of the poorly sewn dress Anabel wore.

Anabel came quickly to her side. "Megan. Did ye nay tell yer mother ye were with me?" She glanced back at the hall. Lady McDoon had sent her in and hurriedly climbed the stairs to see to Dylan.

"Anabel!" Megan, chagrined by the implied scolding, held a hand out to stop her as she came closer. "I havenae forgiven ye. Why are ye here?"

"Yer brother, Dylan, fell sick whilst spyin' on me and Elspeth."

Megan's frown deepened. "Who? Where?"

"At the hidden castle. Elspeth is a maid from Castle Caladh. She's been … well … since ye're gone … Jack brought her as a help to me and … and to keep things proper." Anabel stood looking down at Megan, her eyes roaming to her ankle. "Jack's been stayin' the nights to protect me from … from yer brothers. But he was gone when Dylan came back." She pushed up the sleeve of her dress and showed Megan the bruise that had already formed there. "And Benjamin grabbed me." She nodded toward where she thought Lady McDoon had disappeared. "Dylan has an illness I havenae seen afore." She took a step forward. "I swear to ye, Meg, 'twas nay fault of mine what happened to Dylan … and Jack's nay been around yet this day."

A mournful scream from high in the tower came to their ears. Megan jerked up to her feet then collapsed back onto the seat. She grabbed a bell from the table next to her and rang it several times. A maid rushed in from the hall, her spine curled like a shrimp's, her skin as mottled as porridge.

"Ginny," Megan said, "go up and see what made me mother scream so."

"Right away, Miss," the maid said. She gave Anabel a quick glance, then did a double-take when she saw the dress she wore. She held her tongue though and left the room holding up her skirts, ready to run up the stairs in her hunched state.

They heard Ginny speak to someone outside the door and then Elspeth burst in. She began to curtsy repeatedly and stuttered, "Mis-, Mis-, Mistress, he's lying there still as a dead man. The brother and the mother be wailin' so. We must leave afore they think 'tis our fault." She stopped the curtsying, saw Megan on the chair, and bowed her head. "Pardon me, Miss. Pardon me."

"I suppose this is Elspeth," Megan began. "What do ye mean, Elspeth? What might be yer fault?"

"I'm so verra sorry, Mistress ... the young man ... I believe he's gone ... he's passed."

Megan's face went pale. "Me cane. Where's me cane?" She hopped up and steadied herself with a hand on the back of the chair, her injured foot held up. "I must go up. Will ye help me? Both of ye?"

Anabel hesitated, looked at Elspeth, and then back at Megan. If they helped her, they'd be further into the McDoon stronghold, up the tower, and under their authority. If Dylan was dead, they'd be blamed, held in the dungeon until a judgment was made.

Anabel cleared her throat. "I think ye should wait for Ginny. We must be on our way. I doan believe an illness could take yer brother so quickly. We'll pray fer his recovery, we will. Come along, Elspeth." Anabel walked out of the room, head high and with purpose and ignoring Megan's sputtering response, but once out of Megan's line of sight, she linked arms with Elspeth and they ran to the door. Another sound reached their ears as they exited: a strangled groan from up above ... and a laugh.

***

JACK SPOTTED THE wagon and his heart fell. He was almost to the end of the shady lane, slowing Soldier, and already getting his feet out of the stirrups. He halted his horse, jumped down, and let Soldier walk on to greet his stablemate. He strode to the entry, glancing around to see if Benjamin or Dylan were near. He couldn't imagine a reason for his wagon and horse to be here, but if the McDoons spirited Anabel and Elspeth here, where were the McDoon horses? Had the lasses come here of their own volition? Perhaps to check on Megan? It confounded his mind to come up with a reason.

He looked up at the front tower and squinted. When he lowered his head, he was surprised to see the lasses come running out.

"Oh, we are saved. 'Tis Master Jack," Elspeth shouted, dropping Anabel's arm and clasping her hands in a prayer.

Anabel ran ahead, straight into Jack's arms. He held her tightly, but turned in the same motion and started walking her back toward the horses.

126

"What happened? Why are ye here?"

Anabel blurted the story out in short sentences, interspersed with Elspeth's urgings to leave now, to leave at once, to hurry on.

Jack still didn't understand it all, but between Anabel's face and Elspeth's warnings, he wasn't going to make them stand here and explain any more.

"Ye'll ride with me," he told Anabel. "Ye can handle the wagon, aye, Elspeth?"

He helped her up into the saddle and sat behind her.

"I dinnae ask ye. Can ye ride, Anabel?"

"Only in a carriage, on a seat."

He felt how much she was trembling, but it might also have been from the recent ordeal.

"Ye needna fash. I'll hold ye tight and keep Soldier to a walk. Ye're a brave lass and I love ye." The last three words he whispered in her ear before reining his horse onto the narrow private road.

They were down the lane and out from under the shade of the old oaks soon enough. For those few moments, with Anabel in front of Jack, his arms firmly around her, he asked a couple questions and she explained, in more coherent sentences, what had transpired. When the wagon came out behind them, he said to Elspeth, "Lass, can ye take the wagon to yer family's farm? I'll nay risk the chance of a McDoon comin' back to the castle. Do ye think yer mother would take in Anabel if she thought she was a common maid runnin' from an evil master?"

"Aye, sir, she's nay wearin' fancy clothes and her fingers are stained from the garden. Me mum willna have any trouble believin' she's poor. She'll allow her to stay especially if she thinks I'll be stayin' home as well." She raised her brows and let the tiniest of conspiratorial smiles form.

"Of course, Elspeth. Ye deserve some extra time with yer family."

"Thank ye, sir. Shall I show ye a quicker way around the loch?"

***

MEGAN FELT AS if she been slapped in the face yet again when she limped to the window and watched Anabel fall into Jack's arms. Ginny came noisily into the room.

"Ah, Mistress Megan, ye must get back in yer chair and put yer poor foot up on the stool. I'll brew ye some sassafras tea with mint and me grandmother's secret ingredient."

Megan mumbled, "I've had enough of secrets." Then more loudly she asked, "And what, Ginny, was me mum shriekin' aboot?" She hobbled to the chair and let the girl help her down and pad the stool with a folded blanket.

"Aboot yer brother." She lifted Megan's foot ever so carefully and placed it on the blanket. "He had a sudden case of the chills. He was all a-tremblin' in the bed and Lady McDoon thought he was aboot to cross over into the glory land. Master Benjamin ..." she trailed off, one hand on her back to help herself straighten up.

"Go on, what did Benjamin do?"

"Yer mum ordered him to disrobe yer brother and cover him with a quilt. His shirt had the smell of sickness and when Master Benjamin shook it, a berry fell out. He musta mistaken the poison kind fer the good kind and ate too many."

"Poison berries?"

"Aye, they plant them around graves to keep the ghosts away. The fairies like'em though, fer their pretty flowers." Ginny relaxed and her shoulders stooped over again.

Megan shook her head, but pondered what Ginny said as the girl hastened out to make the tea.

She knew in her heart that Anabel and Jack had nothing to do with Dylan's illness. Frankly, it served her brothers right to suffer a wee bit for all the times they'd been nasty to her. A little stab wound for Benji and an upset stomach for Dylan were small punishments. And if Dylan had gone back to the castle to kidnap or otherwise harass Anabel, then she had no sympathy for his contracting some mysterious ailment from graveyard berries.

Her thoughts turned to Jack. She wished things could have turned out differently. Who were her choices now? She would have to find a way to overcome this ankle pain so she could attend the games and have her father show her off to the other clans' leaders. She was in competition with Orla and Shona, wasn't she? Of course, she wasn't concerned about Clara's future—the unsightly lass was destined to be what Lady McDoon called 'unclaimed treasure.'

"Here ye are, Mistress Megan." Ginny ambled slowly into the room with a cup of steaming tea. "I made some fer Master Dylan as well. I best go up with it right away."

"Aye. So ye're sure me brother dinnae die?"

"He was still breathin' when he had the shakes. But if he had too many berries then he's nay long fer this world." She tisked her tongue and shook her head as she set the tea down. "I'm sorry fer me honesty."

Megan wondered if she should go up and see for herself if Dylan was dying. "Wait, Ginny. Where's me cane? Have ye seen it?"

"Aye, Miss, yer mother dropped it by the door. I'll fetch it when I come back down."

"Nay. Fetch it now, Ginny. And then help me up the stairs."

"Oh, Mistress, I'll spill his tea fer sure then."

"I have to see me brother now, Ginny. Help me up the stairs. Ye can come back fer the tea."

Chapter 14

JACK WOKE RESTED and ready for the opening day of the Highland games. After Anabel was installed at Elspeth's—he'd watched from the trees as the lass walked Anabel up to their modest home—he'd tied Soldier to the back of the wagon and drove it on to Castle Caladh, noticing when he arrived how many more people had set up camps. The stable lad unhitched the wagon while Jack tended to his faithful horse. There was talk of adding a horse race to the third day's events and he might do well with Soldier. Once inside the castle, the new cook served a hearty meal to him, his father, and his brothers separately from what the ladies and the lad, Colin, had. He went straight to bed afterwards, tired and anxious, but not worried about Anabel and that meant he could fall asleep and stay asleep until dawn.

He stretched and threw the covers off, went to the window, and looked out at the fields, now populated with wagons, tents, people, and animals. He could hear the buzz of low talking even this high up.

The barely yellow early morning light promised to expand into a clear, sunny day. He already sensed the excitement in the atmosphere; it was electric with anticipation as competitors and spectators roamed the fields or sat around cooking fires or practiced a skill one last time.

A pounding at his door meant one of his brothers was anxious to get going. Logan burst in holding horn and drum. He was dressed in full Scottish regalia, from the feathered cap on his head to a new fur sporran at his waist to his thick woolen socks and buckled shoes. Under his red and black vest, he wore a pleated white linen shirt. His kilt swung as he strode into the room exclaiming, "What? Ye're nay dressed, brother. Do ye need help? And a nanny to wipe yer arse as well?" He laughed and set the drum on the nearest chair. "Ye best hurry as Keir has told the bagpipers to start the parade as soon as they hear ye beat the drum." He tossed a small knife onto the drum. "And doan ferget to tuck this *sgian dubh* into yer sock. 'Tis tradition." He turned on his heel and left the room.

Jack found a fresh shirt in his wardrobe and silently blessed Elspeth's early preparation; hanging next to the shirt were all the rest of the pieces to outfit him in matching garb. The three McKelvey brothers would strike an imposing picture as they marched about the field.

As soon as he was ready, he met his brothers in the great hall. Laird McKelvey stood at the door, arms folded, and assessed his sons, finally letting a Gaelic word of praise escape his lips followed by a proud smile. "Out wi' ye. Let the day commence." He pulled open the great door himself and his sons walked through, Logan holding a horn under one arm and Jack ready with the drum.

Keir walked straight to the iron gong which had been brought down from its usual place in the high tower. He struck it hard leaving time for the reverberations to die away between the second and third strike. Then Logan blew the horn loud and long and Jack let loose with a rumble of drum beats. The waiting bagpipers lined up behind Jack while Keir grabbed the pole that held their coat of arms. The three McKelveys, followed by the musicians, marched out of the bailey and into the fields.

The excitement was palpable. Men lifted banners and shouted, falling in step behind the pipers; children ran in circles and women cheered and clapped as they passed. A mixture of cooking smells added to the excitement and anticipation and soon there was also the clamor of metal spoons banging on pots as the oldest in the crowds added their enthusiasm and delight to the parade.

On the third pass, Jack saw Hannah and Eleanor at the gate, arm in arm, observing their husbands with the broadest of smiles on their faces. He'd been grinning himself, but then his face fell as he thought of Anabel having to forego the festivities. He'd noticed two missing banners as they marched around. Neither the MacLeods nor the McDoons were present.

131

He was sorry for the MacLeods as Will and Alpin were undoubtedly searching frantically for their sister, but it was relief he felt that Dylan and Benjamin McDoon were absent. He didn't wish them ill will, but there might have been a fight or two had they shown up. Of course, there were several days for the games and they might yet appear. He couldn't believe that Dylan might have died or that Benjamin was too badly injured from the knife he threw at him.

He beat harder on the drum and tried to smile at the next group he passed. *Och,* the flag of the Kilmahews. He scanned them for the scrawny lad, Hamish Kilmahew, who would only wed Anabel over Jack's dead body. Where might the lad be? He spotted the clan leader, but … wait … could that bull of a lad be Hamish? All grown up and muscled up? He'd be a worthy opponent in the tug-of-war. Jack cursed under his breath. The young man was attracting the stares of several young women, lasses who had always favored Jack with their smiles. He remembered the Kilauea heir from the Beldorney Ball … how was it possible Hamish changed so much in the two months since?

In front of him Logan blew the horn again, the skirl of the pipes echoed a last time, and the parade ended without Jack beating out the rhythm he'd always imagined doing. He was still staring at the Kilmahew tribe and feeling quite glad that Anabel wasn't here after all. Then the crack of fireworks made him and several others jump.

***

ANABEL DIDN'T KNOW how much work there was in readying breakfast, but she was learning quickly and with a rare smile on her face. Elspeth took her by the hand—and it was Elspeth's gentle spirit that oozed through that touch—and led Anabel to the small shed where she could learn to milk the cow. They'd already collected eggs, fed the chickens, gathered firewood, and carried water in. She'd slept in the frayed dress, but had slept more soundly than any night at the hidden castle. She had fewer worries now and it was delightful to be a part of Elspeth's warm family. Her younger siblings were sweet, her mother welcoming, and her father exuded a manly confidence in his ability to keep his family safe and fed.

"This be Lottie, named after the queen of England," Elspeth said as a way of introduction to the cow.

"Ye name the beasts? I thought only horses had names." Anabel stayed well back of the large animal.

Elspeth spilled a laugh then quickly sobered. "I dinnae mean to laugh at ye, Mistress."

"Shh, 'tis fine. Ye mustna call me Mistress. Remember, we told yer mum I was Annie."

"Aye, Annie."

"And doan curtsy, Elspeth."

"I shan't ... here ... ye must sit on this stool ... Annie."

Elspeth taught Anabel how to squeeze the teats and fill the bucket. Just as they finished with the early morning chore, they heard the sounds of bagpipes, their distinctive hum carrying well on the August air.

"The games have begun," Anabel sighed.

They commiserated a few moments that they must miss such excitement. Elspeth had hoped to be a part of it, having never been before, she was most eager to see them up close. As a servant at Castle Caladh, she would have been in the midst of things.

"Ye can still go," Anabel urged. "Ye needna be me guardian here. Ye must go. And tell me how Jack does."

At that moment the cracks and booms of fireworks startled them.

"Are ye sure, Mis— ... Annie? I did promise me little sisters they could come for one of the days. Today ... well, I might be of service."

"Aye, 'tis a grand idea. Tell me what else I need to do to help whilst ye're gone."

Elspeth stared at Anabel a moment without speaking, then, as if it had just occurred to her, she said, "Mistress ... ye could go too. Ye'd nay be recognized. Ye could wear me hooded cloak again." She looked her up and then down. "Oh, and ye must use me old slippers. Nary a maid I ken has shoes so nice."

Anabel looked down and smiled. "I could pretend to be an aunt. Would yer sisters call me Auntie?"

***

MEGAN FUMED. SHE was being made to sit by Dylan's bedside and tend to him while the rest of the household went to the Highland games. They were late leaving, due to Benjamin's injury starting to bleed again, but her father, Patrick McDoon had little sympathy for his sons and much ire toward the McKelveys. He insisted any in the McDoon clan who could walk would attend. Making an entrance after the fireworks might be to their advantage. He'd recruited not one, but three distant relatives to replace Benjamin. And now with Dylan lying weak and perhaps on the verge of death, they'd need the three cousins more than ever.

"Jist hold yer fool head up a second more," Megan coaxed. "Ye're nay gettin' enough water to drown a fairy. Drink up."

Dylan tried. Water from the cup dribbled down his chin and wet the sheet that covered his bare chest. Megan began to mumble how unfair it was that her mother and father and brother and Ginny and the stable lad and the shepherd boy and the cook and two of the other servants all got to go. Here she was, her ankle strong enough to walk on with the cane, sitting next to her foul-smelling brother. The only other human at McDoon Tower was the older-than-dirt nanny who stayed in the rain shelter by the sheep pen as she could no longer manage the great number of stairs they had.

"Meggie," Dylan whispered her name as if it were a prayer, "can ye forgive me?"

"Fer what?"

"I'm dyin', Meg. Forgive me fer all the tricks I played on ye."

He seemed sincere enough, but he'd said stranger things in his delirium. "Forgiven."

"And I wanna give ye somethin' I made … ye can be the mistress of that castle."

Megan perked up. "What castle?"

"That hidden one, where Jack keeps Anabel. Look under me bed." He blinked his eyes and groaned. "There's a parchment … names missin' … dates. Help me sit up."

Megan frowned at him. He wasn't making much sense, but she gritted her teeth against the pain of standing and pulling on him and then of getting down on her knees and peering under the bed. It was as he'd said. There was a parchment, rolled up. She pulled it out, dusted it and herself off, winced at the ankle pain, and sat again on the chair she'd been warming for an hour now.

She untied the narrow black ribbon and unrolled the parchment. It appeared to be a deed of sorts, but there were, as Dylan had mumbled, names and dates missing.

"Get me a quill and ink," Dylan sounded a wee bit stronger now that he was sitting. "I saw the name on a headstone … I remember the date." His eyes closed and he relaxed against the pillow, waiting.

Megan studied the parchment further. It wasn't real; it couldn't be. This was another of her brother's malicious tricks.

Nevertheless … she was angry with Jack and with Anabel and if she owned a castle that would make her paltry dowry much more attractive. Could she possibly win back Jack?

Dylan's room was dark and dreary, but there was a desk by the window. She hobbled to it and threw back the draperies. Enough light shined on the desk that she easily found what she needed in one of the drawers. She took two paper weights and held the parchment open with them. Then she sat and uncorked the ink and dipped the quill. "What names go here?"

"Can ye make the fancy letters?" Dylan turned his head toward her.

"Of course. Tell me the names and what should be the date of sale?" Megan dipped the quill in and sat poised, ready.

"The castle belonged to Finnias Caldecott." He spelled out the nine letters of the last name. "And he's to have sold it to our great-grandfather, Abraham McDoon." He coughed as Megan wrote. Then he supplied a date one month earlier than the date he saw in the castle graveyard, just before he ate the poison berries. He grunted at the memory and cursed himself.

"'Tis finished," Megan said, blowing on the document. "But how does it belong to me then?"

"Save it. I fear I'm dying, soon ye'll be the only heir."

Megan huffed. "There's Benjamin."

"He'll nay live through the games. He whispered his plan to me afore they left. It willna work. If the McKelveys doan kill 'im, then the MacLeods shall. Will and Alpin may miss the games, but once Benji trots through the crowd with Anabel, they'll hear of it and he'll be lucky to live out the day."

Megan scowled in thought. "And how will he get Anabel? Jack took her away from here, ye ken."

"Aye." Dylan struggled to get the words out. He'd started to feel better a moment ago, but now he was relapsing. "Benji carried me up and Mother screamed when she thought I'd died. Then I rallied and made

135

her laugh. She let Benji go then and he followed the three of them. Mother watched from yon window tellin' me he took me horse, bareback, and cut across the side field."

"So now he kens the way to the hidden castle." Megan itched a spot on her chin then rolled up the scroll and tied the ribbon.

"Nay," Dylan looked past her out the window at the cloudless day, a perfect summer day for the games. "Jack dinnae take her to the castle. He dropped her near a peasant farm and the other lass walked her there, he said."

The slightest of fears coursed through Megan's frame. She was resentful of Anabel, but she didn't truly want any harm to come to her. But harm there'd be if Benjamin had his way.

***

ANABEL AND ELSPETH walked on either side of Elspeth's younger sisters, who skipped and giggled the entire walk to Castle Caladh.

"I heard Master Keir tellin' his new wife they'd be startin' with the sheaf toss on the first day," Elspeth said, glancing over at Anabel who for all the money in Scotland looked prettier than a princess even in her drab get-up and a little dirt rubbed on her nose. Elspeth could make that comparison as Master Keir's wife was indeed a real princess, though they'd warned all the servants to keep that bit of knowledge to themselves whilst there'd been some Scottish plot to dethrone King George. "Pull the hood down further, Mis—, uh, Auntie." Elspeth showed her what she meant with her mother's borrowed cape. "We may get too warm, but 'tis better to roast than to burn, me mum says." She called to her sisters who'd run ahead, warning them to stay close to them when they reached the field.

Anabel adjusted her hood and tucked back any stray hairs. Elspeth had tied her hair back for her and wasted no time with braids; Anabel rather preferred the simplicity. She'd agreed to come along only because she was certain her father and brothers wouldn't be looking for her here. She was also curious to see Jack in a competitive situation.

"Auntie, sister ..." the older of the wee lasses, ten-year-old Lucy, came running back to them, "there be a man ahead, tossin' balls in the air and children tryin' to catch'em. Libby's there a'starin'. Should I pull her back?"

"'Tis a performer, a juggler," Anabel said.

136

"Aye, a chuggler," Elspeth repeated, her tongue obviously not familiar with the word. She frowned at Anabel. "'Tis safe for them?" When Anabel nodded, Elspeth said to Lucy, "Ye can watch the chuggler, but come when I call ye." Elspeth moved closer to Anabel and asked, "Will the chuggler want a coin from me sisters?"

Anabel shook her head, then pointed. Beyond the juggler and the crowd of children surrounding him were several camps, flags and banners flying, and then the field with contestants gathering in the center. The festivities had begun; laughter and cheering rang in the air.

"I see Jack," Anabel said. He was carrying a pitchfork and two sacks filled with hay, one twice the size of the other. He placed the smaller one before the first man in line and handed him the pitchfork. He left the larger sheaf next to his father. Then he took his place at the end of the line, next to his brothers.

Two men brought out three poles; they were servants, she could tell by their clothing as none of them wore kilts, but rather billowing breeches instead. Two of the poles were notched at successively higher spots so they could place the third horizontal pole in them and make it more difficult to toss a sheaf over.

"Oh, let us hurry on," Elspeth said, sounding excited. "I've seen the McKelveys practicin' and I'm sure they'll best all the others." She grinned at Anabel, tucked her arm in hers, and said, "Come on, Auntie."

They reached the closest sidelines and Anabel resisted going further, but Elspeth whispered, "If we stay in the back, anyone can turn and see our faces. Let us be bold and stand over there." She tugged her up to the front and called for her sisters. When they came running up, she lifted Libby into her arms and hugged her.

Anabel touched Lucy's shoulders as the lass stood in front of her. The child's enthusiasm was contagious even without a skin-to-skin contact.

The event began when Laird McKelvey, sitting on his horse, loudly announced the first contestant. The bar's height was set above the pole holders' heads and the first several men easily tossed the sheaf over. By the time it was Keir's turn, five men had been eliminated. The McKelveys each pitched the sack over and the cheers resounded.

It was a bit of a problem to raise the height, but the servants had practiced a method. They laid the poles on the ground, moved the horizontal one up a notch, and carefully re-erected the contraption. The spectators were equally enthused about their efforts and cheered almost as loudly for them each time.

In rounds two, three, and four every man managed to succeed. They repeated the bar raising process for three more rounds, but on the highest level every single man failed, down the line, until the young Scot next to Keir got it over the bar. His clan's red and gold banner was raised and waved and there were proud cheers from the southern clans. Then several of them started walking through the crowd taking wagers on the outcome.

Next it was Keir's turn and he took a few extra breaths as his brothers yelled encouragement. The sheaf arced over and the crowd made noise. Only two contestants left: Logan and Jack. But they both knocked the bar off the notches when they couldn't pitch the sheaf high enough. There were boos and shouts and Anabel was especially saddened. She watched Jack's face as he joined the crowd and was warmed to see how he now rooted for Keir. She lost sight of Jack as he melted into a group of his supporters.

Laird McKelvey announced, "We've prepared a heavier sack as the poles cannae go higher. Each contestant will get three tries, if neither succeeds, it will be a draw. Keir McKelvey will go second after our guest, Hamish Kilmahew."

Anabel gasped at the name.

"What be wrong, Miss, uh Auntie?"

Unconsciously Anabel squeezed Lucy's shoulders; the lass looked up at her pretend aunt and shook herself free of the grip. "I'm sorry, Lucy," Anabel was quick to say. She leaned toward Elspeth. "'Tis the name of me intended, though he's much changed from … well … he's nay the chinless scarecrow I danced with at the princess's ball."

Elspeth set her little sister down and said to Lucy and Libby, "Cheer for Master Keir. Ye ken I work fer Castle Caladh." The girls began to yell along with others who were stridently cheering on the McKelvey clan. To Anabel Elspeth said, "Do ye wish to leave, Miss? Might he recognize ye?"

"Nay. I've nay worry of that. Oh … he missed."

Hamish stood glaring at the large sheaf and handed the pitchfork off to Keir. Logan and Jack gave him an encouraging slap on the back and shouted a few words from their banner to remind him: strength, courage, valor. Keir nodded at them, gave a slight bow to the crowd, and waved at his wife, Eleanor. He picked up the sheaf, and glanced at his father. Laird McKelvey put a hand up to stop Keir. He stared off to the north.

Everyone else looked that way, too. A hush came over the crowd as a horse-drawn carriage with several servants hanging off the back wound its way through the camps and stopped. Five men on horses passed the carriage and rode out onto the field.

"'Tis the McDoons," someone shouted.

Chapter 15

BRIAN MCDOON'S PRANCING horse was a spectacle on its
own as he rode directly up to Laird McKelvey, with his son
Benjamin and three other men, four abreast, behind him. The
horse halted, but pawed the ground as if it was as enraged as its rider.

The elder McDoon raised a fist and shook it at Laird McKelvey. "Yer
son has wounded all three of me offspring. Where be he?" He searched
the dozens of faces in the crowd.

The Laird drew his sword and angled his horse to prevent McDoon
from moving forward. "I've three sons, McDoon, which one are ye
accusin' and what be these injuries?"

"'Tis Jack I want," he yelled, bobbing in the saddle as he glared at
the crowd, most of whom had either stepped back, fearful women, or put
hands on dirks, apprehensive young men, or stepped forward, clan
leaders expecting a conflict. Jack moved into view and McDoon pointed.
"There. There be the varmint I'll see hanged. He damaged me fair
daughter and stabbed me son, Benjamin." He paused and looked back at
the nearest rider. The crowd made a collective gasp when Benjamin
lifted his jacket enough to show a white shirt stained red and black.
McDoon went on, "And poisoned me other son, Dylan, who now lies
sufferin' on the edge of death's door." A cry came from the carriage,
Lady McDoon's contribution to the interruption to the sheaf toss.

Talking among the spectators started to hum, but a hush came when Jack spoke.

"I brought yer daughter home safely. Her sprained ankle was unfortunate, but nay me doin'. As for Dylan's illness, I doan ken how that came aboot. I'll confess to throwin' me dirk at Benjamin, though" there was a reaction from the crowd, "but it was to defend meself as he held a pistol on me, a'threatenin' to tie me to a whippin' tree."

Someone in the crowd yelled, "Jack was in the right," and another yelled, "Hang'im." A couple of fights broke out then a loud, sharp bang, accompanied by sparks brought everyone's attention to the Laird, who'd sheathed his sword and now held a smoking pistol in the air. Gunpowder, burnt metal, and sulfur overrode the other scents in the air.

"I'll nay have yer lies and tales disturbin' the annual games."

The injured Benjamin reined his horse up next to his father's and shouted. "There be more. I doan see the MacLeods here."

Someone shouted, "They be searchin' fer their daughter. The English stole 'er."

"Nay," Benjamin snarled, "she's been hoorin' with that verra same McKelvey. He has her in an old, hidden-away castle, keepin' her there whilst he was supposed to be betrothed to me sister."

That news set off a flutter of talk. A baby wailed and two little girls turned to their sister and pretend aunt with questions. The two lasses, faces hidden by hoods, huddled close and said nothing.

The young Scot who'd just missed getting his sheaf over the pole, spoke up. "Are ye speakin' of me betrothed? Anabel MacLeod?"

Benjamin stared down at the impressively strong-looking lad. "Ye're Hamish Kilmahew?"

"I am."

Benjamin huffed, but said no more.

Hamish took a step forward. "What is this aboot the English stealin' her?" He looked at Keir and then Jack, then turned his attention and his words back to Benjamin. "How do ye ken she's bein' held in a hidden castle?"

"I've been there. I saw her with me own eyes."

"And ye dinnae rescue her?"

"I promised to keep her sec—" Benjamin hushed himself with a cough, stopped talking, while a look of suffering pain clouded his face. He put a hand to his infected shoulder.

"Where is this secret castle? Take me there. I'll rescue her meself."

Jack, hand on his belt where the axe hung, stepped up eye to eye with Hamish. "I'll show ye, but there nay be any maiden there. I'll admit she was hidin' there, runnin' away from marryin' ye, Hamish. But she's gone now."

Benjamin shouted, "'Tis true. I had her in me grasp at McDoon Tower, when she brought me brother back all sick and dyin'. Then Jack took off with her." He gave a loud laugh and weaved precariously in his saddle. "And I followed ye, Jack. I ken where she be. That wee maid o' yers has 'er at a farm." He pointed over the heads of the spectators, many of whom craned their necks as though they could see the farm through the trees.

Jack's face turned red, then he bolted toward Benjamin as if to fight him then and there, but his real intention was to catch Benjamin as he toppled unconscious from his horse. The horse backed up and Jack laid Benjamin out on the ground. Patrick McDoon jumped from his horse and shoved Jack away. Lady McDoon left the carriage and ran up to kneel beside him, crying, and the three men with them as well as the servants who'd ridden on the carriage surrounded Jack and took their revenge first with shouts and then with fists.

***

ANABEL COULD BEAR it no longer especially with her precious Jack in his present predicament. She threw back her hood, stepped in front of Lucy, and shouted, "I'm here," but no one heard her; most were cheering on the brawl that now Keir and Logan and several others joined.

She tried again. Those closest dismissed her cries as parents shouted to children and families gathered their loved ones and herded them away from the fracas.

The McKelvey clansmen and supporters fought the McDoons' men and servants; the various other clans either took sides or scattered.

Anabel saw the frightened looks on the faces of Keir and Logan's brides and spoke quickly to Elspeth. "Come with me. They'll believe ye, won't they?" She grabbed the hands of both of Elspeth's sisters and hurried toward the McKelvey wives. Elspeth followed, then understood, and ran ahead to reach them first.

"M'lady, m'lady," Elspeth was out of breath, "ye must help. Here be Anabel MacLeod."

Hannah was first to react and automatically curtsied when she recognized Anabel under the plain dress and cape.

"What do ye mean?" Eleanor put a hand to her heart. "Oh, Elspeth, our husbands'll be murdered. We must find weapons. Can ye fetch the pitchfork?"

"We must get their attention," Elspeth yelled. "Here be Anabel," she repeated.

Eleanor gasped. "Ye're the one. Ye were betrothed to Keir ... me husband."

"Aye," Anabel dropped the little girls' hands, "and now I'll nay be forced to marry anyone but Jack. Can ye help me? I must stop this before they kill him."

Eleanor thought quickly. "Hannah, take these children over there, away from the fighting." She motioned for Elspeth and Anabel to follow her. There were several camps lined up along the edge of the field, each with buckets filled with water from the Caladh well. There were other women ready and willing to help them. It didn't take more than a minute for a dozen women to dump gallons of water on the heads of the McDoons, the McKelveys, the Kilmahews, and a few others. The fighting stopped abruptly and Anabel swung her bucket over her head to get everyone's attention.

"I'm Anabel MacLeod and I'm here. Jack is innocent. He found me hidin' at an old ruined castle and brought me food and then Megan came." She took a breath and suddenly was too aware of the stares on her, and the whispers. Her hood was down and her hair undone, a breeze making the loose strands billow out like a mane. "He brought his maid from Castle Caladh," she pointed at her, "and he slept outside to guard us from the McDoons who threatened to come and snatch me." She bit her tongue not to say any more about Jack's nights at the castle. "And then Dylan did come back, but he was already ill and when he fell unconscious, we took him to McDoon Tower." She raised the sleeve to show some bruises. "And Benjamin grabbed me ... to have his way with me. I was most fortunate that Jack came lookin' for us."

She paused and looked at the sorry scene. Most were standing in short grass or mud. The horses were scattered but grazing peacefully. There were bloody noses and black eyes, but no swords or axes had come out in the fighting.

Benjamin McDoon still lay on the ground.

Anabel walked slowly to him and knelt. "May I touch him?" she asked Lady McDoon. She frowned at Anabel, then relented. Anabel put a hand on his forehead and felt the fever. She ran her fingers down his neck toward the wound. She pulled back the neck of his shirt and saw the infection there. Always before she could feel a person's melancholy or joy or anger or peace, and especially pain. From Benjamin she recognized agony, weakness, and something new: indifference. As hard as it was to look him in the eye, she did, and she smiled, pressed her hand a fraction harder against his wound and prayed for healing. His face visibly relaxed and he mumbled an apology.

His mother gulped loudly. "I've nivver heard him say he was sorry fer anythin'." She took Anabel's hand in hers and wiped the blood and sweat off with a kerchief.

Lady McDoon rose and ordered her husband, "We best get Benji home. Yer cousins here can come back on the morrow and compete fer us." To the crowd, she said, "I believe Anabel. She has the healin' touch."

The crowd seemed satisfied. Someone hollered, "Who wins the sheaf toss?"

Laird McKelvey remounted his horse and motioned to two servants. "Set the poles and let Keir give it a go."

Anabel walked stiffly toward Hamish. "I wish ye luck on yer second try should Keir nay get it over the pole." Her eyes wandered over all of him. "I barely recognize ye from the ball."

Hamish bowed and reached for her hand. "M'lady. I thank ye fer the wish of luck. And as fer the ball ... 'twas me cousin standin' in fer me as I wished a report as to the fairness of the match ... and," he laughed awkwardly, "we had a wager on it. By the by, he said ye were quite ... exceptional ... and he was not mistaken."

It was her left hand he'd taken and kissed. She felt something through the touch of his fingers and then his lips, but she couldn't give it a name.

144

She simply smiled back, nodded at Keir who stood nearby, and walked to Jack's side.

She turned and stood silently next to him. Once all eyes switched from her to the sheaf toss, she glanced up at Jack. Water had flattened his hair, his shirt was wet, and he was still visibly shaken. Her fingers found his and suddenly she could give a name to the feeling she'd had from Hamish. She'd never had anyone react to her with disgust, but Hamish had. He must have been quite disconcerted to find his betrothed in peasant clothes, her face dirty, and her hair wild. What a contrast it was to touching Jack. With Jack the feeling she sensed from him was one of complete happiness, not the giddy jubilant kind, but rather the calm, satisfied, all-embracing devotion that was mutual. He placed her firmly in his heart for who she was and not how she looked.

Keir drew everyone's attention. He nodded at Jack and Anabel and then at Eleanor. He pushed the tines of the pitchfork into the heavy sheaf, now heavier from the water it had been doused with, and took a stance in front of the raised poles. The bar had been reset to the highest notch, the height Hamish hadn't cleared. His muscles were still twitching from the adrenaline of the fight, but he smiled to himself, and with a loud *"och"* he tossed the sheaf a hands-breadth above the bar. Up and over.

A cheer went up and Laird McKelvey announced his son as the winner of the first contest.

***

JACK CHEERED FOR his brother, but what was going on in his head was a competition of ideas. He was keyed up over the brawl, but calming down faster with Anabel at his side. His father was now announcing the next event before the expected feast. The smells from the roasting meats being prepared in the castle's kitchen had reached his nose now that the sulfur in the air had settled. His eyes darted around, ready to catch any threatening movement he might have to react to. The touch of Anabel's fingers sparked another sense. And the presence of Hamish Kilmahew was unnerving to say the least.

The men competing in the stone put included nearly every man on the field. The heavy rock Keir had dug out of the ground days ago was first lifted high by the smallest man in the Campbell clan. This was something Jack had not practiced and had not planned on entering. He was thankful for that as he needed to catch his breath and think.

"Master Jack," a soft voice came from behind, "shall I take the lady to the castle?"

He turned to see Elspeth flanked by two dark-haired, wide-eyed lasses staring up at him.

"Aye," he said. Where Anabel should stay was foremost on his mind, now that Hamish was here and Benjamin had revealed things about the hidden castle and Elspeth's farm.

Suddenly his brothers' wives were next to him as well. Eleanor nodded at him and said, "We have things she could wear. We'll see to her, Jack." To Elspeth Eleanor said, "Ye can stay watchin'. Are these yer sisters?"

"Aye, thank ye, ma'am."

Jack eyed the lasses then squeezed Anabel's hand before letting go. He watched the ladies walk along the edge of the field back to the castle then spoke to Elspeth. "Ye've been a good friend. Thank ye. Here, let me put the wee one on me shoulders so she can see."

Laird McKelvey announced the Campbell clan and one of them stepped up to the line and lifted the rock to his shoulder. He moved back three feet and allowed himself a single stride to lift and launch the stone as far as he could. Cheers were yelled only by those belonging to the small clan. Two more Campbells followed, then it was the turn of the McDougals. There were eight of them and it took several minutes for each as they took their time. Between throws servants paced off the distance and marked it with a small stake and the clan's flag. The afternoon seemed long as ten more clans competed before the last clan, the McKelveys, stepped up. Keir and Logan and two of their clansmen, Robert and Dougal, raised their banner as they approached the line. Dougal went first, rubbing the scar on his arm for luck before heaving the stone a good distance, but it didn't reach the marker of the Kilmahews. Hamish Kilmahew had surprised the crowd with a distance of twenty-one paces.

Robert did no better and then it was Logan's turn.

"Put yer back into it, brother," Keir encouraged him. Jack yelled his support in Gaelic and the small child on his shoulder repeated the words to the laughter of those around them.

Logan's style was different from all the others. He squatted, balanced the rock with both hands, holding it against the back of his neck with his

146

head bent down. He jumped up and threw the stone forward, two-handed, with all his strength. The unwieldy thing flew like a startled bird and landed a good pace beyond the Kilmahew flag.

A cheer resounded and Keir slapped him on the back. A servant marked the throw and brought the stone back to lay it at the line.

It was Logan's turn to encourage Keir. Robert, Dougal, and Jack did as well, along with Elspeth and both her little sisters. The lad, Colin, and Eleanor's mother Mary, also shouted out the McKelvey name. Keir used the same technique as Logan and flung the rock hard. It landed squarely between Kilmahew's and Logan's. According to the rules these final three men could opt for a second throw. Logan shook his head, satisfied with his lead, but Hamish and Keir nodded.

Hamish stepped up and spoke to the Laird. "I have a great desire to compete against yer youngest son, Laird McKelvey. Can Jack nay have a try?"

Laird McKelvey's face puckered into a frown and he glanced at Jack. Several of the onlookers mumbled their opinions, most of which reached Jack's ears. His father said, "He's nay had time to practice ..." an odd look changed the laird's expression, "... as he's had to guard the lass who was once yer intended."

"She is still me betrothed nay matter what she may say." Hamish set his jaw and stared at Jack. "But I will break that promise if ye can outdistance me."

Jack set the wee lass down on the grass and folded his arms. There were comments tossed about the air from various people, men and women alike. *"Do it, Jack." "She be worth it." "Come on, McKelvey, send the lad away."*

Jack let the words go over his head as he locked eyes with Keir who gave the slightest of head shakes. He respected his older brother.

"Take yer second put, Hamish. I'll nay be enterin' this contest."

Groans of disappointment came from some, but Hamish smirked and shrugged it off. He took his second throw and landed an inch beyond Logan's. Since Logan had refused a second chance, it was up to Keir to win for the McKelvey clan. He looked toward the castle where Eleanor had disappeared with Hannah and Anabel. Then Keir looked at the crowd. "Fer me wife ... and our bairn."

He squatted down, balanced the rock, and proceeded to heave the heavy thing farther than before, this time with an added grunt that seemed to echo on as the rock rolled through the air.

***

HANNAH RUSHED TO the window. "What a loud cheer! Oh, look, they're raising the McKelvey banner again."

Eleanor scooted over next to Hannah and put a hand to her brow to help her look. "It's Keir. He's won again." Her smile was broad and proud. She patted her stomach and said, "He was carrying that rock around all day yesterday, saying he was building up strength for when the baby comes. I think he expects to throw his son into the air like we've seen Fenella's husband do."

Hannah smiled. "We have much to be happy about." She nudged Eleanor and indicated with a tilted head gesture that she should look over at Anabel.

Eleanor reacted and turned away from the window. "Anabel ... I was once quite envious of you. I knew as soon as I met Keir ... well ... I'm sorry."

Anabel finished adjusting the sleeves on the borrowed dress they'd helped her put on. "Ye've nothin' to apologize fer. I ... I have a gift of sorts. Lady McDoon called me a healer ..."

Hannah motioned for them all to sit on the bedroom chairs. "Yes, we heard her." She glanced at Eleanor.

Anabel went on, "I doan believe I have that talent, but I do sense things ... when people touch me or I touch them. I cannae explain it, but ... when ye were missin'" she looked at Eleanor "and Keir and Logan came to ask fer MacLeod help in searchin' fer ye ... well, I gave the lads some bread and cheese and as I offered some to Keir ... he touched the cheese ... 'twas on the end of me knife ... but somehow it was as if we had a direct touch. I dropped it all because of the powerful impression that came to me ... it seemed to pierce me hand and travel to me heart. I kent at that moment that he loved ye and would nivver love me like that." Her frown relaxed and her face brightened. "And then ... Jack."

Hannah and Eleanor bobbed their heads in understanding.

"You needn't explain," Eleanor said. "We're quite familiar with the McKelvey charm." She gave an especially meaningful look at Hannah.

"Aye." Anabel got up and went to the window. "I'm sorry now I've caused me family to miss the games."

Hannah and Eleanor joined her at the window and watched as the crowd began to move toward the castle.

"What are you going to do about this Kilmahew fellow?" Eleanor asked. "I remember learning that the Kilmahews keep their peasants in greater poverty by encouraging gambling."

Anabel lifted her head. "I'll nay do a thing aboot him. I'll run away again if me father insists on such a horrid union. I belong with Jack." She lowered her voice. "Do ye think anyone will stop us if we join the other couples on the last day of the games … fer the weddin' vows?"

Hannah said, "You could be handfasted first … tonight perhaps … that is, if it's what Jack wants." A smile formed on her lips. "I handfasted with Logan first in a secret tower here and then we wed in a musty-smelling church in England." She giggled. "It was wonderful."

"And I almost married Keir in a secret ceremony in a small kirk near Beldorney Hall, but the priest died before we said the vows," Eleanor explained. "But then we married right here, outside, alongside Keir's sister Rory and her betrothed, Rennie."

Anabel pressed a hand to the sill of the window. "Aye, I did hear of it. It was all Megan could speak of."

Hannah sucked in a bit of air. "Oh, we forgot about Megan. She was promised to Jack."

Anabel puckered her face. "'Tis all so complicated."

"Well, let's not miss the feast. See? The clans are swarming the tables and blankets are being spread for the children." Eleanor held an arm out to Anabel. "Take my arm, we'll soon be linked in other ways. Hannah was once my only friend and now we're family. As soon as you wed Jack, we'll all be sisters and we must learn to love each other like sisters."

A broader smile took over Anabel's features. "I'd like that very much."

Chapter 16

I T CAUSED QUITE a commotion when Jack seated Anabel with his family at the hosts' table for the feast, but talk died down quickly as each clan started to chatter and boast among themselves. Jack had ignored the comments and kept Anabel's attention on him by relaying the rest of the day's events and what she could watch tomorrow: the axe-throwing that he was certain he could best his brothers at.

"What if," Anabel tilted her head, "ye can out-score yer brothers yet a McDougal or a Campbell or a ... a Kilmahew throws better?"

Jack squinted as he considered the idea for a moment. He didn't like that she brought up Hamish's name, but the question brought a lot of feelings to the surface. He glanced at the others at the table—all heavily engaged in conversations of their own.

"When I was a wee lad, I'd watch me father at the games. He won more than he lost. Me brothers, bein' older, started training when I was still too young to lift a hogget, let alone a full-grown sheep." He stabbed a piece of meat with his fork and sliced off a large hunk. He eyed the meat, still too large to fit in his mouth and cut it in half. "Winnin' at the games has been all I've thought about since the last games, as I came in second to Logan twice and once against Keir." He put the forkful of roasted venison in his mouth.

Anabel took a sip of cider and said, "Winnin' was all me brothers, Will and Alpin, have spoken aboot fer months." She looked down at her

150

lap. "I wish there was some way I could let them ken I'm safe and they can come and compete."

Jack swallowed and took her hand, turned himself on the long bench so their knees were touching and he was angled toward her. "Anabel, do ye have any suspicion where they might have gone? North or south? East or West? I could send a man to find them."

"Well, south, I'm sure. They'll look fer Captain Luxbury, thinkin' he has me. They'll follow him to England, I suppose." She stared down at their joined hands.

Keir, across the table, perked up. "Did I hear ye mention Luxbury, that scoundrel?"

"Aye," Jack answered, "the MacLeods were led to believe he escaped with Anabel and now they be missin' the games whilst huntin' fer her in England."

Jack and Anabel twisted back to face the table. Jack let go of her hand and reached for a plate of neeps and tatties, the aroma of which had finally seduced him.

Keir glowered. "I'd've missed these games, too, if that woe-begotten man had run off with me sister."

"'Tis all me fault." Anabel sighed. "I nivver should have left home like that. Who kens what ills me father and brothers have endured tryin' to find me …" She sniffled.

Jack pushed his plate aside and looked at Eleanor and Hannah. "Will ye keep her in yer care a wee bit longer? I've somethin' I must do." Abruptly Jack rose from the table and marched away.

A few minutes later everyone's head turned to the sound of hoofbeats as the McKelveys' fastest steed, the horse Logan had ridden to win a race last spring, galloped across the gaming field, with Jack in the saddle. His kilt flapped back on his thighs, his hat tight to his scalp and head down. The horse was across the field and out of sight in mere seconds.

"South," Keir said. "He's heading south. Dinnae fash, Anabel, he'll be bringin' the MacLeod clan to the games. He may miss the axe-throwin', but I've nay doubt he'll win somethin'." He raised an eyebrow and smiled.

***

ANABEL WAS ABOUT to excuse herself from the table when the empty space beside her was suddenly filled with the shadow of Hamish

Kilmahew. Fierce blue eyes studied her for a moment before his stiff presence melted somewhat and he nodded at Keir and Logan and gave a mild salute to Laird McKelvey who sat at the end of the table. He gave a half bow to Anabel, hat in hand, sword trembling in its sheath.

"Mistress MacLeod," he held her gaze, his face looking handsome yet blank, "I see ye're finished with yer plate. May I seat ye at the Kilmahew table? I would enjoy a few moments of yer company before darkness falls."

She glanced where he pointed. The table had space for her, but there were no women with them. All of his clansmen were competitors, all young. She didn't even see the elder Kilmahew. Perhaps what was proper and usual in the their part of the Highlands was different, but a cursory scan of the guests revealed no other men-only groups. She hesitated.

Hamish offered his hand to help her rise. "Come. Please. Or if ye prefer, we could stroll about the garden."

Keir and Logan rose from their seats. Keir spoke. "'Twouldna be proper."

Logan added, "Aye. Laird MacLeod isna here to give his approval. And if he did, ye'd need a chaperone, someone to walk with ye."

Hamish's expression contracted. He looked to Laird McKelvey. "Sire, 'tis yer right to rule. Ye ken Laird MacLeod has given me Anabel to wed … after harvest time. Surely ye can acknowledge I have the right to speak a bit with me intended. I wouldna object should ye ask one of yer sons to chaperone."

Anabel understood the awkwardness of that request and quickly interrupted. "Dear Hamish, I hope ye'll sympathize … I've had a most tiring day and Mistresses Eleanor and Hannah meant to help me get installed in Castle Caladh fer a time … until me father returns. So I must do that … uh … perhaps we could walk about on the morrow if ye're nay competin'."

Hamish slowly shook his head. "And yer mother? Could I nay escort ye to yer home that ye could show her ye are safe and well? Certainly the McKelveys have a carriage and a driver we might use."

Laird McKelvey rose. With deepening tone, he said, "Hamish Kilmahew, we'll be endin' the day as we began it … with fireworks. The ladies will be watchin' from the castle towers, safe from the sparks and debris. I'll certainly allow ye some time to get better acquainted with yer intended … after me son, Jack, returns with yer intended's father, as I'm sure that's who he's gone off in search of. I'll send a carriage in the morn to fetch Lady MacLeod. I cannae think of a more appropriate chaperone, can ye?"

With three McKelveys now standing at the table Hamish seemed to shrink in posture. He dropped the hand he'd previously kept near his sword's hilt. A reluctant smirk formed on his lips and he bowed, this time more deeply, and backed away from the table.

***

JACK WASTED NO time in his actions. He added a large number of coins to his sporran before hastily saddling the fastest horse they owned. He sped across the field and took the only road that went straight to the southern border to cross into England.

Last spring when he had tried to court Hannah, he'd had many long talks with her as they picked flowers or rode horses or sat in the garden, and one thing he'd learned was that she and Eleanor had met Captain Luxbury at Ingledew. Jack's barely-thought-out plan included a stop there, for if Laird MacLeod was tracking Luxbury in order to rescue Anabel, then he may have reason to go there at some point. It was the best he could think of to start his search.

It was a poor time to begin a journey. The sky was still bright enough to see, but there were pink edges to the horizon and the sun would set soon. He intended to ride through the night.

He reached a high hill at dusk and looked back across the highlands. A moment later sparkles glittered in the sky above the land far off. Fireworks, he thought. He was regretting his decision to dash away on a whim, but there was something about Anabel that made him want to give her everything and fight anyone in his way. He had an overwhelming desire to provide for her, to make any sacrifice for her, to defend her and to please her. Perhaps he had overreacted to her sniffles, but her sadness and guilt at causing her brothers to miss the games seemed like good enough reason for him to rectify the situation. His feelings were powerful and complex and he'd go to these lengths for her. There'd be plenty of years in the future for him to compete in the Highland games.

He patted his horse. "Och, I'd do anythin' fer her. I'm completely smitten with the lass." The horse replied with a whinny and Jack gave it another rub. "Rest up a bit. We've a long night ahead of us."

153

He watched the distant fireworks for a few more minutes then tapped the horse's ribs to start him off in an easy walk. As long as they kept to the middle of the road, he thought they'd be fine. He wished he'd brought a servant or at the least young Colin, someone to talk to, but the horse would have to do.

It was nigh unto midnight when the full moon brightened the road and he heard voices. He could easily make out the moving shapes of three riders coming toward him. There was an argument growing louder among them and Jack drew his pistol, keeping it out of sight as he slumped in the saddle and tried to appear non-threatening.

"But it's too unlikely a story to believe him," one was saying.

"He had nay reason to make it up, we had him doubled over in pain. He was wretchin' up his guts and nay aboot to lie," a second deeper voice responded.

The third voice cut in, "Heyo! Will, Alpin, draw yer pistols. There be a rider ahead. Look aside fer others hidin' in the weeds."

Upon hearing the names given, Jack immediately stopped his horse. "Heyo! 'Tis I, Jack McKelvey, come to fetch ye three MacLeods." He tucked his pistol back in its holder.

The three so-named men trotted up and stopped.

"Fetch us? What mean ye?" Old Bram MacLeod kept his weapon out and his eyes on the road edges. "Have ye found our Anabel? The Englishman swore he dinnae take her. He claimed she was the one who let him loose and then ran away."

"Anabel is safe and well … at Castle Caladh."

Alpin reached over and punched Will's arm. "I told ye she was the one to let that animal outta his cage. Then she musta run off to that secret place of hers."

"What secret place?" their father left off watching for robbers and scowled at his sons.

Alpin shrugged his shoulders. "A meadow? She's always sittin' on a rock pluckin' petals off o' flowers when I fetch her."

The moonlight glinted off silver hair as old MacLeod shook his head.

"'Tisn't a meadow," Jack said, reining his horse around to face the same direction, "'tis an old abandoned castle once belongin' to me mum's ancestors. I … I found her there. But she's safe with me brothers'

154

wives now. Ye needna fash. She longs to see ye compete. Ye missed the first events, but ..."

Will and Alpin began to swear and argue over what day it was and who was right and who should have known about the secret castle and on and on, as the four of them trotted forth, Jack next to old Bram MacLeod.

Eventually the argument fizzled out and the quiet of the road surrounded them. Only the clip-clop of the horses' hooves filled their ears, until the early morning birds began to sing.

Jack thought of a hundred ways to begin a conversation with Anabel's father, but nothing seemed right. But when Bram finally broke the silence with a question, Jack knew what he had to say.

"Did the Kilmahews attend the first day?"

"Aye, and young Hamish took second in the sheaf toss and the stone put."

"Hmmff. Only second."

"Anabel watched. Ye need to ken that the McDoon lads were pesterin' her. She was hidin' from them as well as ... as runnin' away from havin' to marry that Hamish."

In the faintest of early light, Bram nodded his head. "I ken she wishes a different match. Anabel is special ... as any father would say, I suppose, but she is. Have ye ever touched her and she pulled away ... sick-like?"

Jack pressed his lips tightly together as he measured what words to use. He risked three pistols suddenly pointed at him, but he said it anyway. "Nay, sir. I've touched her and ... and I've kissed the lass. She didn't pull away." He dared to check Bram's expression, held his breath, and tightened his grip on the reins, ready to bolt and race, thankful he'd chosen this horse, and hopeful it wasn't too tired to run.

Bram startled him instead with a huff and then a boisterous laugh.

The relief spread to all of Jack's limbs and he let his breath out. "Sir, I'd ask fer her hand, but there be many complications."

"There's nary a complication I cannae solve. 'Twas a union with the McKelveys I yearned fer since the day she was born and a marriage to a McKelvey is what she'll have." He laughed again and looked back at his sons. "Did ye hear that? Young Jack kissed our Anabel and she allowed it." His further laughter was met with Will and Alpin's confused expressions and scowls.

"Come on," Bram shouted, coaxing his horse into a canter, "we have complications to abolish and axes to throw!"

Chapter 17

ANABEL WOKE TO a knock on her door then Elspeth entered the third-floor guest suite holding a tray of pastries.

"I took me sisters home and came back to help clean up after the feast. I kent they put ye in this room. Lovely, isn't it?" Elspeth set the tray on a table and continued chattering on about the games, the fireworks, what Lucy and Libby thought, and how the morning was breaking bright and dry. "And I thought I'd help ye with yer dress and hair before I go to see to Mistress Eleanor. She sleeps a little later as does Mistress Hannah now that they're both ... uh ... in the puddin' club ... pardon me language, Mistress Anabel."

Anabel stretched and eyed the pastries. "Ye can still call me Annie, at least when 'tis only the two of us. Ye've been a friend to me, Elspeth. I thank ye."

Elspeth curtsied and smiled. "Master Jack returned a few moments ago. There are three men with him. All quite tired as they rode through the night. Cook is servin' 'em in the dinin' room."

Anabel's delicate mouth formed an O shape, but no words or exclamations came out. She stared at the pastries a moment more then jumped out of bed and began to dress.

"'Tis me father and brothers. I must go to them."

"Oh … Annie … ye must let me fix ye up first. 'Twill be a nice family reunion, aye? And Laird McKelvey has already sent a coach fer yer mum."

"Me mum … oh dear, what will I say?" She reached for Elspeth's hand and relished the sanguine temperament that flowed from Elspeth's happy nature.

"Ye'll nay need words. They'll be filled with joy at seein' yer face." Elspeth patted the hand that was still on hers.

***

ANABEL NERVOUSLY RUBBED her hands up and down the apron front of the borrowed dress she wore. Elspeth had led her to the dining room, curtsied at the three men seated across from Laird McKelvey and Jack, and exited toward the kitchen. Anabel wanted to reached out to Elspeth to hold her hand and keep her by her side, but the men all rose at the same instant and she threw her hands to her face instead and began to cry.

Jack moved quickly to her side.

"Anabel!" Bram MacLeod took a step toward her. "We were so worried aboot ye. Do ye realize the danger ye put yerself in?" He flung an arm out in exasperation. "The prisoner mighta taken ye. Why … why did ye do such a thing?"

The lump in Anabel's throat didn't dissolve. She sobbed and grasped at Jack's arm.

"'Tis all right. Ye must tell 'em." He patted her hand. "Go on. I told 'em a wee bit."

"I'm sorry, Father, but I couldn't do it." She kept her eyes down. "I couldn't marry Hamish. I … I love someone else." She lifted her gaze and allowed herself to look into Jack's face.

Bram stepped between them and embraced his daughter. He brought one of her hands to his face and held it there. "Do ye understand me fears?"

Anabel shuddered at the mix of feelings she discerned. Her father had endured great apprehension and trepidation, but there was now a greater sense of relief and gratitude. She perceived his love for her as never before.

Her brothers sank back into their seats and continued eating as if nothing were happening.

"I understand," Anabel whispered.

Her father's eyes softened as he looked at her. He hugged her again and then turned to face Laird McKelvey. "Can we speak in private?"

The two lairds left the dining room and Jack motioned for Anabel to take a seat. "Will ye break yer fast with us?"

She sat and took a napkin from the table and dabbed at her eyes. Her brothers ignored her as they took another helping of porridge and bread. With a full mouth Alpin said, "'Tis the caber toss today, aye?"

Jack nodded. "And the axe-throw."

"I'm so tired I can barely lift this spoon." Alpin gave a laugh. "But it willna do to let a Campbell or a Kilmahew take the win. Or a McDoon."

Jack nodded, but kept his attention on Anabel. He whispered, "'Tis good our fathers be talkin' it out."

Anabel heaved a sigh and looked at Alpin. "Brothers, were ye truly worried aboot me?" She reached a hand across the table to put a finger on Will's wrist."

"Aye," Will said, "we were ready to take that captain's life, but Father believed him when he didn't confess to anything other than usin' the key ye flung at 'im."

She was satisfied with the sense she gleaned from her brother's fierce and spirited soul. There was a hint of love there, though she suspected it was more a kind of obligation than affection. She knew the burden was on her; she had withdrawn from others all her life … until Jack.

She sat back in her chair and smiled at him. "Thank ye, Jack, fer findin' me brothers and father. Ye made a terrible sacrifice. Ye mighta missed the axe-throwin' and ye've been practicin' so hard."

Alpin snorted. "He'll nay win with us MacLeods now here. We can hit the target at sixty paces. Isn't that true, Will?"

"Mm," Will uttered, another pastry stuffed in his mouth, "if I doan fall asleep waitin' me turn."

***

"WHAT ARE YE wearin'?" Lady MacLeod went from happy tears and hugging her daughter fiercely to a scowl and haughty words. "Ye must nay be seen in such rags."

"Shh, Mother, this was once a dress belongin' to Elsie McKelvey. I'm most thankful they offered me somethin' that fit. 'Tis fine enough to watch the axe-throwin' and caber toss today. Why, look around, Mother.

Do ye see anyone wearin' anythin' as fancy as ye have on? Even Laird McKelvey's intended is wearin' an ordinary day dress. We're to be outside all day."

The hushed argument went on a moment longer until Lady MacLeod put her shawl around Anabel's shoulders, adjusted the girl's bonnet to shade her forehead better, and hooked arms with her to walk to the chairs set out for special guests.

Once seated Lady MacLeod looked at all the banners around the field. "Ah, there's the Kilmahew flag and ... oh my ... is that young Hamish Kilmahew? He's quite a handsome man. Ye're a lucky lass, Anabel."

Anabel glanced to the left where Hannah and Eleanor were seated about twenty feet away. She was grateful they were far enough off not to hear them. She looked directly at her mother, but didn't dare touch her for fear of the sentiments she was about to evoke. "Mother, I wasna—"

"Oh, look, he's comin' this way. Most likely he'll want yer blessin' afore he throws. I wish yer brothers were here to compete."

Anabel huffed. "Mother. Look." She pointed across the field where Will was raising the MacLeod crest while Alpin stood spinning his axe in the air.

Lady MacLeod nearly came out of her seat. "What? The carriage driver merely said ye were at Castle Caladh. I assumed a McKelvey found ye and yer father and brothers were still out searchin'."

"Mother, ye best ken. I wasna abducted. I ran away to a secret place and woulda stayed away till the betrothal was broken. I willna wed Hamish Kilmahew. Me heart belongs to Jack McKelvey." Her knuckles went white in her lap and she held her mother's gaze.

A long moment passed between the two during which a silent resolution was set. Her mother looked back at the field. "I'm glad me boys are here to compete. When will they start?"

A trumpet sounded then and Laird McKelvey came galloping out onto the field. Hamish reversed directions reluctantly and did not come any closer to Anabel, but joined the other competitors on trampled grass. A moment later Bram MacLeod walked up behind his wife and daughter and stood. He bent low to his wife and whispered something in her ear. Lady MacLeod stiffened then slumped her shoulders.

160

Laird McKelvey rode around the edges of the field and waved to the onlookers. He tossed coins to the children, then reined his horse in and stopped by the throwing line. In a thunderous voice he called for the contestants for the axe-throwing event.

Five targets were set up and five rows of men, anticipation ripe among them, lined up behind a ribbon strung between two points. The sun beat down on the field, and the smell of sweat and dirt already permeated the air. The contenders were each dressed in traditional kilts and plaids, with their shining axes held high in their hands, the blades sharp, the handles polished smooth. As they waited in line, several clanged their blades against their own clansmen's axes. They laughed and joked with each other, their deep Scottish accents ringing out in the air. They took turns practicing their throws, the axes slicing through the air with a 'whoosh.'

Keir, Logan, and Jack were last in their lines and took no practice throws.

First up were two Campbells, a McDoon cousin, a McDougal, and Will MacLeod. The first Campbell threw his axe so hard it split off the top corner and sent a hunk of wood flying as the axe rotated once more and thudded on the grass a few feet farther. A mix of cheers and boos went up among the spectators.

"A miss!" Laird McKelvey shouted. "Ye're out!"

The second Campbell hit the target, as did the McDoon cousin and Will, but not McDougal. The men stepped off to the side and the second group went up to the line. Some threw carefully with studied aim, others seemed to let their muscles react as soon as the laird called "Throw." It took quite a while to get through each row of competitors. Anabel held her breath when it was Hamish's turn.

"A hit!"

When Jack went up against his own brothers she nearly passed out from lack of air. But each man's axe found the center of the target and their father called out their success with equal volume.

The air was filled with a sense of anticipation and excitement as well as the scent of fresh cut pine. The targets were moved back. The remaining men took longer to ready themselves to throw at the new distance.

Grunt. Hiss. Thump. "Hit!" Cheer.

161

Grunt. Hiss. Thud. Groan. "Miss!" More groans.

The morning proceeded with a steady repetition of the same calls; there were more misses than hits. By the time the targets were moved to sixty paces only eight men were left competing: the McKelvey brothers, Hamish Kilmahew, Cameron McDoon, Hubert Beldorney, and the McDonough twins. The crowd cheered and clapped in appreciation. The finalists waved to the crowd, and the noise died down. One of the McDonough twins went first and missed. His brother did no better. Then came McDoon. The silence was broken by the sound of his axe slicing through the air.

"Miss!"

McDoon left his axe on the ground, stomped to his horse, and left the games.

Hubert Beldorney set up to throw next and the McKelvey brothers gave encouraging words to him.

"Make Fenella proud," Keir said.

"You can hit it," Logan and Jack said together.

Hubert aimed and threw.

"Miss!"

The McKelveys slapped him on the back and said a flurry of Gaelic words.

Hamish was next, but he bowed to Jack and offered him his spot.

Jack nodded and took his stance at the line. He glanced across the field to Anabel and lifted his chin in a secret acknowledgment. He eyed the target. Was it farther than he had practiced in the field next to *Castle Falaichte*? He smiled to himself that he was thinking of the name Anabel had given it. He closed his eyes and centered his breathing and his focus. There was a hush among the crowd except for the wail of a baby and the snort of his father's horse. That only made him concentrate more. He drew back his arm and hurled the axe. It seemed to spend too long in the air as it spun toward the target.

"Hit!" Laird McKelvey shouted.

Anabel cheered along with most of the crowd. Her mother stayed in her seat and shook her head.

Again, Hamish relinquished his spot to the next brother. Logan waved at Hannah and quickly took his spot, raised the axe, and threw it with all his might. It whizzed past the edge of the target.

"Miss." The laird was not as enthusiastic as when he called out other misses.

Hamish smirked at Logan, who left the area to stand behind Hannah.

Keir refused to go next. "Ye are our guest at these games, Kilmahew. I shall go last." He left no room for argument. Hamish raised his axe and stepped to the ribbon.

"Fer me bride." He raised his eyebrows and tilted the axe toward Anabel who looked down. He narrowed his eyes and faced the target. He took very little time to aim and throw.

"Hit!" Laird McKelvey said.

Keir shook his head. "I am truly impressed." He made a little bow to Hamish, but winked at Jack. He lined up the target and threw his axe.

"Hit! Move the targets back five more paces. They will all throw on my mark."

Hamish picked the middle target with Keir on his left and Jack on his right. "A wee wager, Jack?"

Jack shook his head and took his stance.

Laird McKelvey rose up in his saddle and shouted, "I shall say 'mark, ready, throw' and ye shall obey as if ye were in battle." He looked to the clans and added, "Brave warriors of Scotland, remember how we showed the English our strength and courage! Let them hurl their axes as we did in war, striking fear into the hearts of our foes!" He turned back to the men.

Jack looked to Hamish and quickly said, "Winner stays, loser leaves." Hamish nodded.

"Mark, ready, throw!"

Anabel's eyes were wide. Two axes missed the mark. One stuck deep into the target.

***

ANABEL COULD NOT stop thinking about the games during the carriage ride home. Keir had been favored to win the axe-throw, but Jack's axe was the only one to hit the target and stick. She was so very proud of him. Hamish had stomped off, gotten on his horse, and left the other members of the Kilmahew clan without a word. She assumed he'd return on the morrow for the tug-of-war, but he missed this afternoon's event, the caber toss. Jack and Logan cheered Keir on to victory and then Jack ran over to bow to Lady MacLeod and ask for a moment's walk with Anabel. Her mother wouldn't allow it and Jack politely went off to ready the carriage for them.

"Anabel, pay attention. Ye havena heard a word I've said," her mother grumbled as the jarring of the carriage smoothed out when they turned onto a wider lane.

Anabel could see her father and brothers out the carriage window, trotting alongside the coach. She'd been trying to listen to their words and not her mother's since her father's criticism of her brothers' performance was far more interesting than her mother's comments about the Highland games and the riffraff it drew.

"We'll have to withdraw if we cannae find a seventh man," her father was saying. "The blacksmith joined the McDonoughs when we left to go after yer sister." Her father had calmed from his earlier remarks that his sons would have had better luck throwing their axes blind-folded, but now he seemed to rile up again talking about the tug-of-war event.

Will's voice came through shrill and high. "But we can compete with six. We're as strong as bulls and all three of the Northern MacLeods competin' with us are as big as that blacksmith."

"Aye," Alpin piped in, "ye cannae make us sit along the edge. We may as well nay go at all."

Will gave a snort. "Did ye ferget, Alpin? Ye were bent on gettin' yerself wed to Shona. Were ye goin' to leave her to be snatched up by some sailor? I saw a few standin' by the trees, eyin' the lasses."

Anabel leaned toward the window to hear better. Before she ran away, she'd heard her brothers scheming about 'catchin' a bride' at the games.

Her mother pulled her back against the bench seat. "Doan ye be gettin' ideas. If ye think I'll stand fer ye weddin' up with that McKelvey lad in a field full of sheep droppin's, ye be sadly mistook." She huffed. "Nay daughter o' mine will say her oaths in front of a travelin' vicar." A small smile increased the number of wrinkles on her face. "But I'll nay object to Alpin gettin' hitched to Shona Buchanan on the morrow. The lass brings a substantial dowry with her."

"Shona?" Anabel whispered the name. She wondered what other plans there were for Orla and Clara, not to mention Megan. It suddenly occurred to her that Megan might show up after the tug-of-war and insist that Jack uphold his father's promise. The ceremony would be a confusing jumble of pairs, some who'd been handfasted before and now expected a blessing on their unions, and others who would make a sudden and irreversible decision to wed after drinking too much ale or fermented cider. She'd heard of women being grabbed by exhausted tug-of-war contestants who, after losing their match, went looking for any unattached lass to convince they'd make a worthy husband. It was almost an event in itself, with giggling maidens hiding under hooded capes being hustled to the front of the crowd of brides while the final tug-of-war took place. What if … oh, she should not dwell on it. She had the sudden and horrible thought that Hamish … no, no, she would only think on more pleasant things, like going home to a bath and her own clean clothes.

They hit a bump in the road and she was jostled into her mother who said, "I dinnae see the McDoons at the games, other than that strange one in the axe-throw."

Anabel replied, "They appeared yesterday, much affected by their most unfortunate circumstances. Megan suffers from lameness and her brothers are ill. The older one, Benjamin, fell from his horse and had to be taken home."

Her mother gave her an odd look and said, "Megan is betrothed, ye ken, to the young lad ye couldna take yer eye off."

"Jack willna wed her." She took a deep breath. "And I willna wed Hamish, Mother. Ye cannae force me to."

Lady MacLeod shook her head. "Ye think ye'll sneak into the weddin' crowd and give yer troth to Jack, aye?" She shook her head more. "'Twillna happen. Ye are our only daughter and ye'll be wed in a fine kirk to a man who will cherish ye fer the treasure ye are and nay fer any large dowry." The muscles around her mouth twitched and she turned her head away from Anabel to peer out the other window. "We're almost home. I see the gates."

Chapter 18

MEGAN TESTED HER ankle with a few more steps. There wasn't even a twinge this morning; she could walk unaided. The maid had told her that her brother Dylan was recovered, had eaten, and was already on his way to Caladh, but her other brother, Benjamin, was confined to bed with a poultice on his wound.

"Mother!" she shouted as she walked down the hallway toward Benjamin's room. She stood outside; she'd never dared to enter before and there was a putrid smell wafting out of the open door—a sure warning to stay out.

"Aye? I'll be right with ye, Megan," her mother called back. More words, soft and soothing, were uttered at Benjamin's bedside, but Megan couldn't distinguish their meaning.

"Mother," Megan said as soon as her tired-looking mother came out, "I wish to go to the games. Someone must be there to cheer Dylan on."

"Aye, his recovery was most miraculous. But ye'd have naught to cheer for as he'll most likely only be a spectator. Even with our sheep herders we're down a man. The McDoons may have to withdraw." She looked down at Megan's slippers. "Ah, ye've regained yer footing, I see. I am glad fer ye. But yer father ordered us to stay with Benji, so ye'll nay be goin' off to the games."

"'Tis the final day, Mother," Megan whined. "And there'll be weddin's. Orla and Shona might ..."

Lady McDoon put a hand up to Megan's mouth. "Ye'll nay be watchin' nor indulgin'. 'Twas a most disagreeable fallin'-out we had with the McKelveys and though I couldna stop Dylan from goin' this morn, I will forbid ye, Megan McDoon. Now, off to yer room and back to yer sewin'." She turned abruptly back to the door, went through, and closed it behind herself.

Megan stomped her foot, then regretted it.

She had a thought then: if her brother Benjamin was going to survive and Dylan was quite recovered as well, there'd be no hope for her to inherit anything. She limped toward Dylan's room and searched out the false deed to the hidden castle. She tore it up, threw it into the fireplace which hadn't burned a thing in two months, and lit the parchment pieces from a candle Dylan had thoughtlessly left burning on his desk.

***

JACK SLEPT LIKE a rock and woke ready for the final day of the Highland games. The energy and excitement had not abated. Tartan plaids, bright colors, kilts, and bonnets as well as dresses and swords and buckles and rings all added to the cheerful and lively atmosphere. The music of the bagpipes, drums, and fiddles had echoed through the night and there'd been a bonfire to cast a warm glow over the tents and wagons around the field. The smell of wood smoke still lingered and since Jack's windows were open, he took in the scent and added it to the pleasant memories he would one day look back on. He only wished his mother had lived to see her sons compete together. He was also sorry his three sisters were in too delicate of a condition to travel, though he wouldn't be surprised if Rory made an appearance.

He got dressed and left his room, immediately greeted by new aromas: freshly baked bread and roasting meats. There was much pressure on the Castle Caladh cooks to produce more food than previous years and more variety as well. They were not disappointing anyone. He reached the great hall and went out into the courtyard where tables were laden with breakfast treats. He chose carefully, aware of how certain foods might make him sluggish. Winning the tug-of-war was his main concern as he considered the fruits and baked goods. He filled a trencher and took it the table where his brothers sat with four other men, Robert, Dougal, Ian, and Ethan, who were part of their clan's team for today's final event.

"And a blessed guid mornin' to ye, little brother," Keir said. "We're happy ye found the strength to open yer eyelids."

"Aye," Logan added his own sibling insult, "and happy we'll have yer bonnie face at the front of the rope to scare the competition."

Jack flung a few of his favorite Gaelic cuss words at them and all the men laughed.

"We were jist sayin'," Dougal put a large hand to his mouth to wipe away some crumbs, "that yer father, Laird McKelvey, will be the first in line fer the weddin's."

"Aye," Jack answered, "he intends to lead the parade with Mary Macfarlane."

"And ye're to follow, I ken, with a certain McDoon lass," Dougal teased.

"Nay, I'll nivver wed Megan," Jack hurried to say, "'twas the arrangement made earlier this summer, but 'tis null and void now."

"Of course 'tis," Robert guffawed. "What clan would have ye after ye poisoned and stabbed her brothers?"

Ian slapped Robert on the back and so did Ethan. Keir and Logan exchanged looks while Jack tried to laugh off the embarrassment. He was about to correct Robert's pronouncement and say he had nothing to do with Dylan's poisoning, when he caught sight of the MacLeod carriage coming to a stop at the gate. When only Laird and Lady MacLeod stepped out, followed by Will and Alpin, who both nodded at the McKelveys, Jack's heart dropped to his shoes. She hadn't come. He was afraid of that. The way Lady MacLeod had refused to let him take Anabel for a stroll, was a clear indication of their absolute rejection of a union between the families. Jack grabbed Logan by the arm and pulled him away from the table.

"She's been left behind. They mean to keep us from marryin'. Did ye ken of this? I thought our father had made a contract with ole MacLeod … the other morn … when off they went to speak in private." He scowled, his frown lines going deeper, and his fingers digging hard into his brother's muscle.

"Easy, lad," Logan plucked Jack's fingers off him, "doan get yer feathers up. As Keir and I can tell ye, all things work out fer the best. Ye'll see." Logan gave Jack a nod and then a push. "On with ye. I see the piper headin' to the field. 'Tis time to haul out the anchor rope and ready ourselves for the tuggin'."

***

"STOP, MISTRESS, LET me do that." Anabel's maid was mortified. "'Twas shockin' when ye helped with the bath water last night. Yer mum will have me whipped if she finds out I let ye dress yerself and do yer own hair." She stood, on the verge of trembling, next to the dressing table in Anabel's bedroom.

Anabel smiled more to herself; she liked who she was becoming. She'd been so closed off to people for so long it was no wonder she was perceived as haughty, snobbish, and arrogant. It cost her nothing to be kind and helpful and patient though she still was careful not to touch a hand or bump an elbow.

"Well, I'll nay tell her. I'm sorry, Kayla, fer all the times I've been rude to ye." Anabel took the brush from Kayla's hand and ran it through her hair until the auburn locks hung in soft waves. "See? This is how I want it. There is one thing ye can do fer me ... can ye fetch me old boots?"

"Mistress, ye cannae be thinkin' of takin' a walk."

"Aye, I am. Or rather, we are."

"But we're to stay here. 'Twere yer father's orders. 'Tis why I let ye sleep away the morn. It seems ..." she mumbled the next few words, "they've made a prisoner of ye, as a way to punish ye."

"Indeed. But I'm sure ye wanted to attend the games and ye've had to miss every day on my account. I am releasin' ye from yer obligation to stay here and guard me. Ye're me maid and I'm givin' ye new orders. Ye're goin' to the games. It's a bit of a walk, but I ken ye hoped to wed our stable lad and today's yer only chance."

Kayla dropped her gaze. "Aye, he left a pony cart hitched fer me."

"The cart? Oh, that'll be better than walking. We may make it in time to see the last event."

***

EACH CLAN CAST lots to determine the first round of competition. Jack drew for the McKelveys and they were matched against the Campbells. Laird McKelvey signaled the trumpeter and at the sound of the final note, the stronger clan jerked the rope and the poor Campbells fell forward. It was no contest at all. The onlookers, who had begun to

169

make noise and yell, laughed heartily as the Campbells picked themselves up off the ground and hurried to disappear into the crowd, humiliated.

Following that first contest, there were matches between ten other clans. The sun beat down and various men began to take their shirts off. Sweat glistened, boys cheered, women held children up to see, and a line of young wives wrung their hands and rooted for their husbands. Laird McKelvey was the referee for each match and then allowed a quarter hour for resting while jugglers and acrobats performed.

The next round featured the six winning teams competing against each other. The McKelveys went against the McDougals and won. The McDoons, with Dylan looking quite recovered, were still in it after their match against a clan that included Tavish and his son Malcolm, two people who had once helped Keir. The final winning team was comprised of six McDonoughs and the blacksmith. They had dug in against the MacLeods and made the anchor on the team, Alpin, lose his grip and stumble.

Another rest period was announced and a fire dancer ran into the center of the field. The crowd roared in an exuberant mix of shouts and warnings. He began with a flourish, spinning and twirling colorful sticks and then lighting them. The flames danced in a mesmerizing show of skill and danger as he made patterns with the flames while doing unusual tricks and contorting his body without catching on fire or burning himself. The children were in awe and the crowd continued to buzz with energy as he doused the flames in a bucket and ran around collecting coins tossed to him.

Laird McKelvey explained to the crowd that since each of the final three teams had won two matches, they would draw to see which two would face off first. There were a few boos when the McKelvey clan drew the first spot, but those detractors were the shamed Campbells who had lost early on. The McDonoughs won the second spot and were set to take the other end of the thick ship's rope when the crowd started to divide as to whom they would root for.

The seven strapping young men on the McKelvey team stood with one foot on the rope and both hands on their hips. Their kilts fluttered in the breeze; muscles twitched and flexed. The Laird called for both teams to pick up the rope and take their positions. The Laird himself held the center of the rope where a ribbon was tightly tied. The team who could get that ribbon over the line on their side would win, but the Laird warned he'd award a foot's advantage to one team if he felt the other team begin to tug before he started the contest.

The McKelveys' and the McDonoughs' hands were already turning pale with their tight grips, but no man had begun to pull yet. The Laird looked to his sons and nodded, then to the McDonoughs' team. In one swift move he let go of the center ribbon, yelled, "Go," and stepped out of the way.

Jack dug his heels into the soft grass, Logan braced himself along with the other four helping them, and Keir, at the end, clutched the rope and pulled with all his strength.

The McDonoughs did the same. The borrowed blacksmith had the anchor position on their team and kept yelling, "Pull together, men! Put yer backs into it."

Meanwhile, Keir was more calmly telling his men to keep their feet planted and hold their ground. Then Jack spotted a mistake the middle man on the McDonough team was making and, as practiced, he signaled the others to let the rope go forward for a fraction of a moment followed by a mighty jerk. They dug their feet in and began to pull the McDonoughs toward them. Each step made the quivering ribbon a foot closer to the line.

"Heave," Jack yelled. "Heave! Heave! Heave!" The jerking and jarring stunned the other team and even with the blacksmith leaning as far back as he could, the McKelveys managed to overpower them. The McDonough clan became confused and started pulling to the side instead of back. Once they lost focus it was all over. The ribbon crossed the line and the McKelveys dropped the rope and cheered.

The brothers slapped one another and grinned ear to ear. Keir and Logan looked to their wives and waved; Jack looked to the MacLeod clan, but of course Anabel wasn't with them and Will and Alpin were still bemoaning their loss, but it looked to him like Laird and Lady MacLeod were pleased with the McKelvey win.

The crowd was yelling for the final tug match to begin, but Laird McKelvey had already gestured for the step dancers to find their spots. After exerting so much energy in a short amount of time, it was necessary, to be fair, that the winning team should have another rest. The Laird had already arranged for these intervals of entertainment.

The rope was coiled and set aside and the step dancers were cheered on.

***

ANABEL AND KAYLA jounced along in the pony cart all the way to Castle Caladh. They could hear a cacophony of sounds long before they arrived, cheering first and then the notes of flutes and the hum of bagpipes reached their ears.

"They must be dancin'," Kayla said. "Oh, Mistress, I'm so excited. And I thank ye so much fer allowin' me to wear yer fancy dress."

Anabel smiled. It was an ordinary day dress, but to the maid it was a ball gown and the perfect thing to wear to marry her beloved stable boy.

"Ye look lovely, Kayla. Ye'll be the prettiest bride."

"Thank ye, Mistress. I'm nay sure aboot that, but I am sure I'll be the best-dressed. Exceptin' fer the new lady of Caladh, o' course. I heard that she and Laird McKelvey will be tyin' the knot along with the commoners."

Anabel noted the cheering in the distance and nodded. "Aye, there'll be a large number of couples promisin' to love and obey. I'd hoped to be …" She let the words go as they suddenly hit a bump.

She had hope the day would turn out as planned. It was why she had her hair down. Who would recognize her like this? She looked like a farmer's daughter perhaps, and not at all like a proper lady who would only be seen in public with braids and bonnet and shawl. She was certain her own parents would look right past her … but not Jack. He'd seen her this way before. She planned to watch from the woods and then join him when the wedding march began.

The road dipped and then they turned into the long lane to the castle alongside of which stood several carriages, coaches, and saddled horses. They came to the gate, but there was no stable hand there to help them. Kayla jumped down and tied the pony to the gate. She helped Anabel down and Anabel laughed when Kayla's palm touched hers.

"Ye are more excited than ye said. Yer face is all aglow." Anabel landed on the grass and put a hand to Kayla's cheek. "Ye look feverish, but ye're jist happy."

172

"Ye look happy, too, Mistress. I hope ye'll nay get in any trouble with yer father. I 'spect ye'll go home in the carriage so me new husband will see to this cart and pony."

"Aye, that'll do fine." She impulsively leaned forward and hugged Kayla. "Ye needna worry aboot me. And Kayla, ye have tomorrow off."

Kayla curtsied and waited to see what Anabel expected next.

"Go on. Find yer man. I'll be all right."

Kayla lifted the hem of the borrowed dress and took tentative but hurried steps through the longer grass, then skirted the bailey, and disappeared.

A medley of smells made Anabel's mouth water. She took the same path Kayla had, but more slowly. This was going to be her wedding day and she wanted to savor every aspect of it, from the bugs on the bushes to the birds in the air to the smells and sounds of the Highland games just behind the castle. She picked her way along, breathing deeply, calming herself, and imagining … oh, the most wonderful things. Like Kayla, she could barely contain her enthusiasm and wondered if her own cheeks were just as rosy, the freckles warm, her eyes aglow, the smile fixed.

"Mistress Anabel." The voice was full of surprise. "What are ye doin' here? Ye should be with the others."

She looked up from the path to see Elspeth carrying a tray of cakes. "Oh, Elspeth. It's so good to see ye." She beamed at her. "Do ye need help carryin' that heavy thing?"

"Nay, Mistress," Elspeth managed to put one foot behind the other and attempt a small curtsy, "'tis a light load. These are the cakes to break over the brides' heads. There be one more tug o' war and then we'll have the parade o' brides to end the games."

"Are the McKelveys still competin'?"

"Aye, Miss, they won all their matches and have only to best the McDoons." Her sweet face scrunched at the name.

Anabel gasped first with glee and then dread. "Oh … all the McDoons?"

"Master Dylan, his father, their shepherds, and a bull-like man I dinnae ken."

"Well, they wouldna be competin' if Benjamin had died."

"Nay, Miss. Benjamin isna here, nor is Lady McDoon or Mistress Megan."

Anabel was glad of that. She did not want to face Megan today. "One last thing," Anabel asked as she peered toward the area set up with a wedding arch and decorated with flowers, "do ye think ye could get a message to Jack that I'll be waitin' fer him, uh," she looked back where she'd come through the bailey, "behind the statue."

"Aye, Miss, if I cannae tell him meself, I'll send young Colin. He's been hoverin' around the kitchen between events." She tried to curtsy again and Anabel smiled at her, turned toward the bailey, and retraced her steps.

There was an immovable stone bench beside the statue and she sat there. It seemed to be a good choice, out of the way, and hidden. But she only sat for a few seconds before popping up and pacing around. Should she try to find a place where she could see the competition? The music was enticing. She knew the tune, had learned to step dance long ago, but her mother had forbidden her to practice and had fired the maid who taught her. She twirled once and tried a few of the intricate steps and quick footwork. She'd forgotten so much and now she really wanted to see what was going on on the other side of the castle.

Chapter 19

JACK AND HIS brothers did not sit on the ground to watch the step dancers as so many did. They slowly walked around the perimeter, savoring the encouragement of those who wished them to beat the McDoons.

"'Tisn't fair," one old man said to Jack, "there only be two true McDoons in the bunch."

Another man, who'd been rooting for the McDougals before, whispered, "I've placed me wager with Kilmahew that ye'll win in under two minutes. Doan let me down."

Jack's head whipped around to look for the Kilmahew flag. He'd noticed it before, but thought it had been left hanging by the oaks, forgotten when Hamish rode off yesterday. Now he could see a small group around Laird Kilmahew, but no Hamish. It seemed too good to be true that Hamish hadn't come back. Then it hit him: maybe he was with Anabel this very moment. She hadn't come with her parents. He'd assumed she'd be brought by a stablehand in time for the nuptials. Didn't a lass need all day to prepare? His sister had taken weeks. But what if the MacLeods had honored the betrothal and allowed Hamish to take her away?

He scanned the crowd again. No, no Anabel. He stopped walking and let Logan, Keir, and the others continue on. He doubled back to where the MacLeod clan was sitting, considering what he might ask. Then he saw young Colin skipping along the edge, looking like he was going to join the dancers. He stopped twice to try different bits of footwork. The boy seemed to want to do anything and everything that others did. Jack stopped where he was and gave the lad a wave of his arm to call him over. He planned to have the lad ask for him as he wasn't sure his tongue would form the right words.

Colin came close and Jack thought of something else to say to him first. "Heyo, Colin, we'll get ye a proper kilt and sword and teach ye the steps."

"Can ye do them?"

"O' course, but as we McKelveys are yet competin', 'tis only the other clans that be scunnerdancin'." He tousled the lad's thick hair. "I'll come to yer new home at Strathnaver Castle this winter and teach ye meself."

Colin grinned. "We'll be goin' there tonight. All the work's been done. We were only waitin' on the weddin'."

Jack nodded back at him as the bagpipes played their final notes and the dancers formed a circle.

"I guess me rest is over. Wish me luck and the help of the fairies."

"Ye willna need it, but I wish it anyway. Oh, I almost fergot to tell ye. Elspeth ..." he gulped, "Elspeth said to tell ye there be a special present fer ye waitin' at the statue in the bailey. Do ye want me to fetch it fer ye?"

Jack shook his head. "Nay. Jist ye stay here and root fer a McKelvey win." He fished in his sporran for a few coins and handed them to Colin. "And go over to the Kilmahews and bet on us."

Colin stared at the money in his hand and slowly turned. He made a whooping hoot and ran toward the red and gold flag.

***

ANABEL PEEKED AROUND one corner of the castle. She looked up at the high tower and considered how good a view she'd have from there, but though she'd spent some time in Castle Caladh, she'd never seen the door to this second tower's stairs. Could there be another door, an outside door? She walked around the circular structure and discovered just such a door. Unfortunately, it was locked.

The dancing music concluded and her attention shifted to the field. A few more steps and she'd be in view of the activities and anyone out there could look here and see her. She took those steps and stayed perfectly still to stare. It didn't take but a second to pick Jack out in the crowd. He was talking to a young boy who then headed toward a red and gold banner. Her heart skipped a beat in sudden fear. That was the Kilmahew flag. Yesterday she'd seen how Hamish Kilmahew, dishonored by his loss to Jack, had ridden off in a rage. A moment ago she would have dared to walk closer, but now she thought it best to stay out of sight. At least the tug-of-war would take place on the high ground; she'd be able to see Jack compete from here. The shadow of the tower would help to shield her should anyone look this way.

The McDoons took their stance, spreading themselves well apart. The McKelveys, on the other hand, got into position and spaced themselves quite close together. Keir was in back, she could see. She had no feelings toward him though they'd been engaged for a few weeks. As handsome and strong and noble as he was, he wasn't the man for her. Jack was. Her mouth curled up just thinking about Jack. Even at this distance she could admire his fine physique and how handsome he was with those piercing eyes, strong chin, and expressive mouth. He also was noble, and he was praiseworthy, principled, and certainly honest—all characteristics she admired. And she was going to be his wife in a matter of hours, if not minutes.

Her stomach did flips and her heart fluttered. She startled at the sound of a trumpet. Laird McKelvey held the center ribbon in one hand and put his other hand high in the air. When he dropped it, the battle began. The crowd shouted, their voices reverberating in the air. The teams seemed equally matched, straining to pull on the rope, their heels sinking further into the ground, the ribbon in the middle moving neither right nor left.

She knew it wasn't all up to Jack; there were six other men as strong or stronger pulling with him. She could see how red their faces were getting even at this distance.

"Come on, Jack!" She didn't realize she'd yelled until she heard her voice echo back, somehow resonating off the tower roof. She yelled again. And again. Her cheering made her feel a part of the clan. She lifted her skirts and ran forward, up the field, toward the chairs Hannah and Eleanor had just leaped up from.

Once she reached the women, she pushed between them, linked her arms with theirs, and shouted along with them.

177

The ribbon still did not waver. The tugging from both sides had taken on a rhythmic pulse as both teams yanked. Dylan's face reddened as he burst every blood vessel in his face. His father faltered and the shepherds who could pull a ram up a cliff with one hand lost their grip. The rope creaked and groaned on its own until ever so slowly the advantage went to the side more determined to win. The other team lost its unity and after several more minutes of the long struggle, the McKelveys pulled the McDoons over the line, sending the crowd into an uproar. Anabel jumped up and down along with her new friends.

***

THE CHEERING FOR the tug-of-war win did not last as long as after other events, particularly because so many couples were anxious for the ceremony. Bonnets were tightened, sashes repinned, kilts straightened, sweaty faces wiped, and best wishes given as shy lasses met up with eager lads, or handfasted pregnant women came arm in arm with farmers, and even widows and widowers had someone to walk with in the parade to the castle gardens.

Laird McKelvey dismounted and took Eleanor's mother Mary, his intended, with him to lead the couples forth. They stopped at the entrance, beside two topiary bushes that had been trimmed into the shape of long-eared rabbits. They stood to either side and greeted every couple before sending them through to stand before the vicar for a blessed and legal union. Other guests had gone around to the sides of the garden, some to watch, some to break cakes over the brides, and some to shoot an acknowledging pistol into the air. Children screeched, babies cried, young lasses held their hands over their ears, and young lads pinched those same lasses.

Logan and Keir came last holding Jack by his arms between them. Their wives, Eleanor and Hannah, reached them a moment later, escorting a very nervous and beaming Anabel.

Laird McKelvey knit his brow and shook his head. "Nay. Stand aside, Jack. Ye'll watch yer old father wed afore ye get yer chance." He gave a slight bow toward Anabel, then waved her father forward. The two fathers bowed to each other and Laird and Lady MacLeod pulled Anabel away from Eleanor and Hannah.

"Come along, lass," Laird MacLeod said to her.

"But, Father, I'm to wed Jack. Now. Today. I insist."

178

"Ye'll follow me and make nary a complaint." He wrapped his arm fully around her and nearly lifted her off her feet.

Jack started toward them, but Laird McKelvey put his hand out in front of his son and said, "Jack, obey me as ye would obey the Good Lord. Trust me. I need ye to be me witness. All will work out." He gave a sly look to his other sons, who helped him by steering Jack into the garden. The other brides, grooms, and guests had moved on into the courtyard where tables were set with yet another feast.

Jack stood angrily fuming, but held his tongue, listening as the vicar took his father and Mary through the ceremony. The parchment was signed, the cake was broken over a laughing Mary's head, and the Laird himself shot his pistol into the heavens.

"Now, Jack. Now ye may go. Ye're to follow the vicar to the kirk beside Strathnaver Castle. There ye'll meet yer bride."

Jack looked over his shoulder to where Anabel and her parents had trailed off to the carriages. He puckered his forehead and scowled at his brothers who laughed uproariously before moving next to their wives.

"The joke's on ye, Jack. 'Tis payback fer taggin' along all these years and fer bein' the obnoxious baby of the family. But 'tis also a reward fer leadin' us to victory, as I kent ye would, in the tug-o'-war. Yer horse and one fer Anabel are hitched to the vicar's wagon," Keir said.

"Aye," Logan piped in, holding Hannah's hand up to his lips and kissing it before he went on, "ye best hurry on. Ye dinnae want to be late to yer own weddin'. The Laird and Lady MacLeod will be yer witnesses."

They didn't need to explain the details. Jack was quick to accept the jest and the intricate plan. "And Dylan McDoon? Ye heard what he said at the start of the tuggin'. He promised to snatch Anabel and take her to England."

"Dinnae fash. The lad left with his tail between his legs."

Jack looked to the vicar who was waiting patiently, holding a Bible and a sack full of parchment papers.

"Sir," Jack said, a relieved and buoyant smile tugging at his mouth, "do ye have the stamina fer one more weddin'?"

***

ANABEL STRUGGLED AGAINST her father's strong arms at first as he took her away from Jack, but it was her mother's unexpected words that made her hold her tongue and limply acquiesce.

"Daughter, ye'll have a proper weddin' in a proper kirk, as yer father and Laird McKelvey have agreed to. Calm yerself. Ye'll be seein' Jack in a few moments' time." She smirked. "I had the hardest time holding' me tongue."

They were soon out of sight of the reveling crowd, most of whom had started feasting. They didn't have far to walk before they came to the gate.

"Is that our pony cart?" her father said.

"Aye. Kayla and her new husband will return it."

Her mother laughed. "I kent she'd find a way here." Then she took a firmer tone as they reached the MacLeod carriage and she stood aside to let Anabel climb in first. "I doan ken what we can do to make ye more presentable. Yer hair ... yer dress ..." She huffed and shook her head.

"I'm fine, Mother." Anabel said as her mother sat across from her. "Am I really goin' to a kirk to be married?"

"Aye. Laird McKelvey arranged it all. It's a kirk that sits on a hill beside Strathnaver Castle. He planned to have his own weddin' there to surprise his new lady, but she, it seems, insisted on a public vow-speakin' as there was some doubt concerning her first weddin'." She let a puff of air pass through her lips. "'Tis a wee bit of gossip that she may have been the wife of the disowned son of King George the Second."

Anabel was barely listening as she watched out the window. Her mother continued to rattle on about other snippets of things she heard at the games like how much money the Kilmahews lost by betting against the McKelveys. She explained how Laird McKelvey sought out her father as soon as they arrived at the games this morning, "The good Laird was in possession of a letter of renunciation from Hamish. 'Twas hand-delivered with another letter fer the Laird, claimin' favoritism and schemes against the Kilmahews. Yer father spent a while workin' out the details. He thought we'd have to send our carriage back to fetch ye, but we saw Kayla wearin' yer dress and she confessed ye were here." Her voice softened. "Me darlin', I'm happy ye're gettin' wed to someone ye care fer."

A smile crept across Anabel's lips as she turned her head away from the window. She leaned forward. "Thank ye, Mother." She rested her fingers on her mother's hand and read the honesty and love through that momentary touch.

She sat back and closed her eyes. Could everything be about to work out as she wanted? Were they really taking her to meet Jack and to take her vows in the Lord's house? She took a deep breath and let her fears flow out as she exhaled. She had no more reason to worry about Dylan or Benjamin or Hamish. She was sorry her friendship with Megan appeared to be over, but she'd made new friends in Eleanor and Hannah and Mary and even Elspeth.

The carriage jostled and came to a stop. Her eyes popped open and the first thing she saw was a quaint stone kirk. There was so much peace and quiet here. After all the noise and clamor of the games it seemed like heaven. Her father opened the carriage door and she stepped out first. She didn't wait for her mother, but hurried up to the open door. Inside the kirk was filled with the late afternoon light coming in all the open windows. She took a long moment to observe all the details of the interior, the intricate carvings on the altar, the ornate paintings on the walls, the stone columns, and the wooden pews with their engravings. It smelled richly of the late summer flowers that decorated the kirk: foxglove, sweet William, and heather.

There was a small table at the door and a crown of flowers lay upon it, a head covering meant for Mary, she realized, but she picked it up and placed it on her own head. She'd always been told she was beautiful, but in this moment, she felt beautiful on the inside.

She sat in the last pew, folded her hands, and closed her eyes to say a prayer of thanks.

Minutes ticked by, but it wasn't long before she heard a wagon stopping outside. Voices. Greetings. Hushed tones.

A hand on her shoulder.

Her mother helped her up and led her to the altar then sat with her father in the first pew. The vicar and Jack strode up the aisle, both smiling, and the vicar went around to the other side of the altar while Jack faced her and took both her hands in his.

He whispered. "'Tis the last moment. Ye can still run off, but be assured ... I'll run after ye."

The lump that formed in her throat dissolved. "I feel truth in yer words." She squeezed his fingers. "And love."

The vicar cleared his throat and began, "Dearly beloved ..."

Anabel heard every word twice, once through her ears, and a second time through Jack's touch. She understood how precious the words were to him.

"... I require and charge you both, as ye will answer at the dreadful day of judgment when the secrets of all hearts shall be disclosed, that if either of you know any impediment, why ye may not be lawfully joined together in matrimony, ye do now confess it."

They shook their heads in unison. Jack said, "There be none."

Anabel heard her mother weeping and realized the matching tears were her own. Jack's eyes looked equally wet. The joy in her heart swelled. They repeated the sacred vows and Jack added, "In God's eyes and in front of yer mother and yer father, I swear I'll honor ye in all ways, forsake all others, and keep meself only onto ye, me beloved Anabel."

The vicar finished with a lengthy prayer and held the parchment out for them to sign.

***

THE LATE AUGUST sun did its best to take the edge off the cool morning. Jack McKelvey, shirtless and barefoot, finished pulling the last bucket out of the well at Castle Falaichte where he and Anabel had spent their wedding night. His arms felt like rubber after all the exertion of the last few days, but that wouldn't stop him from carrying as many buckets as needed to prepare a bath for his bonnie new wife.

The Highland games were already a memory that was fading fast. He'd practiced the hammer throw and the caber toss so hard, hoping to master the events and make a good showing, but it mattered not a bit now. He'd won the lass and that was a victory that overshadowed any other, even the final McKelvey team win.

"There ye are," Anabel called as she came around the first bend of the maze. "I thought ye might be drawin' water fer us."

"I'll be heatin' it, too." He appraised her loveliness as she stood there in her night shift, her hair as mussed as his, her cheeks red, her lips so inviting. "Come closer," he urged as he put the second filled bucket at the base of the well.

Anabel blushed deeper and closed the gap, pressing her chest against his, and running her fingers through his thick dark hair and down to his bare shoulders.

"I love ye today more than yesterday," she murmured, holding his gaze.

"If those be the last words I hear before I die, I'll die a happy man," Jack said before he kissed her.

The kiss stretched on and on before Anabel finally needed to catch her breath. "Ye doan mean to die on me, do ye?"

"'Tis jist an expression. I love ye too much to die."

She put both hands on his face. "I missed ye when ye left our bed this morn. Leave the buckets and come back with me now."

Jack grinned and lifted her into his arms to carry her out of the maze and toward the door that she'd left open. He didn't bother to bar the door, for setting her down for the seconds it would take to do that, meant having her out of his embrace for too long. That rubbery feeling he'd had in his arms earlier was gone. He was as strong and hard as an ox.

"Lady McKelvey of Falaichte, is there anything else ye wish fer?"

"Nay, Jack, I have everything if I have ye."

THE END

MORE BOOKS by this author writing under the pen names of Debra Chapoton, Boone Patchard, and Marlisa Kriscott:

Young Adult and Adult:

THE HIGHLANDER'S SECRET PRINCESS
THE HIGHLANDER'S ENGLISH MAIDEN
THE HIGHLANDER'S HIDDEN CASTLE
THE HIGHLANDER'S HEART OF STONE

SECOND CHANCE TEACHER ROMANCE – Christian romance series written under the pen name Marlisa Kriscott:
AARON AFTER SCHOOL
SONIA'S SECRET SOMEONE
MELANIE'S MATCH
SCHOOL'S OUT
SUMMER SCHOOL
THE SPANISH TUTOR
A NOVEL THING

EDGE OF ESCAPE Psychological Thriller - Innocent adoration escalates to stalking and abduction in this psychological thriller. SOMMERFALLE is the German version of EDGE OF ESCAPE

THE GUARDIAN'S DIARY Young Adult Coming of Age - Jedidiah, a 17-year-old champion skateboarder with a defect he's been hiding all of his life, must risk exposure to rescue a girl that's gone missing.

SHELTERED Young Adult Paranormal - Ben, a high school junior, has found a unique way to help homeless teens, but he must first bring the group together to fight against supernatural forces.

A SOUL'S KISS Young Adult Paranormal - When a tragic accident leaves Jessica comatose, her spirit escapes her body. Navigating a supernatural realm is tough, but being half dead has its advantages. Like getting into people's thoughts. Like taking over someone's body. Like experiencing romance on a whole new plane - literally.

EXODIA Dystopian Biblical Retelling - By 2093 American life is a strange mix of failing technologies, psychic predictions, and radiation induced abilities. Tattoos are mandatory to differentiate two classes, privileged and slave. Dalton Battista fears that his fading tattoo is a deadly omen. He's either the heir of the brutal tyrant of the new capital city, Exodia or he's its prophesied redeemer.

OUT OF EXODIA In this sequel to EXODIA, Dalton Battista takes on his prophesied identity as Bram O'Shea. When this psychic teen leads a city of 21st century American survivalists out from under an oppressive regime, he puts the escape plan at risk by trusting the mysterious god-like David Ronel.

THE GIRL IN THE TIME MACHINE Young Adult Time Travel - A desperate teen with a faulty time machine. What could go wrong? 17-year-old Laken is torn between revenge and righting a wrong. Sci-Fi suspense.

THE TIME BENDER Young Adult Alien Sci-Fi - A stolen kiss could put the universe at risk. Selina doesn't think Marcum's spaceship is anything more than one heck of a science project ... until he takes her to the moon and back.

THE TIME PACER Young Adult Alien Sci-Fi - Alex discovered he was half-alien right after he learned how to manipulate time. Now he has to fight the star cannibals, fly a space ship, work on his relationship with Selina, and stay clear of Coreg, full-blooded alien rival and possible galactic traitor. Once they reach their ancestral planet all three are plunged into a society where schooling is more than indoctrination

THE TIME STOPPER Young Adult Alien Sci-Fi - Young recruit Marcum learns battle-craft, infiltration and multiple languages at the Interstellar Combat Academy. He and his arch rival Coreg jeopardize their futures by exceeding the space travel limits and flying to Earth in search of a time-bender. They find Selina whose ability to slow the passage of time will be invaluable in fighting other aliens. But Marcum loses his heart to her and when Coreg takes her twenty light years away he remains on Earth in order to develop a far greater talent than time-bending. Now he's ready to return home and get the girl.

THE TIME ENDER Young Adult Alien Sci-Fi - Selina Langston is confused about recurring feelings for the wrong guy/alien. She's pretty sure Alex is her soulmate and Coreg should not be trusted at all. But Marcum … well, when he returns to Klaqin and rescues her she begins to see him in a different light.

TO DIE UPON A KISS Gender-swapped Retelling of *Othello* - Several teenagers' lives intertwine during one eventful week full of love, betrayal and murder in this futuristic, gender-swapped retelling of Shakespeare's Othello.

HERE WITHOUT A TRACE Young Adult Parallel World - Hailey and Logan enter a parallel world through hypnosis in order to rescue a girl gone missing.

LOVE CONTAINED Christian Suspense - Trapped in a shipping container, sinking to the depths of the ocean … but this isn't the worst thing that's happened to Henry … or Max.

SPELL OF THE SHADOW DRAGON Epic Sci-Fi Fantasy - Four hundred years after colonizing a planet ruled by dragons, the future of the human race hangs in the balance once again.

CURSE OF THE WINTER DRAGON – Epic Sci-Fi Fantasy – Sequel to SPELL OF THE SHADOW DRAGON

A FAULT OF GRAVES – young adult thriller - A disastrous fall into the depths of our planet turns into a desperate fight for survival.

Non-fiction:
35 LESSONS IN THE PSALMS Ready to use Sunday School lessons and/or personal Bible Study Workbook

PRAYER JOURNAL AND BIBLE STUDY FOR MEN

PRAYER JOURNAL AND BIBLE STUDY (for women)

PRAYER JOURNAL AND BIBLE STUDY (the 4 Gospels)

GUIDED PRAYER JOURNAL FOR WOMEN

OLD TESTAMENT LESSONS IN THE BIBLE Sunday School lessons and/or personal Bible study

NEW TESTAMENT LESSONS IN THE BIBLE Sunday School lessons and/or personal Bible study

TEENS IN THE BIBLE Sunday School lessons and/or personal Bible study

MOMS IN THE BIBLE Sunday School lessons and/or personal Bible study

ANIMALS IN THE BIBLE Sunday School lessons and/or personal Bible study

HOW TO BLEND FAMILIES This guide gives step by step advice from experienced educators and also provides several fill-in worksheets to help you resolve family relationships, deal with discipline, navigate the financials, and create a balanced family with happy people.

BUILDING BIG PINE LODGE A journal of our experiences building a full log home

CROSSING THE SCRIPTURES A Bible Study supplement for studying each of the 66 books of the Old and New Testaments.

300 PLUS TEACHER HACKS and TIPS A guide for teachers at all levels of experience with hacks, tricks, and tips to help you get and give the most out of teaching.

HOW TO HELP YOUR CHILD SUCCEED IN SCHOOL A guide for parents to motivate, encourage and propel their kids to the head of the class. Includes proven strategies and tips from teachers.

HOW TO TEACH A FOREIGN LANGUAGE Tips, advice, and resources for foreign language teachers and student teachers.

200 Creative Writing Prompts Workbook

400 Creative Writing Prompts Workbook

Advanced Creative Writing Prompts Workbook

Beyond Creative Writing Prompts

BRAIN POWER PUZZLES Volume 1
Stretch yourself by solving anagrams, word searches, cryptograms, mazes, math puzzles, Sudoku, crosswords, daisy puzzles, boggle boards, pictograms, riddles, and more in these entertaining puzzles books.

BRAIN POWER PUZZLES Volume 2
BRAIN POWER PUZZLES Volume 3
BRAIN POWER PUZZLES Volume 4
BRAIN POWER PUZZLES Volume 5 (Spanish Student Edition)
BRAIN POWER PUZZLES Volume 6 (Math Edition)
BRAIN POWER PUZZLES Volume 7
BRAIN POWER PUZZLES Volume 8 (Bible Theme)
BRAIN POWER PUZZLES Volume 9
BRAIN POWER PUZZLES Volume 10 (Christmas Edition)

BRAIN POWER PUZZLES Volume 11 (Word Search Challenge)

Children's books:

THE SECRET IN THE HIDDEN CAVE 12-year-old Missy Stark and her new friend Kevin Jackson discover dangerous secrets when they explore the old lodge, the woods, the cemetery, and the dark caves beneath the lake. They must solve the riddles and follow the clues to save the old lodge from destruction.

MYSTERY'S GRAVE After Missy and Kevin solved THE SECRET IN THE HIDDEN CAVE, they thought the rest of the summer at Big Pine Lodge would be normal. But there are plenty of surprises awaiting them in the woods, the caves, the stables, the attic and the cemetery. Two new families arrive and one family isn't human.

BULLIES AND BEARS In their latest adventure at Big Pine Lodge, Missy and Kevin discover more secrets in the caves, the attic, the cemetery and the settlers' ruins. They have to stay one step ahead of four teenage bullies, too, as well as three hungry bears. This summer's escapades become more and more challenging for these two twelve-year-olds. How will they make it through another week?

A TICK IN TIME 12-year-old Tommy MacArthur plunges into another dimension thanks to a magical grandfather clock Now he must find his way through a strange land, avoid the danger lurking around every corner, and get back home. When he succeeds, he dares his new friend Noelle to return with him, but who and what follows them back means more trouble and more adventure.

BIGFOOT DAY, NINJA NIGHT When 12-year-old Anna skips the school fair to explore the woods with Callie, Sydney, Austin, and Natalie, they find evidence of Bigfoot. No way! It looks like his tracks are following them. But that's not the worst part. And neither is stumbling upon Bigfoot's shelter. The worst part is they get separated and now they can't find Callie or the path that leads back to the school.

In the second story Luke and his brother, Nick, go on a boys-only camping trip, but things get weird and scary very quickly. Is there a ninja in the woods with them? Mysterious things happen as day turns into night.

THE TUNNEL SERIES 12-year-old Nick escapes from a reformatory but gets side-tracked traveling through multiple tunnels, each with a strange destination. He must find his way home despite barriers like invisibility. When he teams up with Samantha they begin to uncover the secret to all the tunnels. (6 books in series)

Follow me for new book releases:
https://www.amazon.com/stores/author/B003MX4NCS

Made in the USA
Middletown, DE
29 May 2024

55033851R00108